C O L D
COMFORT

C O L D COMFORT

Stories of death and bereavement

**E D I T E D B Y
J A M E S L O A D E R**

Library of Congress Catalog Card Number: 95-68391

A catalogue record for this book is available from the
British Library on request

The right of the individual contributors to be acknowledged as
authors of their work has been asserted by them in accordance
with the Copyright, Designs and Patents Act 1988

Copyright © 1996 of the individual contributions remains with
the authors. Compilation copyright © 1996 James Loader

First published in 1996 by
Serpent's Tail, 4 Blackstock Mews, London N4,
and 180 Varick Street, 10th floor, New York, NY 10014

Typeset in 10½ pt Caslon by CentraCet Ltd, Cambridge
Printed in Great Britain by Cox & Wyman Ltd, Reading, Berks.

Contents

To Molly Loader, with
much love and
gratitude

ACKNOWLEDGEMENTS

'The Last Judgement' by Jan Brokken, translated by Tony Briggs, first appeared in *Passport, the Magazine of New International Writing* in 1993.

'The July Ghost' by A S Byatt first appeared in *Sugar and other stories*, published by Chatto & Windus in 1987.

'Close-up of Death' by Slavenka Draculić has appeared in *New Republic*, *Index on Censorship* and *The Balkan Express*.

'A Honeymoon in Los Angeles' by Tobias Hill was first published in slightly different form in *Printed Matter*, Japan, 1995.

'Lust for Loss' by Lynne Tillman was first published as 'Vivre sa perte' in *Visite aux armées: Tourismes de guerre/Back to the Front: Tourisms of War*, edited by Diller and Scofido, FRAC, Basse-Normandie, 1994.

'Assia' by William Trevor first appeared in *Excursions in the Real World*, published by Hutchinson in 1993.

INTRODUCTION

My mother died in the summer of 1957, when I was nine years old. It was a period of odd, fragmentary images: in the days before her death I wandered round the house, poking about in a room which had been my grandfather's, where lumber had been stored since his death. I found a box of toys that had been my father's, quaint things from his own lost childhood – a wooden horse on wheels, a stuffed black doll with a fez – and a Christmas card I had made for my mother, years ago when I was five or six. The babyish scrawl, with its exuberant border of Christmas trees, cocks and hens, embarrassed me. It was not good enough. It belonged to the past.

Her bed had been moved downstairs into the drawing-room. She was very frail, but the process of emaciation had been so slow and gradual that at the time I hardly registered the changes in her. Her laughter had a papery dry sound and a cold sore had broken out on her upper lip. I remember the feel of her scabbed mouth against my skin. Otherwise – quite simply – it was my mother, no more, no less.

She died late on Thursday night. That afternoon we played cricket at school. The teacher preferred to sit in the sun with the boys who had already been out to bat while the game went on of its own accord. We were discussing where we had been born and when I told her my birthplace she repeated the word softly, gazing at me as though there were something else on her mind. I wondered later whether she already knew what was going on, as the other adults did, or whether she was just bored with the chatter of children.

When I got home – relaxed, quite cheerful, a little touched by the sun – and went as usual to see my mother, someone had locked the drawing-room door. People had been 'trying to talk' to me all that week but the message that she was dying had not sunk in. One of my sisters – both of whom had lived for months with the knowledge that my mother was terminally ill – talked to me about God. 'God isn't *cruel*,' she said (I still hear her intonation exactly), but to this day I do not know why she said it, given the facts as she knew them. At the time I took it as a reassurance that my mother would live.

I had slept well enough all that week. Something was obviously not quite right, but my mother had been in and out of hospital before; she had her ups and her downs (she was, I was told years later, frightened of the ambulance when it came for her, because she associated it with the radiotherapy which she loathed). I had no bad dreams, although my fears were beginning to take clearer shape as I became aware of a new quality in the adult anxiety around me.

Our aunt had come to stay with us and, on the last two or three nights of my mother's life, she would come into my bedroom after I had put my light out and sit by me until I was asleep. She spoke to me gently before tip-toeing out with the half-finished orange that I had taken up to eat in bed. She was trying to talk about death in a way that a child would understand.

I lay there wishing she would go. I was tired, longing for sleep, and I could never follow what she was trying to convey; nor did I want to. As I slipped in and out of consciousness I was aware of her hesitancies and understood that she was trying to develop an idea for which she

⊣ **✕** ⊢

could not easily find words. Then the image came to her that would, she thought, make whatever it was she was attempting to say intelligible to me. She said, 'It's like your orange,' and then, gathering confidence, she developed the simile while I drifted into sleep, exhausted and bored by her adult need to find expression for the thing that was about to take place downstairs.

So I never knew why it was like an orange, or even what she had used that image to explain. Was she thinking of a tumour, as she looked at the half-peeled, torn segments? Did the fruit make her think of my mother's destroyed flesh? The orange could have been her metaphor for death, for cancer, but there again it could have been anything, mortality, growth, health, whatever is natural or inevitable, the members of a family clinging together, pain, love or God. Or, I suppose, something absurd, something trashy; something meaningless.

After my mother's death people found more conventional metaphors: flowers plucked from gardens, journeys, things like that. But the orange stays with me because of its mystery, and because it reminds me of the difficulty we face when it comes to saying anything at all about death – what it is really like, what it means, how we react to it or how we should react – that is neither convention nor cliché. I have chosen the writings in this collection because, in their different ways, they address this problem.

James Loader
August 1995

Paul Bailey

DISQUE BLEU

⊣ **i** ⊢

The Arab offered me a cigarette. 'Smoke?' he asked. I shook my head, and smiled to express my gratitude. He had a little boy with him, whose hair he ruffled. 'Girl' was his next word, followed a minute or so later by 'new', then 'baby'. I indicated with a nod that I understood what he was attempting to tell me. He had come to register the birth of his daughter. He had already guessed that I was there to record someone's death. My face had told him as much. He had recognized grief, and acknowledged it with a small gesture of kindness – the only one available to him in the curious circumstances.

That brief meeting took place on the afternoon of March 27, 1986, in a waiting-room in the Westminster Council House. I remember how the Arab tried to contain his happiness by adopting a serious expression whenever our eyes met. I was touched, and slightly amused, by the way in which he manoeuvred the change from obvious delight to awkward sympathy. I desperately wanted to tell him not to bother; that the offer of the rather foul-smelling cigarette had been enough. My name was called first, and before I left I muttered words I thought he might know: 'Thanks', I said, and 'Congratulations'.

'Not *quite* the youngest this week,' the woman who took the death certificate from me remarked. 'There was one yesterday who was only forty-six.' She was stating a matter of fact. I watched her as she read the slip of paper. 'It isn't for me to ask you why,' she observed, writing 'cirrhosis of the liver' alongside David's name in the large ledger on the table between us. 'Guilt,' I ventured, without explanation. 'I think it was guilt.' I sat in silence until she finished. When I rose to leave, she advised me to enjoy the rest of my life. Her tone was almost brusque. 'Yes,' I heard myself answer.

As soon as I got home, I telephoned the undertaker nearest to the hospital in which David had died. 'It's Easter in a few days time,' said the man I talked to. 'We're pretty heavily booked.' Could he have my number? He would see what he could do. He rang back the following morning. 'You're in luck, Mr Bailey,' the fruity voice announced. 'There's been a last minute cancellation.' I nearly laughed, but managed to say something absurd, like 'Good', instead.

The owner of the fruity voice had a rubicund face to match. 'I'm a failed actor,' he informed me. I had noticed a copy of *The Stage* on his desk. 'You need to be a bit of a thespian in this job.' I accepted his invitation to 'take a pew'. 'Shall we run through your requirements?' We began with the most basic. Was it to be a burial or a cremation? On hearing it was the latter, he recommended Mortlake, for its 'atmosphere'. I replied that Mortlake was perfectly suitable. What kind of coffin did I prefer – plain wood, or walnut perhaps, or even mahogany? 'Plain wood,' I replied. 'Very practical, Mr Bailey. Very sensible. It's going to be burnt, after all.' He cleared his throat and inquired if my 'late companion' was religious. He was a lapsed Catholic, I told him. 'Plenty of those,' he said, and chuckled. 'In that case, will you be requiring a clergyman or priest?' We were virtually soul mates by now. 'Good God, no,' I said. 'Very sensible, yet again. You've saved yourself £120.'

A secular service presented no problems, he assured me. 'I'm afraid it's restricted to thirty minutes maximum,' he added. He suggested that a rehearsal might be in order, given that I intended to read some Jane Austen, play a couple of tapes of Mozart arias, and have a friend address the mourners. I'd already revealed that I'd once been an actor. 'Timing's of the essence, Mr Bailey.'

Mr Bailey heeded his advice, and rehearsed the readings from *Pride and Prejudice* and *Persuasion*. The funeral director made sure that the trio from *Così fan Tutte* and 'Porgi amor' from *Figaro* came in and out on cue, and the publisher who praised David did so with feeling and wit and brevity. My red-faced adviser had proposed that everyone should depart in advance of the coffin's disappearance. 'Such an upsetting moment. Sliding away behind those curtains. Much too *final*.'

After the service, which had been a celebratory affair, my unlikely soul mate took me aside and confessed that the publisher's speech had moved him deeply. 'I have to tell you, Mr Bailey, that I too am gay,' he said in a near-whisper, and then wagged an admonitory finger: 'Not a word to the staff.' He was ashamed to be dishonest – but, well, there it was. His guarded confession was the more poignant because I was certain that the people who worked with him were fully aware that he was homosexual. I found, and still find, his innocence beguiling, and his unnecessary discretion both comic and sad.

'The ashes are in my office, safe and sound,' he phoned to say. 'Come along when you're ready.' It was weeks, months, before I was ready. He was as cheerful as ever on the day I called to collect the urn that contained them. 'Do you remember the joke I made, Mr Bailey?' He'd made so many jokes, I wasn't certain which particular one he had in mind. 'The cancellation joke,' he reminded me. He proceeded to quote himself, in a fruitier voice than his customarily fruity one: ' "You're in luck, Mr Bailey. There's been a last minute cancellation." ' Of course I remembered it. 'I was testing you,' he confided. 'I try it on all my clients. You hesitated, and I knew you wanted to laugh. If you'd reacted differently, I'd have treated you more *solemnly*.' I said I was glad he hadn't; that his jokes, his performance, had been a comfort. I couldn't imagine him being solemn. 'It's well within my range, solemnity,' he intoned.

I had a novel to complete and, in the immediate period after David's death, I wrote the closing fifty pages in a kind of haze. It was as if I had no life except the life in the book, the life I'd been living with for over three years. I was driven; I was inspired, I suppose. With the last words committed to paper, I was no longer protected from the real life of absence and emptiness I knew was awaiting me.

⊣ **ii** ⊢

David and I had been living together for nearly a decade when his mother died of Huntington's disease. He visited her at her home in Abergavenny some weeks before her death, and was so distressed at the spectacle of a middle-aged woman shaking involuntarily that he found any number of reasons not to return. She was already exhibiting signs of senile dementia. He had to hold a cup to her mouth so that she could drink the tea she had asked him to make.

He heard, later, that she had called out for him on her deathbed. She had stared at his sweet-tempered younger brother and told him to fetch the son she really loved. How I wish that Arthur had kept this piece of information to himself, for it came to haunt and unnerve David. He hadn't seen her die, and there were times when he found he could barely live with the fact.

I discovered by accident that he was drinking heavily. I was in his workroom – he was a costumier by profession – looking for a piece of material a designer required when I chanced upon dozens of empty gin bottles, mostly halves and miniatures. His secret exposed, he began to drink openly, knocking back his first gin and tonic at breakfast.

It was his misfortune not to endure hangovers: he would rise each morning in what seemed to be a state of glowing health.

I realized that he was committing suicide, slowly, and tried to talk him out of it. David was tirelessly kind to others when they were unhappy, but showed no such consideration to himself. Years passed before the effects of his determined self-punishment became obvious. It was typical of him that when a doctor shouted at him that he would die if he didn't stop drinking he stopped at once. In his final, abstinent months he underwent major surgery and bore indescribable pain, clinging on to the life he had previously hated.

Ours was a stormy, unpredictable relationship, of a kind I could not be part of again. I accepted a fellowship at a university in America, I understand now, in order to be thousands of miles away from the furnace we had created in London. I came back to it, however, because it was warm.

Grief was not merciful with David. I sat with my newly dead mother for an hour, holding her cold hand in mine, and I cherish the memory of the peace that had settled on her features. David had no such last meeting to sustain him. He sank into a black pit of guilt, from which he would emerge – improbable as it may sound – in a mood that was often the cause of hilarity in those who loved him. It still pains me to recall that he could be the funniest person in the world.

I sometimes dream of David, and it's always the demonic aspect of his complicated nature that asserts itself. I awake in panic, convinced that he's there in the room with me. Then I calm myself with the knowledge of his death; with the certainty that his terrible agony is over.

⊣ **iii** ⊢

The gently courteous Arab, the brisk registrar of births and deaths, the histrionic funeral director will continue to be vivid presences in my life. Each of them was distinctly thoughtful, distinctly solicitous.

'Your late companion was fortunate in his friends,' said the funeral director when I went to collect the ashes. 'A most impressive turn-out. He must have been a popular chap.'

'He was.'

'Unlike some I could tell you about.'

He told me about a rich old man who had written 'reams and reams of dire epic verse'. The 'poet' had arranged that his service should run for an hour and a half – the time it took the funeral director to read his masterpiece aloud: 'An appalling piece of doggerel, Mr Bailey. I performed it for what it was worth, which – alas – wasn't much.'

The chapel at Mortlake was filled with the old man's relatives, who listened to the doggerel with feigned interest. Some gave up the effort, and fell asleep. 'There was a woman in the front row *snoring*.' They were there in anticipation of the versifier's will, which was read the same day.

'Theirs was a wasted journey, Mr Bailey. Not a sausage did he leave them. Not a single *sausage*. Everything was left to charity.'

I carried the urn home with me, but did not keep it. I arranged for it to be sent to Abergavenny. What remains of David is buried in his mother's grave.

Jan Brokken

THE LAST
JUDGEMENT

Translated by Tony Briggs

He used to read in the lavatory; he could spend hours there. He did not feel safe in the sitting-room. True, the manse was quite a way away from the dyke, but the market gardeners' practised polder eyes were still able to focus sharply on his slightly bowed shape. If he was reading they thought, 'Dominie has time.' They rang the door bell and sat in the light of the reading lamp and told of bad crops and God's wrath embodied in the shape of excess rainwater. He listened, an impatient finger laid on the cover. The study at the back of the house seemed a better refuge. But the telephone was there too. Its ringing could not be heard from the toilet. That lay at the end of the passage, under the stairs, far from the inhabited world. You saw him slip inside with a book under his arm, sniggering like a truant schoolboy. Once the door was locked, he did not allow himself to be distracted any more. You could knock and bang, he would not budge. Sometimes he pinned a note on the door: AWAY, TRAVELLING.

'Shall we get on with it then?'

He sits perched on the edge of the sofa. His hands rest on the ivory knob of the walking-stick standing between his knees. He has a dark blue suit on, with a waistcoat, a dark purple Macassar silk tie and black shoes. His cheeks are the colour of bad quality paper – yellowish with a brown spot here and there. The Zealand clock above the dresser strikes three.

'We could drink another cup of tea.'

'No, no, no. I don't want to have to hurry later.'

He gets up but falls back on the sofa immediately. His joints will not co-operate. Or is he tired by the leave-taking? Perhaps he longs to rest even more than I.

It is raining outside. The sky is grey as only a South Holland sky can be grey, seven different tints of grey, painted by a manic-depressive God. No wonder, when at Portland, he turns to books by Friedericy.

Ploughland stretches out at the front and the back of the house. A narrow path runs from the dyke to the front door, as muddy as Russian steppes in spring. The house is practically identical to the manse, just as big, just as lonely and just as chilly.

'One more try, son.'

A hollow attempt at cheerfulness. His face tells a story, but I do not know exactly which. Expressions slide like masks one over the other. He gets to his feet shakily and shuffles to the door, centimetre by centimetre.

'You walk like Sartre.'

His response is a snorting sound, indicating assent.

'Sartre and I have one thing in common, we have sat too much during our lives.'

And smoked too much, I want to say, and drunk too much, but I keep silent; he is old, and the old have a right to be agreed with.

We walk along the passage.

'Let me take your arm.'

I give him my arm. Since Olga's death, three weeks ago, his knees sometimes suddenly swerve to the left and before you have had time to realize it, he is lying stretched on the floor with an astonished groan, like a child.

'One metre, h'm?'

He had understood. After the funeral I had sometimes

thought he was deaf, or was at least playing deaf, but this much had got through. He has understood he has to leave the house.

'Yes, just one metre.'

He pushed open the door of the study with his stick. I let go his arm and turn the heating on. His eyes travel around the room, a high, long room with hundreds of books on the walls, thousands . . . sixty metres of them. He nods at the bindings, shuffles to the leather armchair standing in a corner of the room, lets himself fall into it and reaches for the cord of the reading lamp in an automatic gesture.

'Start at once?'

'Yes. There.'

He points top left. But before I have taken the first book from the shelf, he says he feels like having one.

'A proper one, if you please. Not watered down.'

I half fill the gin glass from the bottle in the kitchen and top it up at the tap. When I give it to him, he gives me a searching look. His hands are shaking. He swallows it in one gulp. The contents produce a disconsolate grimace round his lips.

'Water in South Holland tastes of chlorine.'

I feel caught out.

'Top left then,' I say, as breezily as possible.

'In the Indies,' he mutters, staring at the empty glass. I know the tale. In the East Indies he had a gigantic library, a good ten thousand books. The war broke out and he was marched off to a camp in the north of Celebes. He returned four years later to find a pile of ash on the study floor. A Macassar Bible lay on his desk. The other books had been burnt by the Japs.

'Thank God your mother managed to hide a couple of hundred before she was arrested two days later.' He looks at her photograph on the desk. She sat on the veranda of a white palace, surrounded by magnificent bouquets of flowers.

'Shall I tell you about Olga again?'

'Later . . .'

'I thought . . . I could tell another story . . .'

'Now don't go being awkward,' I say and I hear my voice break shrilly.

He lays his head back on the antimacassar.

'If you give me another drink, then I won't. Then we can start.'

He smelt of books. It amazes me I never developed a dislike of the smell of ink, paper and dust which rose from his clothes. Perhaps the reason was his modesty. If conversation moved to books, he was no missionary. I have never heard him deliver a long speech in praise of a book. He left the subject untouched, except when you yourself began, and even then he kept himself reined in. Possibly he was afraid. In the eyes of the village reading was the same as lazing around. Dominie and the gentry read, others did not. The Bible was the only book to the market gardeners. Books for study gave you a swollen head and literature was filth. Reading novels – to them that was nothing more than 'tittie-squeezing.'

It was not till after his retirement that he dared talk about books.

'*The Confessions of St. Augustine.*'

'I'm taking that.'

Barth. Barth. Barth. Berkhoff. Several lesser gods. And then Kierkegaard, Kierkegaard, Kierkegaard, Kierkegaard.

'I never knew you had so much Kierkegaard.'

'Do I rise in your estimation?'

'Considerably.'

'In that case I might have risen in your estimation a long time ago. I had those books long before the war.'

I open one of them, a German edition of *Stages on the Road of Life*, Berlin, 1928.

'I seem to remember you having much more Barth.'

'I only began on Barth half-way through the 'thirties. Kierkegaard was earlier, that was at the beginning of my time at Leiden. I was mad about Kierkegaard then and I've never been able to let him go completely since. Books,' his voice drops to a whisper, 'they're like women. First loves are always the greatest.'

I turn back a page and see the inscription. 'Pour ton vingt-cinquième anniversaire. Genève, 28 mai 1934. Olga.'

'Mama gave you this.'

'In Geneva. I had come over from Holland. We walked along the lake in the evening. The night was clear, serene, with moon and stars, without alcohol. She wore a long white dress and a wide hat. No gloves. I took her hand at the bridge, her bare hand, and that was quite something in those days. She gazed at me for a long while. Then she said, ' "I've bought a present for you ... the *Stages*." I'd already got it. But what can one do in a case like that?'

'Keep your mouth shut.'

'And take her in your arms, enraptured.'

He laughs boyishly.

'What language did you speak to each other?'

'German and French, you know that. She spoke beautiful French, with a strong Russian accent. French is an elegant language when spoken by foreigners. Not when the French speak it, they weld the words lovelessly together. Olga gave each syllable its own tone. I don't mind telling you now that I fell for her voice first, and then for her freckles and then for her lips, they had something gluttonous about them ... most women had parsimonious lips in those days, in Switzerland too.'

He turns to the photograph on the desk again.

'This one too then, the Kierkegaard?'

'Of course.' He pushes his spectacles higher up his nose. 'But not that other one, otherwise I'll have to do too much thinking. Kierkegaard always makes you think hard.'

'Seems an advantage rather than a disadvantage to me.'

'Not when you're old. Give me his *Epilogue* a moment. Here, "a. A logical system can be given. b. But no system of the existing can be given." I don't know what you do with that, but I can spend two days thinking about it ... and I haven't got many days left to spend thinking.'

He had been more optimistic two months ago. 'Creaking carts carry on longest' was what he had said then.

When he was away, I used to tiptoe into the study. I would light the fire, find a book and sit with a rug pulled over my knees. I read. Especially about the East Indies. I escaped, out of the village, far away, away to the firm breasts of a fourteen-year-old Macassar princess. My hand kneaded my trousers. Time disappeared. Sometimes I would take a girlfriend with me and show the books to her. I told her of the whispering, mysterious world that lay behind the bindings. It had something secretive. It was as if there, on the shelves, a treasure lay, shining gold in the midst of the polders. The fire crackled. The flames flared. Everything gleamed.

'Be your father's son. Have one too.'

I fill two glasses to the brim.

The rain has meanwhile turned to hail. The hailstones clatter against the window.

'Geniuses are like a thunderstorm,' he is quoting Kierkegaard, 'they travel against the wind, frighten people, clean the air.'

Calvin's *Institutes* lies on the table, published by Van Schenk Brill in Doesburg in 1889, a reprint of the 1650 edition published by Paulus Aertz van Ravesteyn in Amsterdam, with an introduction by the grand old man of Dutch Calvinism, Abraham Kuyper.

'I read it three times, this tome ...' He nips at his gin

and wipes his lips. 'Never saw any lightning, never heard the thunder.' His words have a melancholy tinge.

'One evening on the Red Sea. Olga was sitting in a sagging cane chair on the stern deck. I leant against the railing . . .'

Photographs taken at the time show a tall, thin man with dark blond combed-back hair and small round spectacles.

'The desert slid by in the distance. The screeching of palm court strings rose from the bowels of the ship. Olga longed for her Bechstein . . . I'd promised her a Bechstein . . . one she could play Mozart on whenever she pleased. "Never anything but Mozart," I said, teasing her. She gazed at me wide-eyed. "But ee eez a gen-i-us." "Tell me why then." "Because," she said, "his music is clever, light and transparent." '

He chuckles.

'I had to think of Calvin at that moment. A clever theologian, but his works are heavy, dark and humourless. Quite the opposite of Luther. At least Luther generously admitted to having had his greatest inspiration, the Two Kingdoms Thesis based on Romans, 13, when sitting on the lavatory. It's no more than an incidental circumstance, but it does make someone come to life.'

He used to sit on the lavatory for hours. Fortunately the manse had two, one down and one up, in the bathroom. The second one was often occupied by my second brother, Mikhael, who always sat reading *Catcher in the Rye*. Olga would sometimes scream in fury, 'Does nobody do anything but sheet in this house?' 'Shit' my brother would then correct her from behind the door, which only served to double her fury. She was proud of her Dutch and did not wish to be reminded of minor imperfections in her pronunciation. One day she took revenge. She carved deep grooves in the wooden toilet seat with her scissors, grooves which rasped your buttocks viciously. However, when she emerged from the toilet two months later with a blood-stain on her skirt she had new seats installed. Father thanked her with a bunch of roses.

Two hours later we start on his Oriental collection. A 1901 German language edition of the Koran. Studies of Islam in the East Indies. The collected works of the Dutch Islamic scholar Snouck Hurgronje. Conrad, of course. Couperus. Kipling. Multatuli. Du Perron. Terborgh's poems. *The Forbidden Kingdom*, Walraven's letters. Between all these *Travels among the Toradjas of Sa'dan and Mamasa* and Guides to Batavia and Macassar. Paatje Daum. Bep Vuyk. Vicki Baum. Székely-Lulofs. H. J. Friedericy . . .

'I expect you want that.'

A Mirror of the East Indies by Rob Nieuwenhuys. *A Passage to India* by E. M. Forster. ' "India",' he mutters, ' "a hundred Indias – whispered outside beneath the indifferent moon." '

He shakes his head.

'Europeans in the tropics. They wrote with pens brimming with curiosity. Great literature is often written by exiles, by foreigners looking for a foothold in unknown territory. Conrad. Slauerhoff. Forster. *A Passage to India*. That title in itself . . .'

He gets out his handkerchief with a slightly embarrassed gesture.

'Olga thought it was a masterpiece. She used to read a lot in those days. I was sometimes away for months, travelling. She couldn't always play the piano, go riding or dancing the charleston.'

Dancing the charleston?

There's a lot I can imagine her doing. I can see her humming, playing the piano, conducting choirs, cycling across the polders, giving a cursory tug to her nylons, standing in front of a mirror in a black suit, washing my back, brushing my hair ... but dancing the charleston? At the Assembly Rooms? In a short dress with a kiss-curl falling across her eyes?

'People have been talking a lot about Olga the last few days,' he says, guessing my thoughts. 'To me they have been talking about a different Olga.'

A more demure Olga? A more frugal Olga?

I dare not ask. When their parents are involved, children suddenly become prudish.

He sits staring at the photographs of the liner *J. P. Coen* in *A Passage to the Indies* by Rudy Kousbroek. He has difficulty in keeping his eyes dry. I have come to the shelves of foreign literature.

'Sixteen volumes of Goethe.'

'All of them or not a single one.'

'Then I am afraid it'll have to be not a single one. I have to be strict.'

'When I used to be strict, you would say, "One person has a soul, the other doesn't."'

I hasten to the following book.

'Malraux.'

'The French bard. Thank you. I don't like baritones.'

'Mauriac.'

'For heaven's sake, no. I may never have been a real Calvinist, but Mauriac is too Catholic for me.'

'Sartre.'

'*The Roads to Freedom*. No, better not. Only *Les Mots*. Provided it can go with a volume of Goethe's letters. And Flaubert's letters. D'you hear me?'

'Schiller.'

'I said, Flaubert.'

'Spengler.'

'H'mm? Is that in my bookcase?'

'Wederkind.'

'I say, what's the time? I'm hungry.'

*

We ate. Bortsch and fried rice. A peculiar combination. Olga assembled the strangest dishes and all of them had in common that they were burnt. She played the piano while doing the cooking. Mozart was only abandoned once smoke billowed from the kitchen. Father's back was bowed. He wolfed his food down, his nose approaching ever closer to his pile of fried rice. Something seemed to be getting at him. Olga asked whether he could not eat a little more decently. He put down his spoon and said, without lifting his eyes, that there had been complaints at the congregation council meeting yesterday evening. In an instant Olga was transformed into a Tartar. Sniffing and snorting she enquired what had happened. His back seemed to bow even lower. Mikhael giggled. Pieter launched a grain of burnt rice at the lamp above the table. I tried to make myself invisible.

They had complained. They said he was too modern. They said he read too much.

'That you drink too much,' Olga corrected.

No, that he read too much.

He looked at his thin hand, the one he had wanted to strike the table with the previous evening. He had not done it. Red patches appeared on Olga's throat. All of us sat waiting for her tirade against the Hollanders.

Father got up from the table.

After our pudding I slipped into the study. He was sitting in front of the bookcase, a stiff tot of gin in his left hand. He was not aware of me behind him. He swore softly. It was the first time I had heard him swear. All of a sudden he said, with hopeful tone to his voice, 'Bobbers'.

Upstairs, in my room, I looked it up in the dictionary. All I found was 'bobber' – a float used in angling, also bob-fly.

'Why have you always read so much?'

I have started on a new shelf, a shelf of psychology, while he probes a hollow tooth with a matchstick.

'Why ... why. I don't think a person need analyse his passions.'

The matchstick breaks. He tosses it in the ashtray and asks for a cigarette. The doctor has strictly forbidden him to smoke, but I give him one all the same.

'Once', he says, inhaling the smoke deeply, 'I often dreamt I was missing the boat. I've succeeded in keeping that dream as a dream for fifty years. Explaining the dream would destroy the myth.'

I pull *Die Traumdeutung* from the shelf with a sarcastic grin.

'You can leave it there. Though I still deeply respect Freud. What style! That man should have written novels.'

The book goes back on the shelf.

'All the same,' I persist, 'all the same I've often wondered why you read so much.'

I sense an undertone of disapproval in his muttering.

'The thing that has always surprised me is that people read so little. I am normal, the others aren't. I'm an ordinary person ... curious ... always in search of other worlds ... other opinions. What's strange about that? I never thought I read much. Thousands of masterpieces have eluded me. He who reads is soon filled with regret at having missed so much. When you are young you think you can catch up, but there's never an end to it.'

'You were bored. That's it. You were bored here in the village.'

'Nah, course not.'

He takes a quick drag at his cigarette. His eyes light up.

'The talk in books is a distillation, that's what has always appealed to me. Even a slip of a book has been worked on for a year. In the space of one evening you consume the fruits of a year's thought. A matter of impatience. I've always loathed chitter-chatter. Of course writers waffle sometimes in their books, but you can skip the crap. No greater liberty than the reader's. Readers are churlish people really. Bored by a book? Toss it aside. But blathering visitors can't be got rid of without further ado.'

The room has begun to smell of dust. The hail rattles at the window again.

'I think you were dissatisfied. Dissatisfied with life.'

'Who isn't? I can repeat what Slauerhoff said, "I imagined life would be different to this ..." But that still doesn't provide an answer to the why. I felt happy at Leiden, and at Macassar too. And yet I read kilometres of books in Leiden and Macassar. Disappointment came in Portland. I was working on my thesis on "Islam on Celebes" in Macassar. The Japs burnt all my notes. Thousands of filing cards ... years of work. Before the war I thought I would end up at some kind of institute in the Indies. It became the manse at Portland. At the beginning I quite liked it, I grew up in Rotterdam, didn't know the countryside of Holland, neither did your mother, we often said "Chekhov" to each other. Darn it, yes, it was a completely different world, Olga feasted her eyes on it, she loved it, suddenly being the wife of a village notable. But after a year or so had passed I knew all the stories backwards and Olga said, "Just like Chekhov's, they get boring in the long run." '

He stubs out his cigarette. What he is telling is not new to me. Only, he has never told it so succinctly.

'We should have moved, but you children were at the Lyceum and Olga was tired of moving house. She was three when she began, from Petersburg to Berlin, and she changed cities thirty-seven times after that. In the early 'sixties I received a call to the ministry of a church in Perth, Australia. Perth, well yes. I felt like going, but Olga said, "Not another language again, another climate, another house." Once alley cats have nestled in a spot of their own, they never want to leave it. And she was scared to death that you children would become alley cats. She was suspicious enough when you talked about the Indies so often and that Mikhael went looking for his grandfather's house in Leningrad . . .'

He did not find it. He picked up a stone on a derelict site. Once back home he gave it to Olga. He told her that he had found the stone in the garden behind her birthplace. She did not look pleased with it. She slipped it into her apron pocket and rushed off to the kitchen. But when she collapsed, dead, she had it in her hand. Mikhael and I had great difficulty in unfolding her hand. While we were prising her fingers loose, Mikhael told me it was just some old stone he had found somewhere. Grandfather's house had disappeared.

'*The Gift*.'
  'Take it.'
  '*Spring in Fialta*.'
  'Yes, yes.'
  '*Speak Memory*.'
  'A pearl.'
  '*War and Peace*.'
  'Well of course. And *Anna Karenina*. And *Crime and Punishment*. And *Resurrection*. And *Fathers and Sons*.'
  'Not too many, Pa.'
  'What?'
  'Not too many. Just one metre.'
  'But those are your mother's books.'

She read about a country she had hardly known. She brought it back with the help of Pushkin, Tolstoy, Dostoyevski, Gogol, Turgenev, Chekhov, Nabokov, Pasternak, Bjelyj. Piece by piece she mapped out the land of her birth. Father selected the books for her and underlined the passages she should not miss. I sometimes suspected him of projecting his love of Russian literature on her. Or was it that she, still, after so many years, was strange to him and he needed to find an explanation? 'Why,' I can hear him ask it still, 'why does she always want you to call her Olga, never mother?' It would remain a mystery to him. To me too for that matter. Rare were the moments Father permitted us a peep into his soul, and Olga practically never did. You could laugh with her, you could romp with her, but never did she become intimate.

Olga read the books in Dutch. She had forgotten just about all her Russian, though as her life drew to an end all sorts of childhood pet names began to re-emerge in her memory. She read the books five, six times. I was to do the same later on. My East Indies are drawn from books. We both created our native lands ourselves.

And Father?

Father had always disavowed his native land. He rarely read books by Dutch novelists. If they had not been to the Indies, they were good for nothing. He dismissed the literature of his own nation as 'black prose'. On St Nicholas' Eve one year I gave him Wolkers' *Return to Oegstgeest*. His left eyelid quivered with disappointment. Wolkers, that was Holland, that was what he saw around him every day. Olga saved the evening by playing Tchaikovsky's *In the Troika*.

'Gogol.'

A deep sigh.

'Never understood him. A beautiful writer, but I could never sit face to face with him. For a brief moment, sometimes, but then he got up and rushed outside. The man is matchless. Possessed. When I read Gogol, Russia constantly eludes my grasp. Endless plains, somewhere in the east, peopled by invisible devils.'

His right hand clamps the arm of the chair.

'One evening Olga and I were out walking on the dyke. It was a chilly evening. She turned the collar of her coat up and pointed at the polders. She didn't utter a word but I knew what she meant. She was wondering what she was doing here really. She felt lost. Can you follow me?'

He does not wait for an answer. Seemingly without effort he gets up. He stumbles to the toilet, more hastily than his limbs wish.

He withdrew, to the end of the passage. She took her bicycle and rode to the river. I cycled after her. I found her near the old ferryman's house. She was leaning against the wall sunk deep in her raincoat and with her left leg crossed over her right. I kept an eye on her from behind a bush. The wind made me catch my breath. She had told me so often about her uncle who had thrown himself in the Neva ... or had that tale come from a book too? Her upper teeth bit into her underlip as it curled inward. She gazed toward the bend in the Meuse. It was an abrupt bend. Ships appeared. They slid without warning into sight from behind the willows. Only then did you hear the stamping of the engines. Their bows towered up high above the polders. Once they had completed the graceful sweep round the outside of the bend they came straight at you. Small tankers and coasters ... to Olga they were probably mail packets, black like the ships of the KPM. I saw her come to her feet as a ship appeared on the horizon. But once the coaster was close she shut her eyes.

Remembering and forgetting come from a common spring.

'What must we do with these Gogols?' I ask once he is sitting opposite me again.

'Oh, give them to Mikhael. Or to Pieter.'

The clock in the sitting-room strikes eleven times. He yawns, I skip three shelves.

'A couple more books, there, in the corner of the bookcase.'

Left. I only need to stretch out my hand.

'Heinrich Mann. Thomas Mann, Kurt Tucholsky.'

One by one I take the yellowing copies from the shelf.

'On May 5th 1933 I travelled to Berlin.'

I want to interrupt but realize it may well be the last time he tells me of his German adventure.

'Germany to my generation was what America is to your generation. I spoke fluent German, corresponded with a Prussian student of theology who, just like me, was interested in Islam. We had met at a congress in Brussels . . .'

He swallows a couple of times. There are deep shadows under his eyes.

'Am I boring you?'

'No.'

Colour comes into his cheeks, betraying the tale's end.

'He invited me for a visit in the spring of 1933.'

Silence.

'And then?'

'He had booked a room for me at a hotel off Unter den Linden, not far from the university. We ate every evening in town. But he didn't want to go outside on the evening of the tenth of May. He behaved rather nervously, said there were all kinds of rumours going round town. I was a bad newspaper reader, politics didn't interest me . . . I read books. Yes, in those days I led a cloistered life. I ate that evening at the hotel. I can see myself sitting there, in the bare dining-room, a book next to my plate. Naïve, just a boy of course, but that's easily said with hindsight . . . I went up to my room about nine. I lit a cigarette and went on reading. The room soon filled with smoke, so I pulled the sash up a little. It was getting on for ten when I heard an incredible hubbub in the distance. I put a scarf on and walked outside. The noise drew me to Kaiser-Franz-Josef Platz, the square in front of the Opera. The noise grew louder. Thousands of spectators. Brownshirts, but dolls from the bars too, giggling excitedly. Bands played marching songs. People sang, shouted. I almost joined in, there was something about the spectacle. An atmosphere of 'the end is nigh'. A collective delirium. I saw hundreds of banners in the glare of the searchlights. Torches were thrown on to the paving of the square and blazed fiercely. Waves of an inexplicable sort of joy passed through me. I struggled to get through the crowds. I could hardly manage it. Half an hour later I was at the front of the crowd. Then I saw what was being burnt. Books! Books by Heinrich Mann, Tucholsky – their names were being called out. How they brayed! It was opera of the worst kind. I was deeply ashamed. Later on in the evening Goebbels gave a speech there. But I was back in the hotel by then. I left next morning. Red-faced.'

His eyes screw tight.

'Two months later I was in Switzerland for a short holiday. While there I bought everything by Heinrich Mann, Thomas Mann and Kurt Tucholsky. I unpacked them in the hotel lounge. It was a posh hotel where your grandparents often stayed, with or without their children. It was my second home. I ordered tea, leafed through the books, keen as ever. A young lady came and sat opposite me. With a self-assured gesture, she reached for one of the books, looked in it and said, "So you are reading them too, the works they have banned in Germany." The waiter laid two cups on the table. "Yes," I said, "yes . . . yes." I told her what I had seen on the square in front of the Opera in Berlin. She talked about her years in Germany. Her voice sang. I asked her her name. She gazed at me a while, then got up hesitatingly, offered me her hand and said, "Olga." She coloured and I saw the freckles on her nose. That same evening I lent her *The Magic Mountain*. That's how it began . . .'

He takes one more look at the yellowing bindings. Then he says, 'Away with them.' His head shakes angrily. He grips his stick and pulls himself up out of the chair. Waddling like a goose he makes his way to the sitting-room, his whole body trembling. I remain in the study. Laid on the desk in front of Olga's photograph are about fifty books. One by one I lay them in the boxes the removal men had brought the previous day. They will be carried into the old people's home the next day. I tape down the lids and light a cigarette. What is a library? A logbook of imaginary voyages. The sediment of a lifetime.

I switch off the light and walk to the sitting-room. He is sitting there slumped on the sofa. The glass in his right hand is shaking.

'I have feared this moment for years,' he says. 'It seemed to me it would be worse than dying. I can't stop thinking of that old farmer. I sat at his deathbed. He had spent the whole day ranting and raving. But then when the moment came, he smiled peacefully. Before his last breath, he wanted to say one more thing. I held my ear close to his mouth and heard him say somewhere in the back of his throat, "It wasn't so bad." '

Acquiescence? I had expected something else. Something savage.

Two days later. He is on the phone. His voice sounds as if it is being chased by a snowstorm.

'They've nicked my new coat. You know, that one I bought last month at Van Kranenburg's. A brand-new coat. I suspect the removal men. There was one kid with them ... long, greasy hair ... you know the type ... can't be trusted. He was nosing around the whole house, sniffing at the coffee-pot, the cups, the glasses. I kept an eye on him ... though I couldn't follow his fingers all the time. He was everywhere and nowhere at the same time ... in the hall, in the passage, in the sitting-room, in the kitchen. And now I've lost my coat.'

'Come, come.' I had never heard him talk so fast. 'Old

Bram did the moving, didn't he? Old Bram is straight as a die.'

'Times change my boy. A new coat. Quality material. Pure wool. Fitted me like a glove. Van Kranenburg took the sleeves in a little and made the shoulders narrower. Put an extra button on so it wouldn't blow open. It was a beauty. Bought it from my last savings.'

'Savings?'

He had never saved his whole life through. Never. If he had a hundred guilders to spare he caught the bus to Blok's bookshop in Rotterdam.

'Savings, yes. New coat. Nicked. Last savings. Does the story mean nothing to you?'

'Don't shout like that.'

'Does the story mean nothing to you?'

God. Why hadn't I thought of it immediately?

'Gogol.'

'Exactly. Gogol. I've been looking for my coat the whole day. Opened every suitcase and found nothing. Looked under the bed ... in the hall. Nowhere. It gave me the palpitations. Hallucinations. And then I suddenly remembered that story by Gogol. *The Overcoat.* I must reread it, I thought to myself. The devil take it, I can't find the book anywhere.'

'You didn't want to take it with you.'

'What? Nonsense! You're lying. I can tell from your voice you're lying. Not take it with me! The very idea. Me not take Gogol. Where is it? I want to have it.'

'Mikhael took it.'

'That's just fine. Mikhael? He's at a congress in London.'

'So you'll have to wait. He'll be back tomorrow. Or the day after.'

'The day after? Damn it, I'm not going to go waiting for my coat for two days. I want to read it now. Now! It's in volume two of the *Collected Works.* Do you happen to have that in your bookcase?'

'It just so happens that I do have that in my bookcase.'

'Couldn't you bring it?'

'Father ... it's two hours' drive to Portland and there's snow in the air.'

'Oh come on. Please. I ask you. I beg of you.'

'Blast it Pa, it's two hours there and two hours back. That's four hours.'

'I know, I'm just an old neurotic, but I've cured myself of being ashamed of it. Every man has his weaknesses.'

'All very well and good ... but I've got my work ... I haven't done a thing for the past four weeks.'

'Work. Work. Don't let them misuse you. Where are the standards of yesteryear? Your old father ... he'll be dead in a couple of weeks. I can feel it in my feet, they've gone completely cold already, the cold is creeping slowly upwards, my knees are beginning to shiver already ... and if only I could pull that coat over them ... but no coat, coat's gone, stolen by a guttersnipe.'

'Whoa, whoa ... you've had too much to drink. I can tell by your voice.'

He hawks. A gob on the receiver. A curse. A hollow coughing. I can hear death in his throat.

I drive into Portland two hours later. The heat of the old people's home hits me in the entrance hall. I step inside the tiny room. He holds the coat, retrieved, in his hands, and I too am holding one, the other *Overcoat*.

Simon Burt

HEAD SMASHED IN
BUFFALO JUMP

I went to the prairies in the summer of 1989 – the English
summer, a few days before my birthday on 23 June. In my
hosts' garden in Canada the spring flowers were just fading
– and no one would believe that I wanted to see them.
Everyone said, when I got to Calgary, Alberta, where the
Great Plains begin to buckle into foothills before the
sudden wall of the Rockies, that I was mad to want to see
them. Nothing, they said. Go to the prairies and all you
will see is nothing. Mile after mile of nothing but prairie.
Horizon to horizon nothing but prairie. You should go to
the mountains. You'll love the mountains. I went to the
mountains. And they were right. The mountains were very
beautiful. I loved the mountains. I spent a week in the
mountains and it was everything and more than you would
expect the mountains to be. And after a week I went down
on to the plains, and they were right again. Nothing. All I
could see was nothing. Mile after mile, horizon to horizon
of nothing but prairie. It was wonderful. The sky. I'll start
with the sky. The English sky is low, two-dimensional. At
its best an intimate azure canopy. A majestical roof, but
still a roof. At its worst, as it is today – early June. In
gardens in Calgary spring flowers are coming into bud – a
stifling grey blanket, weeping and seeping a matter of
feet above the rooftops. In London at night the streetlamps
absorb the stars. The sky over the Great Plains has depth.
Events take place within it. The cloudscape is not a canvas.

It is a towering, many-layered dimension. All my life I have been afraid of flying. Aerodynamics have never convinced me. A plane in the air is like walking on water, something accomplishable only by faith, and I have no faith. A journey for me is a little death. I never expect anything to be the same after as before it. Each leg of the journey is a gamble with death, and I don't expect to win. If the journey is by air I regard myself as being *in extremis* throughout. Whenever I fly anywhere my visit is haunted by the spectre of the flight back. But a plane in the sky over the prairies looks as if it belongs there. For the first time I could look at a plane and feel that it was flying in the sky. Not across it. Not through it. A dolphin in water. For the first time the spectre took a step or two back, and I could begin to entertain the idea of flying home unafraid of the journey.

My mother died on April Fool's Day, 1984. It was a Sunday, and my mother always got up early on Sundays to go to eight o'clock Mass. She had been complaining for some weeks of a headache, and she was being treated by the doctor for something. I forget what. Something minor certainly. Call it flu. A week or so previously my brother Andrew had organized a trip to the theatre. My brother and I live on opposite sides of London, and my mother lived in Wiltshire. For someone like my mother a far greater spiritual distance than an actual one. My mother did not like to travel. My mother lived virtually her whole life within a ten mile radius of where she was born. She visited me twice. Once with my father when I lived in Edinburgh. Once alone, after my father's death, when I lived in Notting Hill. For her to come up to town for a play was an enormous event. She didn't come. My brother met me at the theatre and told me she had called him. She didn't feel up to it. A dreadful headache. A headache that wouldn't go away. Over the next few weeks we spoke once on the phone, and

I sent her a card. We spoke about nothing much. We were not a family for talking about anything more than nothing much. This and that. She told me what she had been doing. A visit here. A meal there. After my father's death she had bought a café in Warminster, and now she ran it with her second husband. We talked about her second husband. He greatly resented, she said, the fact that the local council would only collect the café's waste if it was left out in a certain sort of plastic bag, this plastic bag costing a few pence more than the usual domestic bag, and obtainable only from the local council. So he would pack the waste into the usual domestic bags, and have it taxied through the town to my mother's house and leave it there for the domestic binmen who were less picky about their bags. That was Brian all over. We giggled about that. We talked about how her head still ached. The card was for Mother's Day. Lots of Love. The usual shorthand. On the Saturday night, my sister-in-law Celia told me, my brother Matthew's wife, she went to my mother's house to collect her daughter who had spent the day there. Now, all my brothers have children. Then Rosie was her only grandchild. My mother was always surrounded by men. She was the only daughter in a family of seven children. Her mother died in 1955. Her four children were all sons. She had ached for a daughter. And finally she had a granddaughter, and she loved her. She loved her for three years with the stored-up love of sixty. And when Celia arrived that evening, at first she found the house empty but for the sound of laughter. Gales and squeals of laughter. She followed the laughter to its source, and found my mother's bottom sticking out from behind a sofa where, with a vivid smile – my mother's smile was huge – and a radiant headache, she was playing chase with Rosie. The next morning, up early to go to Mass, she bent down to pull on her tights, something went in her brain, and she died.

*

We came to the buffalo jump in the late afternoon. We had driven all day. We came down out of the mountains at dawn and spent ten hours on the road, watching the landscape change. The mountains gave way to bush. Lake and pine gave way to scrub and pine. Muskeg and slough and water in the tyre tracks beside the highway reflecting hours of pine. Then, in the roadside diners, farmers in baseball caps complaining of rain gave way to ranchers in cowboy hats complaining of drought. My mother and father were farmers and the children of farmers. Among farmers complaint is endemic. It is a prophylactic, a bulwark against disaster. My mother loathed it. It roused her to panic and futile rage. But she was farmer enough to know that if it stopped then the very thing you were complaining about would happen. If it didn't start again, the dam would burst and you would be engulfed. We skirted Edmonton and turned south. Out on to the prairie now. Yellow flatland, arrow-straight road from sky to sky, donkey jacks pumping gas from under the corn. We stopped for lunch in Stettler. Mennonites in the diner complaining of storms. Barely a week without a storm. There would be a storm that evening, you'll see. Gonna be a big one. Walking through the town after lunch we found a bookstore and read the titles in the window: *Parenting Isn't For Cowards*, *Men Have Feelings Too*, *What Kids Most Need In A Dad*, *Bringing Up Children In A Negative World*. We passed through Brooks. Cattle lots and grain silos and a museum full of sixty years of farm implements. The old schoolhouse, wood, with a roof-high stove, and framed on the wall the reports of long-dead children. Sophie Not-So-Lazy, a good year's work. Jackson Two Bears, could do better. We detoured to take a look at Newell Lake. Brooks depends for its existence on irrigation. Without piped water it wouldn't be there. Without piped water Newell Lake wouldn't be there. Nothing but bald prairie would be there. I loved Newell Lake. An artificial inland sea. On the artificial beach, wind-break trees and beach huts, radios and people struggling with deck chairs. Boats and windsurfers way out on the lake. I saw my first pelican. I walked out on to an artificial spit of boulders projecting into the lake, listened to the waves, and thought that when I came to die, here would be a good place. For as long as I can remember I have been obsessed with death. Almost daily the thought of it stops me in my tracks. I try to imagine it. Wherever I go I wonder, could I do it here? What would it be like if I did it here? One of my first memories is of my father sitting on the edge of my bed listening to me tell him that if I felt myself dying in my sleep I would wake myself up and prevent it. For the first time, on Newell Lake, I could think of dying as something natural. Something I could reconcile myself to doing. Another prairie first, I thought as we drove south. Our next stop was in the badlands at Drumheller, a rift in the plain, brimful of unimaginable heat. Coulees and hoodoos and dinosaur skeletons in the folds of the rock. We circled Lethbridge and dropped down to Writing On Stone on the Montana border, where prehistoric generations of Indians had carved pictures of themselves on the coulee wall, most of them on foot, no horses on the prairies then, and we were told to walk warily, for fear of rattlesnakes. And then we headed north again for the buffalo jump.

Unfortunately, cruelly perhaps, although my mother died on that Sunday morning, her body lingered for some days afterwards, until early on the Thursday morning in fact, with all the ordeal of hope and hope abandoned that such a vigil entails. Cruelly, because it was terrible to watch her insensible body drag on in a travesty of life while gradually, gradually, it was borne in on us that life itself was not going to return, that she was not going suddenly to stretch and roll and wake up, and we were not going to get to say all those things we were standing round the bed planning to say and knowing that we wouldn't say them if she did. Perhaps, because it gave us a space, a hiatus, in which to get used to the idea of her absence. I don't know when it happened, or which of us was the first to say it, but imperceptibly in our endless conversations over the next days we moved, my brothers and I, from saying 'If she dies' to 'When she dies'. And perhaps that's cruel, perhaps it's not. I don't know. The life I was living then was an odd one. Blurred. My first book had just been published, and my mother, though she knew me well enough not actually to read it, had read all the reviews, and treasured them. I had sort of slipped back into that highly-polished-address book way of life – dancing with boys who'd danced with girls who'd danced with the Prince of Wales – that I hadn't known since the late sixties. I detested my job. For no reason really, I see now, other than that I had been doing it too long. No one should do anything for longer than ten years. And I knew I was dying. I was suffering from AIDS hysteria, a condition separate and different from the syndrome itself but in its own way very unpleasant. You know you are going to die. You wake up, you sleep – if you sleep. Sleep is the brother of death. You do not welcome it – you spend your day in this knowledge. It does not concentrate the mind wonderfully. It is beyond reason. It laughs at reassurance. I kept my skin covered at all times. I couldn't bear to see it. My journey home from work took me along the tube line from Moorgate to Ladbroke Grove. The line from Kings Cross to Paddington is underground. I counted the minutes till it was over. After Paddington the line is overground except for a dip outside Westbourne Park. This dip, fifteen seconds out of the light at most, was almost more than I could bear. For a year after my mother's death this condition rose and rose to fever pitch and beyond. I have no idea how I got through it. No memory of getting through it. I remember only that I had a dream and it was over. I dreamed I met a pack of dogs, ravening, slavering dogs, and I whipped my way past and through them, and when I woke up I no longer knew that I was going to die. Then, though, I knew it. And my sister-in-law called me in the morning. Midmorningish, and I was laying the table, knowing it. I had guests coming for tea that afternoon and I like to have all the preparations for that sort of thing out of the way well in advance. I like the room cleaned and swept, the table laid, the kitchen stripped for action, and then to spend an hour or two reading before it's time to cook. And Celia called to say that my mother had been taken ill and was in hospital in Bath. She was going to take a few things over in a case. I went back to laying the table. A couple of hours later Celia called again. Things were not looking so good. Maybe I had better come down. My brother Andrew and I travelled down together. We met at Paddington where there was a message for us from my brother's wife. My mother had been moved from Bath to Frenchay Hospital outside Bristol, the best hospital in the west of England, apparently, for whatever it was was wrong with her. At this stage we didn't know. My brothers Matthew and Mark would meet us at Bath station. On the way down we talked. This is beginning to look serious, we said. The only other thing I can remember our talking about was hairlines. The hair gene in our family, Andrew said, seems to get less and less tough as it goes down from brother to brother. My youngest brother, Mark, is twelve years younger than me. At that time he was twenty-five and already bald. I remember thinking that Andrew was being none too observant, as my own hairline was receding, only too obviously to me, into great bays above my forehead. I remember, too, remembering how, when my father died in 1972, Andrew had been there, and when I arrived from Edinburgh, I found the words *And Death Shall Have No Dominion* written over and over on the telephone directory. How it was Andrew, too, who had taken my father's beloved corgi, Josephine, on her final journey to the vet a couple of years later, and how Josephine, so old now and pain-filled and prone to convulsions, perked up when she got to the vet's, and went grinning, ears pricked and tail wagging to her long home. Matthew and Mark met us at Bath. My mother was settled into the hospital and sleeping. There was no point in going there now. We would drive back to Matthew's house and spend the night there, and go across to Frenchay the next morning. When we got to Mark's car we found that we were locked out, the keys nowhere to be found. Panic and dither. Cursing and slapping of pockets. In the end we decided to go back into the station and call a garage from there. More cursing, and Mark found the keys where he had left them, in the lock. I remembered, as we drove to Matthew's house, how, when my father died, I flew down from Scotland, and in the evening we opened a bottle of champagne to dispel the gloom, and the five of us sat long over dinner, yelling with laughter.

A buffalo jump is a killing ground. Numberless buffalo have died here. In the centuries before the horse arrived on the plains and revolutionized their methods, the Indians hunted herd after herd and killed them here. The ingredients of the kill were simple, if not so easy to come by. You needed, apart from your own stealth and cunning, a cliff, a rift in the prairie, a long slow slope up to the lip of the cliff, and a herd of buffalo correctly positioned so that they could be panicked into charging, deceived into charging over it. The correct positioning of the buffalo alone took days of gentle herding. The migrations of both Indian and buffalo were not predictable events. They did not coincide at the buffalo jump regularly. Sometimes years passed without their coinciding. But when they did coincide it was always fatal for the buffalo. It had to be fatal for the buffalo. It was essential that not one buffalo escape. Partly, one suspects, as a display of logistical prowess. Partly because there could be no witnesses. Not even buffalo are that dumb. A survivor would spread the word across the plains that here were deception and death, and the jump would be avoided. Cliffs on the prairie are not many. They must be treasured. The provinical government has turned the site into a visitors' centre. The Peigan Indians run it, calling it, with typical terse accuracy, Head Smashed In Buffalo Jump. The centre is a beautiful place, built into the face of the cliff, symbiotically at home there. You enter at the bottom, and climb up through halls filled with light and prehistory, much like the plains themselves, and the mysteries and rituals of the hunt are explained to you: the week-long herding, the identification of the hunter with his prey, the better to understand him, the better to deceive him. The lead hunter, with the help of disguise and ecstasy, becomes a buffalo, and the herd follows him. The moment when the disguise is thrown off, when leader becomes hunter, and the bewildered herd charges. The long run up the gentle, imperceptible, treacherous slope till the ground vanishes. You come out at the top, on the lip of the cliff. Not at the actual jump. The jump itself is a hundred yards or so away to the left. Walking along the cliff to the jump, looking out over a skywide sea of grass, you can see how the buffalo were deceived.

The next morning we discovered the depth of our illusion. We were still at the few-things-in-a-bag stage. We arrived at the hospital with chocolates and magazines, expecting I don't know what, my mother asleep possibly, her head in bandages, concussion and a darkened room maybe. What we found was a living corpse. And here I was going to describe my mother, to try to give you some idea of what it was whose loss we were so suddenly presented with, but I find I can't. Long ago, when I was nineteen, twenty, I wrote a story about her and showed it to a friend. We were not getting on well at the time. We often didn't get on well. We were very similar, and she could be a fiend. And the story reflected this. My friend read it, and congratulated me wryly on my cruelly accurate portrait, of his mother. We do not know what we write. People read what they want to read. It matters little to you that my mother was a tiny, explosive woman, with a long history of nervous illnesses, skin complaints, stomach complaints, you name it, who passed on to me her teeth and her feet, her anger, her dissatisfaction, her panic. My God but my mother could panic. I have seen her world fall apart because the salt was not in its accustomed place on the breakfast trolley. I know too, because she passed that on to me too, how alone she felt in her panic, and my sympathy takes, as hers did, the form of anger. She also gave me her tendency to dwell on horrors, her predilection for the worst-case-scenario, her conviction that, if it's good, it won't last, if it's bad, it's always going to be like this, and her hatred of an untidy room. And, on the day she died, on the very day her body died, each of her skin conditions. Her courage, alas, her gift for love, her energy went elsewhere. But none of this means much to you. The word Mother has deafened you to it. I say My Mother and the image is so potent that all you see is yours. Mothers have that power. Over the next three days we drove to the hospital daily. Halfway through the forty-mile journey there was a toll bridge, with a toll of sixpence. Twice a day we handed over our two and a half coppers. On the way home on the second day my brother Andrew hesitated on the access road to the M4, and a policeman pulled us over. What's all this then? Are you lost? Yes, officer, we are lost. There was nothing for us to do. My mother's body was in a coma. A condition which bears no resemblance, in its early stages at least, to the simulacrum of peaceful sleep that is its popular image. My mother's body was hideously mobile. It blinked. It yawned. It stared. Its hands, one of its hands, scrabbled at the sheets, the air. It twitched. It started up. It sweated. Nurses came with fans to cool it down. They spoke to it. Jean, they said, lifting her up and flipping her over, we're just going to turn you. Jean, they said, we're just going to flash this light in your eyes, scrape this point across your feet. We're just going to change this bag, this tube. There, Jean, they said, stroking her hair. There, Jean. It's hot, isn't it, poor Jean. My mother's name, I was going to say, but the words wouldn't come out, for those that love her, is Jeannie. Sometimes, I would have held her hand, but the only one available was packed with nozzles and drips. Her mouth was crammed with plastic. Why, I thought savagely, are the supreme moments of our life condemned to be lived in the bleakest ugliness? The hospital was a row of huts. It put me in mind of nothing so much as Sutton Veny army camp, which Sykes Chicks had taken over and turned into a chicken factory, except that chicken factories don't smell pervasively of mashed potato. My mother's room was a dismal green, its window overlooking the next-door hut, the only concession to the non-functional a framed cardboard print of a wide-eyed puppy, and in a mug the orchid my mother's husband had bought to put by her pillow. The room where a harassed houseman, on the run between jobs, told us that she was going to die, although the word was never used. Your mother, he said, has had a multiple cerebral haemorrhage, there is a huge clot in her brain, at best we shall have to operate to remove it, and the operation may damage the brain, the room was poky and shabby and brown, packed to bursting with a random collection of scarred armchairs, the smell of Jeyes Fluid fighting with the smell of dust from the grey net curtains. We spent a lot of time in the canteen. The smell in my mother's room drove us out. No amount of devotion could withstand it. Back at home we called the hospital twice a day, morning and evening. I now know what 'No change' means. It means, 'Your mother is sinking inexorably towards death.' The word was never mentioned. When they called us on the Thursday morning they told us she was gone. My mother was gone. And, for me at least, another ordeal began. I was possessed by the need to say goodbye. I wanted a second or two alone with my mother's coffin. I didn't want to see the body. When my father died – a heart attack. He was fifty-nine. He bent down to pull on his socks, something went in his heart, and he died. I leave you to imagine with what caution I pull on my socks – my brother Matthew and I went to see the body. A mistake. For years my memory of my father was overlaid by this vision of a waxen, pallid thing with an Archaic Smile. A couple of seconds alone with her coffin. I don't know if you've ever tried, but it is impossible to spend a couple of seconds alone with a coffin. They won't let you do it. There are things to do and people to see. There is the hospital, the funeral, the reception. There are doctors, nurses, undertakers, solicitors, bank managers, accountants, registrars, priests, well-wishers, and before you know it, there she is underground. After the reception I went down to the cemetery and touched the grave, where she lies by my father and my uncle Philip. Jeannie Whitworth. Her grave says something else. They wouldn't let us put her name on her grave, so I'll say it here. Jeannie Whitworth.

The prairie is vast. If a storm comes to the prairie, as it came that day, the storm the Mennonite in Stettler had promised would be a big one, you can see it approaching. You can see it hurtle towards you with what seems like a stately slowness, so great is the distance. The greens and browns darken. The sky is dashed with purple and gold, black and cerulean. Bolts of lightning strike nearer and nearer across the plain, and you are in sunlight. In the sky, the prairie sky, which has depth, you can see above the storm. Even when the storm is on you, you can see out past its edges.

*

Of all the things the dead leave behind them the most terrible is their silence. There was a mystery about my mother's death, a minor mystery that the years of silence made grow and grow because it could only remain a mystery. When she had her stroke she was holding something. As she had her stroke her hand, her left hand clenched around something, and remained clenched, and resisted all attempts to unclench it. Throughout the time in hospital the nurses tried desultorily to unclench it. It was not a priority. We speculated about it, but none of us could bring ourselves to try and unclench it. When the body died they tried again to open it, but it would not open. Whatever it was my mother held on to so tightly went with her to her grave. It became a problem for me. I could not stop thinking about it. I worried about it. I never pass up an opportunity to worry. I have it from my mother. The problem grew and grew in my mind until it seemed that I would always think about it. It became, like a persistent tinnitus, the background to everything I thought. I could not guess what the object was. I began by thinking that it had to be something very precious to her for her to hang on to it so steadfastly, and I went through her treasures. They were not many. Her jewels, which went to Rosie. A few pieces of silver which came to her from her mother and which she had salvaged from the wreck when my father's house and land were sold. A pile of letters of condolence for my father. A folder of news clippings from when her horse won the Cheltenham Gold Cup. Her picture from the *Tatler*. A school photograph of a group of girls in gymslips, my mother instantly recognizable by her smile. An envelope full of her children's birth certificates, her family's death certificates, her marriage certificates, Josephine's pedigree. A bundle of letters from her children away at school. A letter from me saying I was on her side about her second marriage. The last letter from her mother saying that they had been to Mrs Robertson's party but she had only been able to drink a spoonful of sherry, that she hadn't been feeling a hundred per cent for the last day or so, but don't tell Pops, he worries. Clippings of her children's hair. Most poignant of all, a florist's label from the bunch of flowers they put on my elder brother's grave when he died, aged one, a month or two before I was born, reading, in my father's elegant copperplate, *Just for a little while Goodbye*. They were not many, and they were all there. I ended up thinking that it had to be something fairly insignificant. Something minimal snatched when the stroke hit her. But I couldn't think what. A Kirby grip maybe. A clasp from her suspender belt. Until I realized that these were images from my childhood, when I would watch her dress, and she had used neither for decades. Of all the things the dead's silence takes with them, not the least terrible is one's own childhood. Great tracts of one's past disappear when there is no one to talk about them with, and they leave only a shadow. For years I nagged my uncles and aunts, my parents' surviving friends, for memories of that early time. But this was worse, because it was a mystery. It left no shadow. It plagued me for five years. Until, at the buffalo jump, it dissolved. On the lip of the cliff there was a plaque. The plaque said that, though the hunt was primarily the work of the men, the women had a part in it too. The men stalked the buffalo, herded them and drove them to their death. The women, at the bottom of the cliff, collected the innumerable bodies as they fell, and butchered them, skinned them and jointed them, did all the things that have to be done to turn death into food. Many women, the plaque said, were killed by the falling bodies. There is mental pain and there is physical, and little to be gained from comparing the two. I compared them then. I came to the conclusion that those people, and I have met many, who told me that mental pain is the worse know nothing of either. But that they did have one thing in common. If you have lived with physical pain, and it stops, for a long time the only sensation you can feel is lack of sensation. The same with mental pain. I stood on the lip of the cliff, looking from down at where the women and the buffalo had died, to out over the plain to the oncoming storm, and the mystery unravelled. Like a knot. You pick and pick until something gives and the knot disappears. So now. Suddenly, three thousand miles away, my mother's hand unclenched in her grave, and my brain sang so loud with the absence of mystery that I didn't even look to see what it was her hand had let fall. Afterwards it didn't matter. The storm came. The storm passed. We drove on, heading for Calgary and bed. Night fell, and as we drove, away from one river which empties into the Gulf of Mexico, towards another that empties into Hudson's Bay, under a sky half dark, half white with reflected light from the polar north, our radio tuned to a broadcast from Santa Fe, New Mexico, the roads became fuller and slower. The last part of the journey we spent behind a Silverado Suburban, a four wheel drive out of Camrose, registration number IAMLOST, and I thought, Can it be? How can it be? That these people, all these people, us, in all this splendour, are simply engaged in the quotidian business of going home.

A. S. Byatt

THE JULY GHOST

'I think I must move out of where I'm living,' he said. 'I have this problem with my landlady.'

He picked a long, bright hair off the back of her dress, so deftly that the act seemed simply considerate. He had been skilful at balancing glass, plate and cutlery, too. He had a look of dignified misery, like a dejected hawk. She was interested.

'What sort of problem? Amatory, financial, or domestic?'

'None of those, really. Well, not financial.'

He turned the hair on his finger, examining it intently, not meeting her eye.

'Not financial. Can you tell me? I might know somewhere you could stay. I know a lot of people.'

'You would.' He smiled shyly. 'It's not an easy problem to describe. There's just the two of us. I occupy the attics. Mostly.'

He came to a stop. He was obviously reserved and secretive. But he was telling her something. This is usually attractive.

'Mostly?' Encouraging him.

'Oh, it's not like *that*. Well, not . . . Shall we sit down?'

They moved across the party, which was a big party, on a hot day. He stopped and found a bottle and filled her glass. He had not needed to ask what she was drinking. They sat side by side on a sofa: he admired the brilliant poppies bold on her emerald dress, and her pretty sandals. She had come to London for the summer to work in the British Museum. She could really have managed with microfilm in Tucson for what little manuscript research was needed, but there was a dragging love affair to end. There is an age at which, however desperately happy one is in stolen moments, days, or weekends with one's married professor, one either prises him loose or cuts and runs. She had had a stab at both, and now considered she had successfully cut and run. So it was nice to be immediately appreciated. Problems are capable of solution. She said as much to him, turning her soft face to his ravaged one, swinging the long bright hair. It had begun a year ago, he told her in a rush, at another party actually; he had met this woman, the landlady in question, and had made, not immediately, a kind of *faux pas*, he now saw, and she had been very decent, all things considered, and so . . .

He had said, 'I think I must move out of where I'm living.' He had been quite wild, had nearly not come to the party, but could not go on drinking alone. The woman had considered him coolly and asked, 'Why?' One could not, he said, go on in a place where one had once been blissfully happy, and was now miserable, however convenient the place. Convenient, that was, for work, and friends, and things that seemed, as he mentioned them, ashy and insubstantial compared to the memory and the hope of opening the door and finding Anne outside it, laughing and breathless, waiting to be told what he had read, or thought, or eaten, or felt that day. Someone I loved left, he told the woman. Reticent on that occasion too, he bit back the flurry of sentences about the total unexpectedness of it, the arriving back and finding only an envelope on a clean table, and spaces in the bookshelves, the record stack, the kitchen cupboard. It must have been planned for weeks, she must have been thinking it out while he rolled on her, while she poured wine for him, while . . . No, no. Vituperation is undignified and in this case what he felt was lower and worse than rage: just pure, child-like loss. 'One ought not to mind places,' he said to the woman. 'But one does,' she had said. 'I know.'

She had suggested to him that he could come and be her lodger, then; she had, she said, a lot of spare space going to waste, and her husband wasn't there much. 'We've not had a lot to say to each other, lately.' He could be quite self-contained, there was a kitchen and a bathroom in the attics; she wouldn't bother him. There was a large garden. It was possibly this that decided him: it was very hot, central London, the time of year when a man feels he would give anything to live in a room opening on to grass and trees, not a high flat in a dusty street. And if Anne came back, the door would be locked and mortice-locked. He could stop thinking about Anne coming back. That was a decisive move: Anne thought he wasn't decisive. He would live without Anne.

For some weeks after he moved in he had seen very little of the woman. They met on the stairs, and once she came up, on a hot Sunday, to tell him he must feel free to use the garden. He had offered to do some weeding and mowing and she had accepted. That was the weekend her husband came back, driving furiously up to the front door, running in, and calling in the empty hall, 'Imogen, Imogen!' To which she had replied, uncharacteristically, by screaming hysterically. There was nothing in her husband, Noel's, appearance to warrant this reaction; their lodger, peering over the banister at the sound, had seen their upturned faces in the stairwell and watched hers settle into its usual prim and placid expression as he did so. Seeing Noel, a balding, fluffy-templed, stooping thirty-five or so, shabby corduroy suit, cotton polo neck, he realized he was now able to guess her age, as he had not been. She was a very neat woman, faded blonde, her hair in a knot on the back of her head, her legs long and slender, her eyes downcast. Mild was not quite the right word for her, though. She explained then that she had screamed because Noel had come home unexpectedly and startled her: she was sorry. It seemed a reasonable explanation. The extraordinary vehemence of the screaming was probably an echo in the stairwell. Noel seemed wholly downcast by it, all the same.

He had kept out of the way, that weekend, taking the stairs two at a time and lightly, feeling a little aggrieved, looking out of his kitchen window into the lovely, overgrown garden, that they were lurking indoors, wasting all the summer sun. At Sunday lunch-time he had heard the husband, Noel, shouting on the stairs.

'I can't go on, if you go on like that. I've done my best, I've tried to get through. Nothing will shift you, will it, you won't *try*, will you, you just go on and on. Well, I have my life to live, you can't throw a life away . . . can you?'

He had crept out again on to the dark upper landing and seen her standing, half-way down the stairs, quite still, watching Noel wave his arms and roar, or almost roar, with a look of impassive patience, as though this nuisance must pass off. Noel swallowed and gasped; he turned his face up to her and said plaintively,

'You do see I can't stand it? I'll be in touch, shall I? You must want . . . you must need . . . you must . . .'

She didn't speak.

'If you need anything, you know where to get me.'

'Yes.'

'Oh, well . . .' said Noel, and went to the door. She watched him, from the stairs, until it was shut, and then came up again, step by step, as though it was an effort, a little, and went on coming, past her bedroom, to his landing, to come in and ask him, entirely naturally, please to use the garden if he wanted to, and please not to mind marital rows. She was sure he understood . . . things were difficult . . . Noel wouldn't be back for some time. He was a journalist: his work took him away a lot. Just as well. She committed herself to that 'just as well'. She was a very economical speaker.

So he took to sitting in the garden. It was a lovely place: a huge, hidden, walled south London garden, with old fruit trees at the end, a wildly waving disorderly buddleia, curving beds full of old roses, and a lawn of overgrown, dense rye-grass. Over the wall at the foot was the Common, with a footpath running behind all the gardens. She came out to the shed and helped him to assemble and oil the lawnmower, standing on the little path under the apple branches while he cut an experimental serpentine across her hay. Over the wall came the high sound of children's voices, and the thunk and thud of a football. He asked her how to raise the blades: he was not mechanically minded.

'The children get quite noisy,' she said. 'And dogs. I hope they don't bother you. There aren't many safe places for children, round here.'

He replied truthfully that he never heard sounds that didn't concern him, when he was concentrating. When he'd got the lawn into shape, he was going to sit on it and do a lot of reading, try to get his mind in trim again, to write a paper on Hardy's poems, on their curiously archaic vocabulary.

'It isn't very far to the road on the other side, really,' she said. 'It just seems to be. The Common is an illusion of space, really. Just a spur of brambles and gorse-bushes and bits of football pitch between two fast four-laned main roads. I hate London commons.'

'There's a lovely smell, though, from the gorse and the wet grass. It's a pleasant illusion.'

'No illusions are pleasant,' she said, decisively, and went in. He wondered what she did with her time: apart from little shopping expeditions she seemed to be always in the house. He was sure that when he'd met her she'd been introduced as having some profession: vaguely literary, vaguely academic, like everyone he knew. Perhaps she wrote poetry in her north-facing living-room. He had no idea what it would be like. Women generally wrote emotional poetry, much nicer than men, as Kingsley Amis has stated, but she seemed, despite her placid stillness, too spare and too fierce – grim? – for that. He remembered the screaming. Perhaps she wrote Plath-like chants of violence. He didn't think that quite fitted the bill, either. Perhaps she was a freelance radio journalist. He didn't bother to ask anyone who might be a common acquaintance. During the whole year, he explained to the American at the party, he hadn't actually *discussed* her with anyone. Of course he wouldn't, she agreed vaguely and warmly. She knew he wouldn't. He didn't see why he shouldn't, in fact, but went on, for the time, with his narrative.

They had got to know each other a little better over the next few weeks, at least on the level of borrowing tea, or even sharing pots of it. The weather had got hotter. He had found an old-fashioned deck chair, with faded striped canvas, in the shed, and had brushed it over and brought it out on to his mown lawn, where he sat writing a little, reading a little, getting up and pulling up a tuft of couch grass. He had been wrong about the children not bothering him: there was a succession of incursions by all sizes of children looking for all sizes of balls, which bounced to his feet, or crashed in the shrubs, or vanished in the herbaceous border, black and white footballs, beach-balls with concentric circles of primary colours, acid yellow tennis balls. The children came over the wall: black faces, brown faces, floppy long hair, shaven heads, respectable dotted sun-hats and camouflaged cotton army hats from Milletts. They came over easily, as though they were used to it, sandals, training shoes, a few bare toes, grubby sunburned legs, cotton skirts, jeans, football shorts. Sometimes, perched on the top, they saw him and gestured at the balls; one or two asked permission. Sometimes he threw a ball back, but was apt to knock down a few knobby little unripe apples or pears. There was a gate in the wall, under the fringing trees, which he once tried to open, spending time on rusty bolts only to discover that the lock was new and secure, and the key not in it.

The boy sitting in the tree did not seem to be looking for a ball. He was in a fork of the tree nearest the gate, swinging his legs, doing something to a knot in a frayed end of rope that was attached to the branch he sat on. He wore blue jeans and training shoes, and a brilliant t-shirt, striped in the colours of the spectrum, arranged in the right order, which the man on the grass found visually pleasing. He had rather long blond hair, falling over his eyes, so that his face was obscured.

'Hey, you. Do you think you ought to be up there? It might not be safe.'

The boy looked up, grinned, and vanished monkey-like over the wall. He had a nice, frank grin, friendly, not cheeky.

He was there again, the next day, leaning back in the crook of the tree, arms crossed. He had on the same shirt and jeans. The man watched him, expecting him to move again, but he sat, immobile, smiling down pleasantly, and then staring up at the sky. The man read a little, looked up, saw him still there, and said,

'Have you lost anything?'

The child did not reply: after a moment he climbed down a little, swung along the branch hand over hand, dropped to the ground, raised an arm in salute, and was up over the usual route over the wall.

Two days later he was lying on his stomach on the edge of the lawn, out of the shade, this time in a white t-shirt with a pattern of blue ships and water-lines on it, his bare feet and legs stretched in the sun. He was chewing a grass stem, and studying the earth, as though watching for insects. The man said 'Hi, there,' and the boy looked up, met his look with intensely blue eyes under long lashes, smiled with the same complete warmth and openness, and returned his look to the earth.

He felt reluctant to inform on the boy, who seemed so harmless and considerate: but when he met him walking out of the kitchen door, spoke to him, and got no answer but the gentle smile before the boy ran off towards the wall, he wondered if he should speak to his landlady. So he asked her, did she mind the children coming in the garden. She said no, children must look for balls, that was part of being children. He persisted – they sat there, too, and he had met one coming out of the house. He hadn't seemed to be doing any harm, the boy, but you couldn't tell. He thought she should know.

He was probably a friend of her son's, she said. She looked at him kindly and explained. Her son had run off the Common with some other children, two years ago, in the summer, in July, and had been killed on the road. More or less instantly, she had added drily, as though calculating that just *enough* information would preclude the need for further questions. He said he was sorry, very sorry, feeling to blame, which was ridiculous, and a little injured, because he had not known about her son, and might inadvertently have made a fool of himself with some casual reference whose ignorance would be embarrassing.

What was the boy like, she said. The one in the house? 'I don't – talk to his friends. I find it painful. It could be Timmy, or Martin. They might have lost something, or want . . .'

He described the boy. Blond, about ten at a guess, he was not very good at children's ages, very blue eyes, slightly built, with a rainbow-striped t-shirt and blue jeans, mostly though not always – oh, and those football practice shoes, black and green. And the other t-shirt, with the ships and wavy lines. And an extraordinarily nice smile. A really *warm* smile. A nice-looking boy.

He was used to her being silent. But this silence went on and on and on. She was just staring into the garden. After a time, she said, in her precise conversational tone,

'The only thing I want, the only thing I want at all in this world, is to see that boy.'

She stared at the garden and he stared with her, until the grass began to dance with empty light, and the edges of the shrubbery wavered. For a brief moment he shared the strain of not seeing the boy. Then she gave a little sigh, sat down, neatly as always, and passed out at his feet.

After this she became, for her, voluble. He didn't move her after she fainted, but sat patiently by her, until she stirred and sat up; then he fetched her some water, and would have gone away, but she talked.

'I'm too rational to see ghosts, I'm not someone who would see anything there was to see, I don't believe in an after-life, I don't see how anyone can, I always found a kind of satisfaction for myself in the idea that one just came to an end, to a sliced-off stop. But that was myself; I didn't think *he* – not *he* – I thought ghosts were – what people *wanted* to see, or were afraid to see . . . and after he died, the best hope I had, it sounds silly, was that I would go mad enough so that instead of waiting every day for him to come home from school and rattle the letter-box I might actually have the illusion of seeing or hearing him come in. Because I can't stop my body and mind waiting, every day, every day, I can't let go. And his bedroom, sometimes at night I go in, I think I might just for a moment forget he *wasn't* in there sleeping, I think I would pay almost anything – anything at all – for a moment of seeing him like I used to. In his pyjamas, with his – his – his hair. . . ruffled, and, his . . . you said, his . . . that *smile*.

'When it happened, they got Noel, and Noel came in

and shouted my name, like he did the other day, that's why I screamed, because it – seemed the same – and then they said, he is dead, and I thought coolly, *is* dead, that will go on and on and on till the end of time, it's a continuous present tense, one thinks the most ridiculous things, there I was thinking about grammar, the verb to be, when it ends to be dead ... And then I came out into the garden, and I half saw, in my mind's eye, a kind of ghost of his face, just the eyes and hair, coming towards me – like every day waiting for him to come home, the way you think of your son, with such pleasure, when he's – not there – and I – I thought – no, I won't *see* him, because he is dead, and I won't dream about him because he is dead, I'll be rational and practical and continue to live because one must, and there was Noel ...

'I got it wrong, you see, I was so *sensible*, and then I was so shocked because I couldn't get to want anything – I couldn't *talk* to Noel – I – I – made Noel take away, destroy, all the photos, I – didn't dream, you can will not to dream, I didn't ... visit a grave, flowers, there isn't any point. I was so sensible. Only my body wouldn't stop waiting and all it wants is to – to see that boy. *That* boy. That boy you – saw.'

He did not say that he might have seen another boy, maybe even a boy who had been given the t-shirts and jeans afterwards. He did not say, though the idea crossed his mind, that maybe what he had seen was some kind of impression from her terrible desire to see a boy where nothing was. The boy had had nothing terrible, no aura of pain about him: he had been, his memory insisted, such a pleasant, courteous, self-contained boy, with his own purposes. And in fact the woman herself almost immediately raised the possibility that what he had seen was what she desired to see, a kind of mix-up of radio waves, like when you overheard police messages on the radio, or got BBC1 on a switch that said ITV. She was thinking fast, and went on almost immediately to say that perhaps his sense of loss, his loss of Anne, which was what had led her to feel she could bear his presence in her house, was what had brought them – dare she say – near enough, for their wavelengths to mingle, perhaps, had made him susceptible ... You mean, he had said, we are a kind of emotional vacuum, between us, that must be filled. Something like that, she had said, and had added, 'But I don't believe in ghosts.'

Anne, he thought, could not be a ghost, because she was elsewhere, with someone else, doing for someone else those little things she had done so gaily for him, tasty little suppers, bits of research, a sudden vase of unusual flowers, a new bold shirt, unlike his own cautious taste, but suiting him, suiting him. In a sense, Anne was worse lost because voluntarily absent, an absence that could not be loved because love was at an end, for Anne.

'I don't suppose you will, now,' the woman was saying. 'I think talking would probably stop any – mixing of messages, if that's what it is, don't you? But – if – *if* he comes again' – and here for the first time her eyes were full of tears – 'if – you must promise, you will *tell* me, you must promise.'

He had promised, easily enough, because he was fairly sure she was right, the boy would not be seen again. But the next day he was on the lawn, nearer than ever, sitting on the grass beside the deck chair, his arms clasping his bent, warm brown knees, the thick, pale hair glittering in the sun. He was wearing a football shirt, this time, Chelsea's colours. Sitting down in the deck chair, the man could have put out a hand and touched him, but did not: it was not, it seemed, a possible gesture to make. But the boy looked up and smiled, with a pleasant complicity, as though they now understood each other very well. The man tried speech: he said, 'It's nice to see you again,' and the boy nodded acknowledgement of this remark, without speaking himself. This was the beginning of communication between them, or what the man supposed to be communication. He did not think of fetching the woman. He became aware that he was in some strange way *enjoying the boy's company.* His pleasant stillness – and he sat there all morning, occasionally lying back on the grass, occasionally staring thoughtfully at the house – was calming and comfortable. The man did quite a lot of work – wrote about three reasonable pages on Hardy's original air-blue gown – and looked up now and then to make sure the boy was still there and happy.

He went to report to the woman – as he had after all promised to do – that evening. She had obviously been waiting and hoping – her unnatural calm had given way to agitated pacing, and her eyes were dark and deeper in. At this point in the story he found in himself a necessity to bowdlerize for the sympathetic American, as he had indeed already begun to do. He had mentioned only a child who had 'seemed like' the woman's lost son, and he now ceased to mention the child at all, as an actor in the story, with the result that what the American woman heard was a tale of how he, the man, had become increasingly involved in the woman's solitary grief, how their two losses had become a kind of *folie à deux* from which he could not extricate himself. What follows is not what he told the American girl, though it may be clear at which points the bowdlerized version coincided with what he really believed to have happened. There was a sense he could not at first analyse that it was improper to talk about the boy – not because he might not be believed; that did not come into it; but because something dreadful might happen.

'He sat on the lawn all morning. In a football shirt.'

'Chelsea?'

'Chelsea.'

'What did he do? Does he look happy? Did he speak?'
Her desire to know was terrible.

'He doesn't speak. He didn't move much. He seemed –
very calm. He stayed a long time.'

'This is terrible. This is ludicrous. There *is no boy*.'

'No. But I saw him.'

'Why you?'

'I don't know.' A pause. 'I do *like* him.'

'He is – was – a most likeable boy.'

Some days later he saw the boy running along the landing
in the evening, wearing what might have been pyjamas, in
peacock towelling, or might have been a track suit.
Pyjamas, the woman stated confidently, when he told her:
his new pyjamas. With white ribbed cuffs, weren't they?
and a white polo neck? He corroborated this, watching her
cry – she cried more easily now – finding her anxiety and
disturbance very hard to bear. But it never occurred to him
that it was possible to break his promise to tell her when
he saw the boy. That was another curious imperative from
some undefined authority.

They discussed clothes. If there were ghosts, how could
they appear in clothes long burned, or rotted, or worn away
by other people? You could imagine, they agreed, that
something of a person might linger – as the Tibetans and
others believe the soul lingers near the body before setting
out on its long journey. But clothes? And in this case so
many clothes? I must be seeing your memories, he told
her, and she nodded fiercely, compressing her lips, agreeing
that this was likely, adding, 'I am too rational to go mad, so
I seem to be putting it on you.'

He tried a joke. 'That isn't very kind to me, to infer that
madness comes more easily to me.'

'No, sensitivity. I am insensible. I was always a bit like
that, and this made it worse. I am the *last* person to see any
ghost that was trying to haunt me.'

'We agreed it was your memories I saw.'

'Yes. We agreed. That's rational. As rational as we can be, considering.'

All the same, the brilliance of the boy's blue regard, his gravely smiling salutation in the garden next morning, did not seem like anyone's tortured memories of earlier happiness. The man spoke to him directly then:

'Is there anything I can *do* for you? Anything you want? Can I help you?'

The boy seemed to puzzle about this for a while, inclining his head as though hearing was difficult. Then he nodded, quickly and perhaps urgently, turned, and ran into the house, looking back to make sure he was followed. The man entered the living-room through the french windows, behind the running boy, who stopped for a moment in the centre of the room, with the man blinking behind him at the sudden transition from sunlight to comparative dark. The woman was sitting in an armchair, looking at nothing there. She often sat like that. She looked up, across the boy, at the man, and the boy, his face for the first time anxious, met the man's eyes again, asking, before he went out into the house.

'What is it? What is it? Have you seen him again? Why are you . . .?'

'He came in here. He went – out through the door.'

'I didn't see him.'

'No.'

'Did he – oh, this is so *silly* – did he see me?'

He could not remember. He told the only truth he knew.

'He brought me in here.'

'Oh, what can I do, what am I going to *do*? If I killed myself – I have thought of that – but the idea that I should be with him is an illusion I . . . this silly situation is the nearest I shall ever get. To him. He was *in here with me*?'

'Yes.'

And she was crying again. Out in the garden he could see the boy, swinging agile on the apple branch.

He was not quite sure, looking back, when he had thought he had realized what the boy had wanted him to do. This was also, at the party, his worst piece of what he called bowdlerization, though in some sense it was clearly the opposite of bowdlerization. He told the American girl that he had come to the conclusion that it was the woman herself who had wanted it, though there was in fact, throughout, no sign of her wanting anything except to see the boy, as she said. The boy, bolder and more frequent, had appeared several nights running on the landing, wandering in and out of bathrooms and bedrooms, restlessly, a little agitated, questing almost, until it had 'come to' the man that what he required was to be re-engendered, for him, the man, to give to his mother another child, into which he could peacefully vanish. The idea was so clear that it was like another imperative, though he did not have the courage to ask the child to confirm it. Possibly this was out of delicacy – the child was too young to be talked to about sex. Possibly there were other reasons. Possibly he was mistaken: the situation was making him hysterical, he felt action of some kind was required and must be possible. He could not spend the rest of the summer, the rest of his life, describing non-existent t-shirts and blond smiles.

He could think of no sensible way of embarking on his venture, so in the end simply walked into her bedroom one night. She was lying there, reading; when she saw him her instinctive gesture was to hide, not her bare arms and throat, but her book. She seemed, in fact, quite unsurprised to see his pyjamaed figure, and, after she had recovered her coolness, brought out the book definitely and laid it on the bedspread.

'My new taste in illegitimate literature. I keep them in a box under the bed.'

Ena Twigg, Medium. The Infinite Hive. The Spirit World. Is There Life After Death?

'Pathetic,' she proffered.

He sat down delicately on the bed.

'Please, don't grieve so. Please, let yourself be comforted. Please . . .'

He put an arm round her. She shuddered. He pulled her closer. He asked why she had had only the one son, and she seemed to understand the purport of his question, for she tried, angular and chilly, to lean on him a little, she became apparently compliant. 'No real reason,' she assured him, no material reason. Just her husband's profession and lack of inclination: that covered it.

'Perhaps,' he suggested, 'if she would be comforted a little, perhaps she could hope, perhaps . . .'

For comfort then, she said, dolefully, and lay back, pushing Ena Twigg off the bed with one fierce gesture, then lying placidly. He got in beside her, put his arms round her, kissed her cold cheek, thought of Anne, of what was never to be again. Come on, he said to the woman, you must live, you must try to live, let us hold each other for comfort.

She hissed at him 'Don't *talk*' between clenched teeth, so he stroked her lightly, over her nightdress, breasts and buttocks and long stiff legs, composed like an effigy on an Elizabethan tomb. She allowed this, trembling slightly, and then trembling violently: he took this to be a sign of some mixture of pleasure and pain, of the return of life to stone. He put a hand between her legs and she moved them heavily apart; he heaved himself over her and pushed, unsuccessfully. She was contorted and locked tight: frigid, he thought grimly, was not the word. *Rigor mortis*, his mind said to him, before she began to scream.

He was ridiculously cross about this. He jumped away

and said quite rudely 'Shut up,' and then ungraciously 'I'm sorry.' She stopped screaming as suddenly as she had begun and made one of her painstaking economical explanations.

'Sex and death don't go. I can't afford to let go of my grip on myself. I hoped. What you hoped. It was a bad idea. I apologize.'

'Oh, never mind,' he said and rushed out again on to the landing, feeling foolish and almost in tears for warm, lovely Anne.

The child was on the landing, waiting. When the man saw him, he looked questioning, and then turned his face against the wall and leant there, rigid, his shoulders hunched, his hair hiding his expression. There was a similarity between woman and child. The man felt, for the first time, almost uncharitable towards the boy, and then felt something else.

'Look, I'm sorry. I tried. I did try. Please turn round.'

Uncompromising, rigid, clenched back view.

'Oh well,' said the man, and went into his bedroom.

So now, he said to the American woman at the party, I feel a fool, I feel embarrassed, I feel we are hurting, not helping each other, I feel it isn't a refuge. Of course you feel that, she said, of course you're right – it was temporarily necessary, it helped both of you, but you've got to live your life. Yes, he said, I've done my best, I've tried to get through, I have my life to live. Look, she said, I want to help, I really do, I have these wonderful friends I'm renting this flat from, why don't you come, just for a few days, just for a break, why don't you? They're real sympathetic people, you'd like them, I like them, you could get your emotions kind of straightened out. She'd probably be glad to see the back of you, she must feel as bad as you do, she's got to relate to her situation in her own way in the end. We all have.

He said he would think about it. He knew he had elected to tell the sympathetic American because he had sensed she would be – would offer – a way out. He had to get out. He took her home from the party and went back to his house and landlady without seeing her into her flat. They both knew that this reticence was promising – that he hadn't come in then, because he meant to come later. Her warmth and readiness were like sunshine, she was open. He did not know what to say to the woman.

In fact, she made it easy for him: she asked, briskly, if he now found it perhaps uncomfortable to stay, and he replied that he had felt he should move on, he was of so little use ... Very well, she had agreed, and had added crisply that it had to be better for everyone if 'all this' came to an end. He remembered the firmness with which she had told him that no illusions were pleasant. She was strong: too strong for her own good. It would take years to wear away that stony, closed, simply surviving insensibility. It was not his job. He would go. All the same, he felt bad.

He got out his suitcases and put some things in them. He went down to the garden, nervously, and put away the deck chair. The garden was empty. There were no voices over the wall. The silence was thick and deadening. He wondered, knowing he would not see the boy again, if anyone else would do so, or if, now he was gone, no one would describe a t-shirt, a sandal, a smile, seen, remembered, or desired. He went slowly up to his room again.

The boy was sitting on his suitcase, arms crossed, face frowning and serious. He held the man's look for a long moment, and then the man went and sat on his bed. The boy continued to sit. The man found himself speaking.

'You do see I have to go? I've tried to get through. I can't get through. I'm no use to you, am I?'

The boy remained immobile, his head on one side, considering. The man stood up and walked towards him.

'Please. Let me go. What are we, in this house? A man and a woman and a child, and none of us can get through. You can't want that?'

He went as close as he dared. He had, he thought, the intention of putting his hand on or through the child. But could not bring himself to feel there was no boy. So he stood, and repeated,

'I can't get through. Do you want me to stay?'

Upon which, as he stood helplessly there, the boy turned on him again the brilliant, open, confiding, beautiful desired smile.

Michael Carson

A WORTHWHILE UNDERTAKING

Friday, 14 September 1990

'What is the name of the deceased?'

'Martin Jon Drury.'

'And what kind of funeral did you have in mind for Martin?'

'Martin wanted the simplest possible funeral.'

The undertaker nods. 'That would be the Warwick.'

'How much would it cost?'

He runs a black Parker down a row of figures, writes on some scrap paper, '£826.00.'

This is more than I'd expected. But I am in no mood to argue. 'That's the basic funeral, is it?'

'That's it. Of course on top of that you'll have the cremation fees. Martin passed away at Mildmay, didn't he?'

I nod. For a split-second I do not believe it. This doubt about the fact of his dying has happened before. When the registrar was filling in the death certificate in her beautiful copperplate, I thought there must be some mistake. I wanted to stop her before she signed it and made us both look silly.

'And will Martin's remains be ready for collection from the Mildmay?'

'No. He's having a post-mortem. I don't know where.'

'We'll find out. There will also be doctors' fees. Two signatures are required. That costs £51.50. That isn't included in the price of the funeral.'

'So that will bring the cost to . . .'

'Just over £950. I'll give you a complete estimate before you leave. We can telephone the hospice to find out where Martin's remains are to be collected from. Did you have any preference for how you want the remains dressed?'

'After he died we put him in his dressing-gown. I think that will be fine.'

The undertaker nods and starts filling in a *Confirmation of Funeral Arrangements* form. While he's doing this he tells me that one has to consider the needs of The Deceased's friends and relatives. They often want a good send-off. It makes them feel better. I tell him I am sure he's right. I sign the form without a thought, anxious to get on home.

The undertaker asks me if I have any questions. I tell him that I want to collect the ashes. 'What do they come in?'

He disappears, returning with a square gold-brown plastic jar with a screw top. I nod at it. 'You could have a wooden casket, but this does the job.'

'It's very small, isn't it?' Martin is over six foot. 'How much do the ashes weigh?' I ask him.

'About six pounds.'

We shake hands.

Outside Hoxton's street market is in progress, the area full of milling people. I walk through it all, seeing it fresh, appreciating the vivacity. Or is it my own vivacity I am savouring? I feel very alive, as if on the eve of something special.

On the way home I open up the Estimate and read the breakdown of charges. I see that it is costing me – or rather Martin:

£202.00 To supply Warwick coffin
£608.00 Provision of hearse, one limousine and four bearers
£16.00 Preparation/hygienic treatment
£110.00 Cremation fees
£51.50 Doctors' fees

This brings the grand total to £987.50. There is a discount of £30 if the account is settled promptly.

I do not like the expense. It does not feel right. Martin left me more than enough to cover it but I had hoped to be able to make a sizeable donation to the Mildmay in his name. The funeral is going to pare this down considerably. Also the limousine is useless. There will be no more than three mourners. Does it take four people to carry a coffin? Does a coffin have to cost £202?

The feeling of something not being quite right persists. When I get home I ring the Co-operative Undertakers and they say their basic funeral, inclusive of cremation and doctors' fees, is £550. I ring friends and wonder if I can get out of the contract I have signed. I try ringing the undertaker but do not get any reply.

Saturday, 15 September

I go back to the undertakers at 9 am and cancel the funeral. I meet a different man. He says that they could have offered me something cheaper. I don't ask him why his colleague hadn't. No pressure of any kind is put on me to keep to the contract. I leave the office without plans having been made for Martin's funeral. When I get home I ring the Co-op, but they are closed for the weekend. Well, I will ring them first thing Monday morning. I feel proud of myself because I know that, by cancelling the original arrangements, I have already saved £400. Martin, I reckon, is pleased.

Sunday, 16 September

A friend from Herefordshire rings his condolences. He asks me how I am feeling. I tell him I am sad but that I think I got through most of my grieving by Martin's bedside during the last weeks. I am quite calm and collected, but very busy writing letters to all his friends. I also mention my problems with the undertaker. 'Why not arrange your own funeral for Martin?' he says.

'How do you mean?'

He tells me about an article he has read in *The Independent*.

'I'll think about it.'

I think about it. I ring friends. Several mention the article, but none has kept a copy. I take a piece of paper and write:

> *Problems of DIY funeral . . . co-ordinating everything . . . can I get the release of the body from the mortuary to go with a suitable appointment at a crematorium? Can I do all the paperwork? What does it consist of? Can I buy a coffin? Martin died of AIDS. Is that a problem?*

Then I get on with writing letters, all the time thinking how good it would be if it works out. I decide to ring Annie at the Mildmay first thing on Monday. She'll be able to answer the questions, or put me through to people who can.

Monday, 17 September

I ring Annie and tell all. She gives me the name and number of the doctor involved in Martin's post-mortem. I tell her that I am worried that the hospital may want the body taken away before I can arrange a cremation appointment. If that happens then he would probably have to be put into the hands of an undertaker. They've cornered the Chapel of Rest business. Annie says she has never had anyone try this before. She wants to be kept informed on how it goes. Of course I will!

The doctor says that the post-mortem has been performed. The hospital can keep the body for up to two weeks at 2 degrees centigrade. No, he is sure I will be able to co-ordinate release of the body with the crematorium appointment. The cause of Martin's death is not a problem. He gives me the number of the mortuary technician. He wishes me luck.

The mortuary technician is especially helpful. He tells me that he has the doctors' form, which must be handed in to the crematorium. The form has already been signed by the doctor at the Mildmay. He will see that it is signed by the doctor who performed the post-mortem. If I come to Reception at the Middlesex Hospital the following day at 1.00 pm, he will give me this paper in return for a half-fee of £20.75. 'The doctor at the hospice has waived hers,' he tells me. Typical.

It looks as if everything is working out. I ring the Islington office of the Islington and St Pancras cemetery in Finchley. I tell the lady, Mrs Rawls, my situation. She asks when I would like an appointment for a cremation service. 'Friday? 2.30?'

'Right you are,' she says. 'Now, what you need to do is bring the form with the two doctors' signatures on it; the green form you got when you registered the death and the fee for the cremation – that's £85 – to our office no later than forty-eight hours before the time of the cremation.'

'I thought cremations cost £110.00.'

'Different cemeteries have different fees.'

'I think I should be able to bring you everything tomorrow afternoon. But I've still got to buy a coffin.'

'Yes, you'd better.'

I phone the Co-op.

'I want to buy a coffin.'

'What for?' the man asks.

I tell him. The phone goes muffled. I hear, 'There's a bloke here wants to buy a coffin!' And: 'Well, tell him he can't,' shouted from some distance away.

'We don't sell coffins on their own.'

'I see.'

I open the Yellow Pages and am about to ring a wholesale supplier of funeral requisites when the phone rings. It is Mrs Rawls from the Islington crematorium office. 'I rang an undertaker. He'll supply you with a coffin for £150.'

'Thank you.' I take down the number. I put the phone down and start to blubber productively. What a kind person!

The undertaker who will supply me with the coffin is located on the Essex Road. I scowl at the statue of The Sacred Heart in the window. The man asks me for the height of the deceased. '6 feet 2 inches,' I tell him. He also wants the full name and the date of birth and death in order to have it engraved on the lid of the coffin. This is necessary, he says, because at the crematorium it is the only means of identification. I am shown the coffin. It is very frilly inside. The bottom is padded, covered in polythene. 'Now, seeing as it is a cremation coffin, the fittings have to be made of plastic. Don't try lifting it by the handles. They won't take it. Don't lift it up on your shoulders either. That's best left to the professionals. Carry it at waist level. How many bearers will you have?'

'Three or four,' I say, though I am not sure.

The undertaker gives me the screws and reminds me to take a screwdriver with me when I pick up the remains. I feel suddenly mean, miserly, the funerary equivalent of Scrooge. 'My friend wanted the simplest possible funeral,' I tell him.

He nods. He seems to understand. 'We could cut down the prices if people would accept a hearse made from an adapted Volvo or Volkswagen. We could get those for twenty grand. And the servicing is cheap. Trouble is that people expect these big flash cars and they cost forty grand and the servicing and spare parts cost an arm and a leg. By the way, how are you transporting the deceased to the crematorium?'

'I'm hiring a van.'

'Right. Well, make sure it's big enough to take the coffin. A Ford Transit or a Bedford should do it.'

Before leaving, I ask him to remove the plastic crosses from the ends of the coffin. He says he will. I say, 'Martin believed in neither carrot nor stick,' not quite knowing why I feel the need to bombard him with such a sentiment. He nods and ushers me to the door. An elderly woman, comforted by a younger one, is on her way in. They have a suit on a coathanger, doubtless to dress the body of their loved one. I hold the door open for them, but they do not notice me.

I hire a Ford Transit from Highbury Corner garage for 24 hours from 4.30 pm on Thursday 19 September. Then I ring the undertaker to tell him I'll pick up the coffin at about five on Thursday. It will spend the night in the Ford Transit outside my flat. That afternoon I take a pile of about seventy letters to the post office. When I have finished I get looks from the people waiting in the queue. It stretches back past the groceries to the door. The postal clerk is very kind and patient. People are.

Tuesday, 18 September

I have two things to do today. I must collect the forms from the mortuary technician and take all the paperwork to the cemetery. I consult an *A to Z* and get my bike out.

The mortuary technician's name is Marios and he is a Cypriot. He meets me during his lunch break. He is taking a course. He gives the lie to every stereotype I have ever harboured about people who work in mortuaries. He is the capital of life.

Marios takes the time to tell me that he thinks more people should do what I am doing. Some months ago he was in Cyprus to bury his father. He and his brothers dug his father's grave and carried his body to it. 'That is how we do things in Cyprus. We do not put our loved ones into the hands of strangers.' I feel as if I am a good person. This does not happen every day. The approval of Marios makes me feel wonderful. I tell him about my 2.30 appointment at the crematorium. He tells me to meet him at the St Pancras Hospital at 1.00 pm. He will help me transfer Martin's body from the mortuary fridge to the coffin. Marios will still be on the course, but he will take a taxi from the Middlesex Hospital to St Pancras in order to be on time.

'So I have everything I need for the Islington cemetery office?'

'Yes.'

I leave him and start cycling towards Finchley. I pass the cinema where Martin saw his last film, a pretty dire effort by John Waters. I blubber again. I don't give a toss who sees and I am not crying only for Martin. Everyone I see now in the Tottenham Court Road seems so fragile. We're all for it. I think of Marios carrying his dad to the grave. It all feels right and proper and commonsensical.

The two angels, Mrs Rawls and Mrs Webster, in the Islington cemetery office say that this is only the fourth DIY funeral they can recall. I am immensely puffed up. I fill in some more forms. I am not sure what my qualifications are for requesting a cremation for Martin. The answer is that I was present at the moment of death. I have brought his passport, so can supply all the information. The only thing I have forgotten is enough money to pay for the cremation. I cycle off to North Finchley and a cash machine.

Outside Woolworths an elderly man in a St John's Ambulance Brigade uniform is collecting for the third-world expatriates forced out of Kuwait and Iraq and pushed into camps in Jordan. Martin and I knew many such people. I stuff a ten-pound note into his box, thinking that the main sacrifice in giving to charity in a public place is exposing oneself to the embarrassment, the mixed judgements of the populace. The man seems taken aback. I leave him in a hurry, recalling the £20 I had given to a beggar in Dalston while on my way back from a day's vigil with Martin. Then I had been trying to placate all those half-forgotten Powers to save his body; now I am giving them a chance to ease his soul.

Back in the cemetery office I pay the fee and the angels tell me that all I have to do is arrive at the crematorium chapel fifteen minutes before the service. I can go up there and have a look if I like. I cycle through the cemetery, following the signs. It really is a very pleasant cemetery. A procession of funeral cars stands outside the front of the crematorium. I take a lap around it. The chimney is not smoking. I know I could go into the chapel, but I don't.

I cycle home and get ready another batch of letters for posting. I telephone Iain and Tony in the evening to ask them if they'll help me carry the coffin. No problem. Tony also volunteers to help me out at the mortuary.

That evening I decide to make a tape for us to listen to in the cremation chapel. The ladies at the Islington office have said that an organ is available. Also a tape-recorder. I take the whole evening up with recording and re-recording a short programme. It will be for me and for the people I duplicate and send it off to. There are people all over the world who have not had the opportunity to share in, to enjoy, the strange relief of grief that I am having. After many false starts I choose:

1. *Africa* – a song by children of the SWAPO school, Zambia

2. *Wants* and *Nothing To Be Said* by Philip Larkin (read by the poet)

3. *The Wild Swans at Coole, Lapis Lazuli, Under Ben Bulben* by W.B. Yeats (read by Cyril Cusack)

4. *A Clear Midnight* and *Now Finale to the Shore* by Walt Whitman (read by Ed Begley)

5. *Hello My Baby* – a song by Ladysmith Black Mombazo.
I listen to the programme I have made several times before going to bed. I drink a bottle of Bulgarian White and

blubber until my shirt-collar is soaked.

Wednesday, 19 September

I send off the rest of the letters, and a few copies of the Funeral Tape I have recorded. I telephone the friend who suggested a DIY funeral and thank him for the idea, saying that it is working like a charm. He asks me how I'm feeling. I say that I am howling a lot but am cheered in the knowledge that I am saving money. I can send £1000 of Martin's money to the Mildmay.

Thursday, 20 September

A bit nervy, worried about picking up the van and putting the coffin into it in full view of the rush-hour traffic on the Essex Road. Still, it will do the populace good and it will do me no harm.

I pick up the van at 4.30. It is not hard to drive. I have planned my route round to the Essex Road. I pull in on the bus lane, mounting the pavement, putting on the hazard lights – doing a pretty good impersonation of the London drivers who irk me daily. *Ford Fast Parts* is written on the side of the van.

Two men help me carry the coffin, placing it in the back of the Transit. They have not taken the crosses off. They assure me that the screws will fit in easily as they have bored starter holes for me. I drive back to the flat and park the van, double-checking that I have locked it properly.

After dark, I take a Malaysian sarong and an Arab head-dress and line the coffin with these friendly items to cover the polythene. I pull off the crosses. They come away easily. They are plastic, even the gold nails are plastic. I know that it isn't important but, as with the funeral tape, I still have the urge to do more. I collect together the many letters and cards sent to Martin during his last weeks. Some photographs too. His spare glasses. These I place on the hall table next to the coffin screws. When the time comes I will put them in the coffin. I search out an electrical screwdriver which seems big enough to do the job. I test it on one of the screws. It fits.

I finish off Martin's bottle of Campari.

Friday, 21 September

The morning gets frittered away worrying about traffic. Tony arrives at noon. We leave the flat at 12.30 and arrive at St Pancras Hospital at 12.45. We drive around the hospital area looking for the mortuary. It is not signposted.

Marios turns up five minutes early and shows us where and how to place the Transit. We take the coffin out and carry it into a depressing yard. There are doors in the wall. A sign warning of infectious diseases. We open the coffin. Marios opens the fridge door. Martin's body is in a grey plastic bag but his face is exposed. His hair is wet through, as if after a swim. Apart from this, he looks exactly as he did at the time of his death. There is no sign of post-mortem scarring. His blind eye is open. His good one closed. Before I can step forward Tony and Marios have pulled him into the coffin in one swift movement. I am weeping. I place the bundle of objects in the coffin. I take my last sight of him. We put the lid on the coffin.

I have the screws about me but we find that the screwdriver is not strong enough to twist them in. I feel foolish. It is typical of me to fail on a technicality, to forget a detail. We lift the coffin aboard the Transit. I place a rainbow scarf on top of it.

We thank Marios and start out towards Finchley. It is 1.15 pm. The traffic is heavy but we arrive within a mile of the cemetery by 1.45. I stop the van and we go off in search of a screwdriver. I also buy three Walnut Whips. I am completely immersed in the practical. We might be delivering a sofa-bed.

Arriving at the cemetery, we pass the Islington office and give the angels a wave. One of them comes out, but she has not recognized me. Then she does. She says she did not recognize me without my bike. She wishes us luck. We drive on, looking for a quiet place. We draw up outside a chapel and Tony goes into the back of the van to screw down the coffin-lid properly. A British Gas van stops behind us, followed by two other vehicles. The occupants get out, light cigarettes. It looks as though they think we are first in line for a funeral taking place in the chapel. Tony finishes, saying that the screws are of different sizes but that he has managed all but one. We smoke a cigarette and then drive on up to the cremation chapel. I park the Transit round the back.

It is 2.15 and another cremation service is in progress. There is an undertaker standing in front of the chapel entrance. He is dressed in a morning-suit and has a cigarette burning furtively inside the cupped palm of his right hand. He asks Tony which undertaking firm we are from. Tony tells him we are doing our own. 'You can put the floral tributes over there,' he says. Along the verge are squares of grass nine feet by nine. There is one with a notice which says, 'Martin Jon Drury'. It is bare. On both sides the spaces are covered with mounds of flowers. POP, MUM, LOVE done in flowers, bouquets in cellophane with purple bows.

'We don't have any,' I say. The man strolls away from us, pulling on his cigarette.

'Why have an expensive car for a funeral?' I ask Tony. 'I bet these people never had one during their lives.'

'Search me.'

'And think of all the money spent on flowers! It doesn't do the dead any good. Much better to send the money to charity.'

'Probably guilt,' Tony says. I nod. I feel very self-righteous. I have pulled money out of the hands of undertakers and florists and pushed it towards where it can do more good. Then I think of the precious, pointless ointment that Mary Magdalene anointed Jesus with. Judas said the money could have been spent on the poor. I think of Jesus's put-down of Judas, *The poor you have always with you; me you have not always with you.* What acres of cloth of gold, tons of stucco, centuries of carving and chiselling, ages of obfuscation that remark has sired! Judas had his share of commonsense. Christians ought to pray for him.

We hide in the Transit as the mourners from the 2 o'clock cremation view the floral tributes. I am nervous. The coffin seemed very heavy at the mortuary. Where is Iain? If he's late, can we manage to carry it into the chapel and on to the catafalque by ourselves?

When the coast is clear we drive up to the front entrance of the chapel. I go inside and hand my tape to the custodian. I ask him to play it once the coffin is in place. We open the Transit and slide the coffin out. I carry the back and Tony lifts the front. It is heavy but we can manage. I think of Marios and his dad. Then I think of Martin, out of sight in the portable dark of the coffin. Then I tell myself that this is not Martin. Only his husk. We stagger into the chapel. I hope we can lift the coffin high enough to slide it on.

Tony lifts the coffin. It gets to the edge of the catafalque and we slide it along. Just then Iain turns up. I cannot stop myself from giving him a look. I may withhold his Walnut Whip. We sit down and the tape starts. The voices of African children fill the chapel. I am sitting by myself and weep throughout. No stiff upper lip required. Just two friends right behind me. No strangers to worry about.

When the final song is finished, Soler's *Fandango* starts. This is the signal for the end of the service. The custodian appears and shows me how to lower the volume of the tape player and close the curtains. I should have found that out ahead of time. Before we go I ask him when I can collect Martin's ashes. He says I can come back tomorrow.

I drive the Transit back – Iain and Tony have gone back to work, taking Iain's car – and have the van checked in with time to spare.

Saturday, 22 September

Taking with me the rainbow scarf to wrap the ashes container, I cycle up to the cemetery. I go straight to the crematorium and ask for the ashes. The man says that he needs a note from the Islington office. The Islington office is shut on Saturdays. I am a bit short with him. The first real hitch. On the way home I seem to remember having been told that I needed a paper. I had forgotten. A screw loose.

Monday, 24 September

I arrive at the Islington office bright and early, so bright and early that the lady I need has not arrived. She has taken the ledger home with her to catch up on entries. I am offered a coffee and sit down, happy to tell Mrs Rawls of my adventures. A man who works at the cemetery comes in and we chat. He says that the Islington section of the cemetery discards 25 cubic metres of flowers each week. This represents a skip about the size of a double-decker bus. The dead flowers cannot be composted because they are entwined with metal, shaped with plastic frames, shrouded in paper. I repeat my opinion that all this costly averting of the eyes from death is unfortunate. Charities could be helped – the bereaved could be helped – if people took a more active part in funerals.

Mrs Webster – the other angel, the recording angel – arrives with her big ledger. I am given the necessary form. I tell them that I am taking Martin's ashes to Ireland, where I will scatter them in Drumcliff churchyard in Sligo, where W. B. Yeats is buried.

They ask if there is any special reason. 'Martin loved Yeats. And on his grave is written:

> Cast a cold eye
> On life, on death.
> Horseman, pass by!

Martin faced his death in that way.' I tell them that the whole experience has helped me a great deal. It may help me to whinge less when my turn comes.

This time I pick up the ashes with no trouble, and apologize to the man for my curtness on Saturday. He says he hadn't noticed. A nice man. Good people.

The ashes are in my rucksack. All that remains of Martin I am carrying on my back. I weep, thinking of *He Ain't Heavy, He's My Brother*, wishing I had included that song on the funeral tape.

Sunday, 30 September

Dusk. After three days hard cycling I have arrived at Drumcliff churchyard. The trip across Ireland has been interesting, but the bicycle was weighed down by luggage and Martin's ashes. I am ready to be lightened, to be rid of them. I have used the rainbow scarf as a piece of brightness to warn drivers and to cover the ashes with a sort of flag.

It is Sunday, but thankfully there is no service going on in the church. No tourists either. I am alone. I take the jar of ashes from my panniers and unscrew the lid. They are silvery-grey. I look around guiltily. I feel as if I am committing sacrilege. I pick up the jar and pour the ashes on and around Yeats's grave. I had expected them to disperse on the wind. Instead, they land heavily, like grain, and I have to scrabble about with my hands, pushing the tiny shards under the white marble chippings that cover the grave. As I am doing this, tens of rooks rise from their nests in the trees overhead, wheel about. I take it as a sign. I close the jar and put it back in the panniers. Then I go to the wall of the graveyard which looks out over Ben Bulben and read *A Prayer for My Daughter* and *Under Ben Bulben*. It is hard to make out the print in the dying light. I cry again self-indulgently.

I return to Yeats's grave, which now doubles as Martin's, and listen to the funeral tape. I notice that a girl has come into the churchyard. I do not move, neither do I conceal my tears. She approaches, then veers away in the opposite direction. She must think I am a devoted fan of the poet.

I leave the churchyard, wheeling my bike. I wave to the girl, dithering by a Celtic cross. She will be Martin's first visitor, though she won't know it.

I find a nice B and B within sight of the tower of Drumcliff church. I tell my hosts, Oliver and Kathleen, why I am here. I am not sure why I tell them. Do I want it to reflect well on me? A couple of times it has occurred to me that perhaps I've done this to star in my own weepy, with a coffin for stage. Still, as *Mixed Motives* is my middle name, I will have to live with that. I also say how worried I was about doing what I did in the churchyard. They say, 'Don't worry about it. This is Ireland.'

My hosts' children are watching a video. It upsets them. It is about a young American boy who died of AIDS.

The jar still contains some ashes. In my haste I was not thorough enough.

Monday, 1 October

Before breakfast I cycle back to Drumcliff with the jar, wrapped in the rainbow scarf. I do not go into the churchyard, but to the bank of the Drumcliff river. I stand on a stone in the stream and wash out the jar. The Atlantic ocean is barely a mile away.

A young man clearing briars from the river-path comes over for a chat. He is a supporter of Aston Villa. He and a bunch of friends often hire a coach and go to England to attend matches. They drive through Northern Ireland to get to the ferry. He says that the British soldiers often stop them to search the bus. They order the Irish Aston Villa supporters off the bus for a body-search and, as they are feeling them up and down, say, 'Fucking Mick!'

'They don't, do they?' I say, screwing and unscrewing the top of the empty container.

He smiles, then says, 'Still, our lads will take care of them.'

'Our lads?'

'The Provos.'

I return to the B and B and Kathleen takes the empty jar from me. She will put it in the bin. I eat a huge breakfast and go to climb Ben Bulben. At the top I sit down, looking back at the way I have come.

Clare Colvin

PIE-DOG

Look at my hands. Those terrible brown freckles. The skin like crumpled tissue paper. They were my best feature then, as we used to say when we awarded women points like horses. At a party a girl read my palm. She held up my hand and said, 'I have never seen such a psychic hand.' She turned it to the light, admiringly. 'So psychic,' she murmured. I thought she was seeing into my soul, till I learnt that it is just a term palm readers use for hands with long fingers. The joints have thickened now, and they are permanently bent, so the length and slenderness have gone. The tip of the index finger is crooked. That was a fall from a horse when I was in India. I was forty then, and I hadn't realized that some of my resilience had gone.

When you are old, incidents that you have not thought of for years come back and haunt you. Curious things that have to do with some failing in you, a decision that you made, or didn't make, which you now realize has marked you. Trivial things that had no effect on the course of your life, yet suddenly they are there again like notches on a tally stick. Sometimes as I move slowly about my flat – my ankles ache and the day is long – a memory will flash into my mind, and I'll say, 'Damn!' or 'Oh God!' or sometimes, when it is particularly painful, I'll only sigh 'Oh dear!' It's as if I'm being asked to decide my place in the hereafter by the notches on the stick.

You never quite recover from being in India. I've not

filled my flat with that Raj junk, I've refused to live in the past. I kept only a few things, like this teapot from Lahore. It's so beautifully moulded, don't you think? One of the best silversmiths. But the memories cannot be ditched like the brass tables and papier mâché trays. I look out of the window at the low grey sky, the suffocatingly green dripping leaves, and there it is again – that memory of the veranda, the glaringly hot day outside, the sound of the crows, harsh, resonant and flapping around in black like ageing shop assistants. And there's my dog Emmie, with her smooth white coat, and her large eyes, watching me. When I look at her, the tail gives a one-two wag, like a greeting, and sometimes she gives a *sotto voce* whimper, which means she wants to be stroked.

Our bungalow was on the edge of the town which is also the edge of the desert. The Thar Desert, cold nights in winter, but a furnace most of the year. The sun's rays penetrate your head like a drill, the heat from the sand hits you under the chin. You spend most of the time indoors, sitting under the fans as they swirl the warm air above your head. We had blinds like rush matting over the windows, and a Heath Robinson device by which water would circulate over them, keeping them wet throughout the day. Walking through the house was like moving through a thick warm soup. You felt physically impeded by the air. You took cold baths, you lay on the bed for a while. Ralph would return from work limp with exhaustion. I made sure there was always a bath full of cold water for him. Unlike the government wallahs we didn't get to the hills in the summer, because the building projects had to go on. Some of the wives went, but I thought it unfair that Ralph should suffer alone.

I always wondered how the pie-dogs survived. The heat of the desert, lack of shade, lack of food. Half wild – you couldn't get near them – but relying on humans for their slender means to live. Scavenging in gutters, tussling over a dry bone. They had an oblique, loping gait that spoke of the stones the children threw at them. A sudden movement and they would shy away as if to avoid a missile. You could see their ribs corrugating their dry sandy coats. Occasionally you would pass by the corpse of one for whom the struggle had ended.

Emmie was a pie-puppy when she came to us. I was in the kitchen talking to Khansamah about the food for the week, when his little boy walked in holding a puppy by the scruff of its neck.

'Shoo!' said Khansamah, and loosed a barrage of Hindustani at the child. He was furious that Memsahib had seen a dog being brought into his kitchen. Later I looked out of the kitchen door. The child had abandoned the puppy and it was sitting lost and alone in the middle of the concrete yard. It looked up at me, and I had the sudden impression it was appealing for help. The short tail wagged twice, the eyes fixed on mine. I bent down and picked it up. I held it to me, and could feel the small heart beating against the fragile ribs. It was warm and living and helpless. I took it in.

No one wanted me to keep Emmie. Ralph said she would attract fleas, lice and other pie-dogs. Mrs Barrington, the area's burra memsahib, wife of the Collector, said she was probably incubating rabies, and we would all end up having a course of injections into our stomachs. The servants didn't like feeding a dog. I would make her the meals myself, chopping up bits of cooked chicken and mixing it with boiled rice. I would put the dish out on the veranda and watch her as she ate. I loved that moment when she wagged her tail at me, as if saying thank you. I would talk to her like a child. Ralph understood, because that was missing from our life. People nowadays imagine they can choose what they want and feel frustrated when they don't get it. But looking at the other wives, I didn't greatly envy them. They would despatch their weeping children to school in England at the age of seven, and then get these small, cold-eyed strangers back once a year. A child, when it wants to survive, learns to cauterize its feelings.

I know it sounds like a proud mother, but Emmie grew to be so pretty – she had some greyhound blood, a lean face, large eyes, a smooth white coat, long-legged and slim. It was not surprising that she began to attract the pie-dogs in the area. That's romanticizing it rather, because it doesn't really matter what a bitch on heat looks like. But what happened *was* really rather romantic. One of the pie-dogs fell in love with Emmie.

He was a black and tan dog – black with patches like eyebrows and a tan waistcoat, cocked ears that flopped over at the end and a busy look about him – as if he had just come from a meeting. We didn't notice him at first among the pack of pie-dogs gathered at our gates when Emmie came into season. Mrs Barrington had a certain *froideur* when she arrived at our dinner party then.

'I never thought I should have to wade through a pack of rabid curs for my social engagements,' she said.

We sat in the dining-room, the fan clanking overhead, in evening dress. Perspiration ran down the faces of the women, the men exuded a faint smell of camphor and sweat. Outside the gates the dogs howled with lust. We talked about the coming Partition, and whether Mountbatten had been pushed by the Attlee Government to such haste, or whether he simply wanted to get back to the superior social life of London. Our area in the Sind was to be included in the new Moslem state. Major Barrington predicted civil disturbance. We could already hear Khansamah and the bearer having a dispute in the kitchen.

Emmie's time passed, and we let her out of the spare room in which she had been locked. The curs had lost interest and gone back to hunting and scavenging. All but the black and tan pie-dog. He was still looking patiently through the gate, and when he saw Emmie, he gave a long, whimpering whine, pushing his nose through the iron bars. I said sternly, 'Emmie,' but she took no notice. The two stared at each other, transfixed. She padded over to the gate, and they stood there, wagging their tails. I remember thinking at the time, 'What a sweet pair.'

She would get out of the garden one way or another, and they would go off together into the desert – their noses tracking the ground for the scent of rodents. It was a game to her, she didn't know that was the way they lived. She would be back for her chopped up chicken in the evening, but she began to leave half of it on her plate and then she would go and look through the gate waiting for him, as if she wanted to leave him the rest of the meal. So I started leaving scraps of food for him, and he would be there waiting. He didn't edge away as if he was expecting a stone, like the other curs. His eyes were hazel coloured, with slanting black pupils, alert and hopeful. I could have put out my hand and touched him, but there was always the inhibition of being told these dogs were carriers of disease.

They called it 'the devil's wind', the mood that swept through the country after Partition. The rumours, the panic, and then the news of wholesale killings, as the country split itself in two, following the official split. Thousand upon thousand of refugees on the roads, Moslems trekking north, Hindus going south, bitterness and fear in everyone's hearts. It was an appalling time and some of us were deeply ashamed that we left India in such a way. I always wondered what Mountbatten felt, or whether he forgot it all once he was back in London.

Our area didn't see the atrocities that happened in the Punjab, but there was violence and rioting in the town. We stayed at home – you could never be sure of not suddenly being in the middle of it, or that the anger might turn against you for being a member of the race that had enabled it to happen. Khansamah, our Moslem cook, who had never been easy to deal with, acquired accusing eyes and a hysterical edge to his voice. Our sweeper was beaten up when he went into town one evening. A few days later, he simply disappeared. I was told that he had left for Gujarat with his family. And then our Hindu bearer, Ram Lal with his nodding head and oversize moustache, came to me and said he had to visit his sick uncle in Bombay, and I knew that this time, unlike the other times he had visited his frequently ill family, he was going for good.

The company Ralph worked for became concerned for the safety of its staff, and any form of construction had ground to a halt. No work was done beyond the day to day matter of keeping going. The Barringtons had already packed up and left, and now it was the turn of those who had till then harboured dreams of staying on and working in the newly founded state.

We had no idea what we would do when we got back to England – it was an unknown and unpromising future. Ralph was fifty-one and he was good at his work, but he was not ambitious, and besides it was too late for that. We were going to stay with my sister while we looked around, and that's about as far as our plans went. I began to pack up our belongings, and as I packed and labelled the trunks, I realized I was packing away the best part of my life.

Emmie followed me around as if she was trying to understand what was going on, trying to get me to explain. She became restless at the upheaval, and when we were out on the veranda having our evening drink, she would lean her body against my legs, as if seeking reassurance. Then Ralph said to me, 'What are we going to do about Emmie?'

What could we do? We had no idea who would take the bungalow after us, or indeed if anyone would. An empty bungalow in the middle of the desert with a dog which was used to getting minced chicken for dinner. Khansamah was leaving, and besides he hated dogs. We thought of taking Emmie back to England, but there was six months' quarantine, and we had no idea of where we would be after that. At home or abroad? We felt like refugees ourselves.

Then Ralph said, 'Emmie's had a good life. She's been happy with us. We can't just abandon her. Either we have to take her back, or we must put her down. It would be the kinder way in the end.'

I knew what he meant by the kinder way. Poor Emmie, one more responsibility and expense to deal with. Emmie in the cold of England after the Indian desert. I knew, of course, he was right.

The next day I got up before sunrise and took Emmie out into the garden. I sat and talked to her for a while, and stroked her, and explained that she was going on a long journey. Then I put my revolver to her head and shot her.

The mali had dug a grave near the garden wall. We lined it with palm leaves and I wrapped Emmie in a shawl, and we buried her. I stayed in my room for the rest of the day and cried for a long time. The sense of loss was overwhelming, as if a child had been torn from my arms, as if part of myself had been torn away.

In the early hours of the next morning I was awake, listening to the silence. There seemed to be a new emptiness about the house, yet I could still hear in my mind the click of her claws on the tiled floor. And then I heard a long, anguished howl that went straight through my heart. It came from the garden outside. I walked out on to the veranda. The night air was thick and warm, and a greyness was spreading through the sky before the dawn. I looked towards the mound that covered Emmie, and I saw a dark shadow standing over it, the shape of a dog. As I watched, it put its nose to the mound, and gave a strange sobbing whine, then it lay down over it as if on guard. The black and tan pie-dog had found Emmie's grave.

He stayed there for three days and nights without

moving from his post. He took no notice of us as we came and went, but sat there as if Emmie were by him and the two were communing together in that silent way they had. I didn't approach him, and avoided doing more than glance at him. I didn't want to meet his eyes. On the third morning I walked out on the veranda and saw that the dark shape was no longer there. Some time during the night he had left. I didn't see him again, and two days after that we left, and took the boat back to England from Karachi.

It's growing dark outside. I can hardly see you now through the gathering shadows. Let me switch on the lamp.

Yes, it's strange that after all the turmoil we witnessed in India, all the things that happened later, that Emmie should come back now and haunt me. It's the notch on the tally stick. The action I should not have taken.

I knew, when I saw him at the grave, how wrong it was to have shot her. She would have survived, you see, for he would have looked after her. She could have lived . . . Oh dear . . .

There's the clock striking six. Well, I think we've had enough of the tea. It's grown quite cold. Time for a chota peg, don't you think?

Slavenka Drakulić

CLOSE-UP OF DEATH

They say that a little girl, A.M., was killed while eating a
pie. It seems that it happened like this: it was morning at
the end of February, bright and chilly. You ask yourself
how that woman, her mother, made the pie in Sarajevo, ten
months after the beginning of the war? What flour did she
use, what oil, what did she fill it with? She must have
baked it the night before – but then again, how? There is
no electricity, or there is but only sometimes. Or did she
do it on an open fire? But there is no wood, all the trees in
the city have been cut down long ago ... In any case, still
half-asleep, the two-and-a-half-year-old girl had been sitting at the table, eating breakfast. At that moment, she
heard the sound of shelling. Maybe she was frightened by
it, so she ran to her mother – but maybe not. The sound of
shelling is normal around here. No, she couldn't have heard
that sound, they say that those who get hit have no time to
hear anything, they have no time to get frightened at all. A
shell went through the roof of their house and landed in
the kitchen. The girl fell to the floor. It all happened with
lightning speed and she was dead before her parents or her
grandfather had time to understand what was happening.
By the time her father took her in his hands and looked for
help, it was all over.

Then – then a TV camera arrives on the scene. Judging
by certain details this happened perhaps only one or two
hours after the shelling. We see the small kitchen already

without the little girl, the floor is covered with brick and plaster debris, scattered shoes, her little boots. The TV camera zooms in on the roof, on the hole left by a shell, as sky and cold descend in the kitchen through it. The father is sitting with his arms on the table, crying. The camera shoots a close-up of his blue eyes and his tears – in fact it looks as if he is crying on camera, so that we, the television spectators, can be sure that his tears are real, that he really cried, the little one's father. He has on a white pullover made of a rough peasant's wool. You do not normally sit in your kitchen dressed warmly like that, but what do we know about the kind of cold that he is suffering from at this moment? From his eyes, the camera moves to that pullover so that we can see a red stain on it, left where he held his girl when he picked her up from the floor – when it was already too late. The blood is not dry yet, the stain is bright red, it looks fresh. I know that raw, hand-spun wool that his pullover was made with. I can feel it under my fingers. It takes forever to dry, soaked blood stays wet a long time ... Looking at this blood is nauseating. Still, the camera returns to it several times. This is unnecessary, but you have no defence from these kinds of pictures – and there is no one to tell how useless it is.

Now we are in the hospital, this is the first time we see the mother too. The reporter's voice explains that she has been wounded in the stomach. Then he (or was it she?) says something absolutely too much, too much in the moment of despair of the woman whose child has just died. The voice says that the young woman probably will not be able to have any more children. She lies on a kind of stretcher, covering her face with her hands. She sobs, her voice comes out as if broken in pieces. The father comes in, in his white pullover with the red stain, and embraces her. It is clear that they meet there for the first time after the little one's death, in a hospital room. On camera – for the first time. The mother lets out something, on some other occasion you could probably call it a cry, a howl. But now it is only a sound of emptiness; with that sound the woman tells her husband that she has just lost everything. This is the end, this has to be the end. The camera can't go any further than the inhuman suffering of the mother who has just lost her child. Neither we, the television spectators, nor the people that we don't see who are standing behind camera – a reporter, a cameraman, a soundman – can stand all this any longer. This has to stop, I repeat to myself while the camera goes on. I don't believe my eyes, but that's how it is: now we are looking at a white sheet with red spots. We have already forbidden this, we recognize that same sign. Red on white, that's the sign of her death. My God, how very bright her blood is, I think, while my whole being cries: enough, enough, enough. I don't want the camera to enter under that cover hiding her small body. But someone's hand surpasses my thoughts and lifts the white sheet. Her face, we see her face. Her small deformed face, no longer human, framed by untidy tufts of her black hair. Her half-closed eyes. We see a close-up of death. Then cut. The funeral. People talking, an off-screen voice, the father, the grandfather, a little coffin in the shallow frozen ground. The report is finished. It has lasted a total of three minutes . . .

A moment later, we become aware that the TV broadcast that we have just seen is the tragedy of one family filmed only a couple of hours after they have lost their child, and that *the whole tragedy has happened on camera*. The only thing we have not witnessed is the moment of death of the two-and-a-half-year-old A.M. (A take from outside, when the shell hits the roof. Then from inside, a scene where the girl falls from her chair, in slow motion, as if she's flying. A piece of pie drops from her hand and rolls on the ground. That's it! The reporter is pleased.). Well – why not? By now we, the public, are mature enough also to stand all in the name of documentation, which we obviously believe in. That is the only thing we have not seen on our TV screens so far. We have already seen beheaded corpses being eaten by pigs and dogs. Eyes gouged out, scattered bodily parts that do not belong to anyone, anything. Skeletons and half-rotten skulls, children without legs, babies killed by sniper fire. A twelve-year-old rape victim talking about it on camera. Day after day. Death in Bosnia has been more and more well-documented. In ten months, Sarajevo has been hit by 800,000 shells. In the city, 80,000 kids are imprisoned – that makes it the biggest children's prison in the world. 5,000 of them were killed or simply died. The rest await hunger and long death, slow death. Fifty years ago this is how Jews suffered. Now it's the Muslims' turn. Do you remember Auschwitz? Really, does anyone remember Anne Frank? Oh yes, we do remember it all, and because of that memory we have the idea that everything has to be carefully documented, so that shameful history can never be repeated, and yet, here they are, generations have learnt at school about concentration camps, about factories of death, generations whose parents swear that it could never happen again – at least not in Europe, precisely because of the living memory of the recent past. *They* are fighting this war. What, then, has all that documentation changed? And what is being changed now, by the conscious, precise bookkeeping of death that is happening in our lives, in our living-rooms, while we watch transmissions of the dying in Sarajevo? The little girl's death is only one horror out of many, in which every previous one has the rôle of preparing us for something even worse.

The biggest change has happened within ourselves, the audience, spectators, public. We have started to believe that it is our rôle in this casting, that it is possible to play the public. As if war is theatre. Slowly and without our noticing it, something has crept into us, a kind of hardness, an inability to see the truth – the signs of our own dying, the close-up of the girl's dead face was one scene too much.

Because it was senseless. The feeling that for the first time it is possible to watch war from so near in its most macabre details makes sense only if, because of that, something can change for the better.

But nothing changes. Therefore, this kind of documentation is turning into a perversion, into a pornography of dying.

Elizabeth Evans

SAYING THE WRONG THING

The hospital appointment was at 10.45 so there was plenty of time. 'You can always park in the road, we'll go slowly' – creeping at a snail's pace and even then it was too much for him. She didn't look at her husband, hearing him cough was enough. On and on this cough, this little hard annoying sound, enough to drive anyone mad. Could he be putting it on? Coughing can be a habit too. Her sister always started to cough when she phoned but then she smoked and people knew she did and made allowances. The sound Rob made was different. He didn't seem to mind, never referred to it. Apart from that he was fine, except for his heart.

They had left the car. Rob drove of course. He was all right just sitting and driving, no effort, he said. He hated her to drive and she always made mistakes as he watched. So he drove all the way and did not cough once but now on the pavement he was reduced, bent over, an invalid plainly on his way to a doctor, shaking and racked with his cough.

'Nearly there,' she said in a new cheerful voice.

'We're not.'

'Yes we are, there's the undertakers, they're opposite the entrance, aren't they.'

'Not quite.' He stopped, leant against a wall.

'I suppose it's useful having them near at hand but a tactless reminder just the same.'

Could a reminder of death ever be tactless? Unwelcome was what she meant. Actually she had never meant to mention the undertakers at all, it was just something to say, to keep him going. Stupid of her.

'Don't *think*,' she cried, knowing him.

If he stood up straight no one would say there was anything wrong. Tall, thick grey hair, firm mouth – well, until lately for he seemed to have let the lower lip droop a bit so that the mouth remained open. Can't breathe, he explained. Lately his breathing had become noisy, peculiar, sometimes it got louder and louder, then died away. Then the pattern started again. At night it destroyed all sleep.

'I can't go on,' was what he said now. There wasn't much to hold on to but he did have the wall behind him.

'It's not far. Try.' But he couldn't.

'I know, I'll get a wheelchair or something.' (Rob in a wheelchair!) But of course you can't take a wheelchair out of a hospital, you might take it home and sell it. Oh don't bother, she cried in exasperation to a person at the reception desk. Anything could have happened while she had been flying about looking for the damn thing but here was Rob standing in the entrance hall looking not too bad at all.

'They made a fuss about the chair.'

'It doesn't matter. I managed.'

Meekly he was led away for his tests and she waited and thought about nothing, just the vast place and the colour of the carpet in front of her chair and was nearly asleep when Rob returned, very calm.

'I don't think there's much wrong with me,' he said. 'That was just panic outside.'

He looked quite happy and pulled out a newspaper. She couldn't read, couldn't concentrate. Three months ago he had gone swimming – alone, the fool – in a nice little deserted bay where the waves had become giants and he had almost drowned. All his own fault because his heart couldn't stand it, couldn't stand anything much really and yet here he was, waiting in the out-patients cheerfully unconcerned. His own fault – she had said this once and couldn't say it again.

When it was their turn an appallingly young doctor came out of a room and shook hands with them. At his age what could he know about anything? He was also extremely good-looking in a pale skin, dark hair kind of way – not Italian or Spanish, something else. Irish perhaps. She did not want to find their doctor attractive.

'Any pain in the chest?'

No, he'd said that before. Nothing much wrong, only breathlessness and a funny cough. Today he had for some reason put on a vest, on a hot day too, and this had to be removed. The worst vest he could have chosen, frayed round the top. Not that doctors bother about such things, she knew that, but his arms looked a bit stringy and his neck more wrinkled than she had ever seen before and red where he had sat in the sun in an open-necked shirt. All in all it was a rather old body and she felt ashamed. Her tall fine husband! He doesn't always look like this, she wanted to say, people think he's barely sixty, no older, he plays tennis still – well, he did.

The young doctor, slender and graceful, was listening and watching so intently that he did not seem to hear the questions she asked. He was on another track. The heart was unchanged but it had taken a lot of punishment, it couldn't cope with what it had to do and needed rest. He smiled charmingly. Some days will be good, some bad, up and down all the time.

All the time? 'Will it get better eventually given rest?' she managed to ask. It seemed not. 'Some things have to be given up.' She almost stopped listening. Walks, long drives, climbing steps to cathedrals, theatres, cutting the grass.

'There will still be things to enjoy,' said the young doctor, knowing nothing. Say he was thirty; he had nearly forty years to play with before he reached Rob's age. Forty!

Of course he could announce confidently that life had to be given up, seventy was too far ahead for him to imagine. Perhaps he felt, if he thought at all, that Rob's main pleasure now should be in remembering the past.

'What things can he do?' she asked.

'Oh, rest, enjoy a book, television, he can go up and down stairs, take little walks, important to move around.'

A heavy silence fell on them. Was this all? All that struggle to get here to be told you couldn't do anything any more. A new drug to strengthen the heart was prescribed. That was something, wasn't it. Hope there. But they had to leave for their doctor was up and shaking their hands enthusiastically. He might almost have been congratulating them.

Rob said 'Thank you' but as soon as the door was closed his wife said 'What was there to thank him for? He was telling you you'd had it.'

'Not quite that.'

'Wasn't it?'

She was upset and angry and didn't care what she said. 'I hate nursing people.'

'You won't have to nurse me. If you do I'll oblige you by dying.'

'I don't want that either.'

What she wanted was to go back to everything as it had been, before the heart became troublesome, before the swim. How lucky we were and didn't know it. Though she used to boast 'we have a lovely life'. Rob had his workshop next to the garage where he made his shelves and music stands, he was thus home and not home at the same time.

'Should he drive?' she had asked the doctor.

'In moderation.'

Carpentry had been frowned on unless a machine did most of the work. 'Everything without strain, that's the idea.'

She wanted Rob to be angry too. Coming out of the

hospital he looked better than he had done, less grey anyway. But how slowly he walked and with every step his shirt seemed to flap up and down. Why was he so breathless now? Really she'd had enough. He must take himself in hand and be like other people.

Their car was hemmed in; they could not move. An enemy had cleverly forced itself into the tiny space in front. On its back window was a sticker saying 'Hoot if you made it with someone last night.'

'Oh Lord, now we'll never get out.' As if the whole long morning hadn't been enough. Rob did not speak, he was too furious. He would never behave like that, he considered other drivers, always had done.

'He's not going to get away with it. I know the type.' He wouldn't sit down but stood rigidly by the bonnet, arms folded. 'I'm ready for the gentleman.'

'Don't go for him, will you. It's not worth it. Promise.'

'Are you telling me what to do?'

'Oh Robbie, don't be so silly.'

Chocolate which usually calmed him was refused.

'We'll just have to wait, it doesn't matter, we haven't got to rush now. In a way it's funny – can't you see it?' She was talking to him out of the window.

'No.'

'The doctor and now this – What did you think of him?'

'Who?'

'Dr Fuller. The one who said you mustn't have any strain.'

He didn't answer. He was waiting.

The warm day clouded over. Inside the car it was hot and airless like the hospital. 'How can they bear it?' How can I bear it, was what she was thinking. If he could not sleep, neither could she. If there was a light burning in the bedroom as she walked up the path, her heart would sink. 'He was all right when I left.' If it was a false alarm, later she would be overcome with exhaustion. And now here was Rob grim-faced, standing stiff with tension. Not what the doctor ordered!

Half an hour went by, she was nearly asleep. Then a man in a baseball cap appeared whistling. He walked swiftly to his car. Rob moved towards him.

'May I ask what sort of game you're playing?' he said.

'Game?' said the man getting in.

'Then why have you deliberately parked so that I am unable to move?'

'Dunno,' said the man, turning the wheel sharply. 'Plenty of room.' After a few extraordinary turns he drove off. 'You're past it,' he shouted.

'What a sod,' she said. 'What a little horror.'

It didn't matter. They could go home now. Rob wrote something on a piece of paper.

'What's that?'

'His numberplate.'

What's that going to do, she thought but did not say.

When they came to their house they went on sitting in the car, it seemed too much effort to get out. The whole day so awful. 'They shouldn't have given us such a young doctor, younger than Peter, much younger. And beautiful. That's what made it all so humiliating, we just seemed like a funny old couple begging for life. And we're not, are we. I thought we were all right before, then I noticed the blotches on my hands and my ankles looked awful and your stomach and our clothes.'

He took notice of that. 'What's wrong with our clothes, for God's sake?'

'I don't know. Something.' Though she had felt rather well dressed as they set out. 'Your torn vest.'

'Forget it.'

They drank coffee at the kitchen table and sat looking at each other. There wasn't anything to do. An afternoon was beginning.

She said, 'Doctors are often wrong, everyone knows

that.' A silly thing to say. He would have no cheering up, never did. A false move.

'We'll eat tonight. I'll get something special.'

He wasn't hungry. He was thinking about the driver who had outwitted him.

'Well, you will be. Let's have a drink, wine's good for you.'

The wine tasted thin and acid.

'Wine's for a celebration, whisky would be better,' and Rob found the whisky. They drank it with hunks of bread and cheese, then he went slowly up the stairs to rest. He could have easily rested on the downstairs sofa but to suggest this might have irritated him. 'You're always telling me what to do.'

On the day of the swim she had called out from the garden of the rented cottage, 'Don't go in the sea alone, wait for me,' as he went off for his walk. Her fault as well as his perhaps.

Late in the afternoon she sat outside the kitchen door shelling peas. The little garden spread around quietly growing; the snapdragons had come into flower while they had been out. She thought of Dr Fuller, not sitting in a garden but playing tennis. Delicious in white flannels she saw him run lightly to the net, jump over it with no effort at all, lie shirtless in the long grass – Do you know, she cried aloud in amazement at herself, I rather fancied him. I disowned Rob. I said, just imagine, 'my father' instead of husband. I think I said father twice, something about what he should or should not eat. Well, Rob did look old, she added to justify herself and hurried upstairs to tell him how funny it was.

Often in their life together she would say to him 'Would you think I could be as awful as all that?' for she had a reputation as someone who spoke first and thought after-wards, and Rob would almost always say 'Yes, yes, I could.' So she came to amuse him now, but he lay on the bed with his heavy shoes on, pale, sweating, clammy. He looked at her as if from a distance; by the time she had phoned for an ambulance his eyes were closed. Don't leave me, she said hanging on to him, I never wanted anyone else, which was another silly thing to say for there had never been a doubt about that.

Duncan Fallowell

SAILING TO GOZO

We are held for two days in Catania port by violent storms. All of Mount Aetna and much of the town have disappeared in a dark turbulence of drenching cloud, out of which a dome, a line of statues or a towerblock might briefly emerge. The winds rage, and whip the rain into diagonals and spirals which sting the face on deck or blow in sudden blinding smears against the portholes if we withdraw inside. Our ship, which is painted the blue and white colours of the Tirrenian Line, is large and has the protection of the basin. But immense waves, so uncharacteristic of the Mediterranean Sea, break against the far side of the harbour wall, sending displays of foam up to a great height. Ever-phlegmatic, the crew play cards in the saloon while the passengers, few at this time of year (only a couple of dozen in a ship which can take hundreds plus cars), stare listlessly out at the chaotic dimness.

Occasionally someone dashes down the gangplank into the deluge, along the harbourside and into the town, to buy the chewy almond cakes for which Catania is famous. In due course he will reappear, sodden but triumphant, with a small elegantly wrapped parcel in a dripping plastic bag. I have already performed this errand myself and the cakes, not too sweet yet dusted in a talcum of sugar, are exquisitely satisfying, especially when taken with tea. But the tea served at the ship's bar is without question the most repulsive I've ever encountered, its taste a mixture of filth and antiseptic, its colour a perturbed grey. And the coffee's not much better.

On the third morning the sky is blue, the light a quivering gold, and the city is visible in meticulous detail. Behind it, the shallow gradient of Aetna slides gracefully to the heavens. All is fresh and new and at last, after half an hour of premonitory throbbing and squirting through its flanks, the ship sails for Malta at 1 pm.

We hug the coast for a long time until blocks of flats appear on the shore, followed by the toytown cluster of Old Syracuse – at the very mention of the name, an enchanted urban felicity arises in the mind: palaces and opera house, cathedral and café, ancient gold stone and young gold flesh, palm trees, sea breezes, handbag snatchers, death in carnival costume, good food al fresco on warm velvet nights, all the sublime and crooked clichés of the south jostling softly together – the locus of another story – not this one.

We tie up alongside the Syracuse esplanade with its string of pom-pom trees and line of grand houses. Scootered or roller-skating kids greet our arrival, then stand mutely staring up at the floating bulk while seven more passengers join the ship – four of them, bent by heavy bags of foodstuffs, turn out to be residents of Gozo.

'Is it like Sicily?' I ask.

'Not in the slightest. Where will you be staying?'

'I rather fancied the sound of the Duke of Edinburgh Hotel – in Victoria.'

'Ah.'

'What do you mean?'

'Do you like character?'

'Yes.'

'Then you'll love it.'

'I haven't booked or anything.'

'At this time of the year it'll be empty.'

We put to sea proper, sailing south-south-west. Everything is fine for ninety minutes – then without warning the ship slides down a steep bank of water into a lurching swell. At first it is almost amusing, in funfair fashion, but one by one the passengers turn avocado green and disappear into their cabins. On deck a pregnant woman collapses in utter disorientation. Legs buckling this way and that, head lolling and eyes rolling as though in the last throes of mad cow disease, and ballooning cargo of unborn flesh threatening to take off into yet another independent direction, she is helped below by companions. Usually I do not suffer from sea-sickness beyond a slightly queasy sense of surprise. I do what one is supposed to do: use the horizon to maintain at least one constant in a world of liquefying references. But eventually I too begin to feel uncomfortable and decide to go below for something to settle the stomach. On the way I pass a splattered mess which looks like half-digested almond cake mixed with tomatoes, and in the cabin my prosciutto e formaggio bread rolls take on a lurid, almost mescalin repulsiveness. Oppressed by the distant, explosive smashing of plates beyond the narrow door, I force down some food and lay my head on the pillow – the very worst thing one could do. Within this tiny coffinlike retreat, all is rectilinear; all reference-points fixed; and yet the entire cabin is pitching about in the most appalling, drunken manner. This disjunction between the evidence of one's eyes (fixity) and the evidence of the other senses (lurcherama) produces swimming of the mind and nausea in the stomach. Really it would be best to go back up on deck but I lack the resolve and so am tossed horribly on the bunk, wondering why the hell I ever left my cosy flat in Notting Hill, or the freezing flat in Palermo.

In fact the reason is quite simple. Curiosity. Through the long coal-black nights of an English winter, I have sat on the floor in front of the fire and pored over the atlas, imagining the world. The large sumptuous legends of escape – Gobi, Venice, Brazil – can send one reeling. But certain small names have a miniaturist allure as of a dream which is exotic but manageable, unusual but wholly gratifying, like a fantastic charm on the bracelet of life. Malacca, Noto, Swaziland, Cochin, Galle, Bordighera. Often there is a misfit quality to these places, crumbling colonial backwaters whose day has gone – if they manage to convey the feeling that the clock stopped in 1929 I can get very excited: nostalgia becomes a form of rebirth. Sometimes it's just the name, the very configuration of letters (especially if it contains a 'z', 'q' or 'x'), which suggests the ideal, forgotten stopping place. Usually they are on the coast or are islands with a quaint capital, and in warm climates – in which case they should be visited out of the hot season (an endless battle with the sun severely curtails the psychic space which these resorts are intended to supply).

In such respects Gozo appeared to have everything. An island off the north-east coast of Malta, it was part of the British colony and occasionally visited by Governors from Valletta by way of recreation. The capital Victoria was named in honour of the Queen on the occasion of her Diamond Jubilee in 1897, and there is in Victoria only one hotel – the Duke of Edinburgh. Gozo's history is very old. Odysseus was shipwrecked there and entertained for seven years by Calypso, the nymph daughter of Atlas – but there are remains of temples built two thousand years before this. It is said to be greener, sleepier, more seductive than its parent island. The inhabitants speak English, make red wine, and drive on the left hand side in the deep deep south of Europe within winking distance of Arabian Africa . . .

Meanwhile, back in the cabin, the torture continues. The particular distress of sea-sickness is not simply the sick feeling but the way it mimics certain forms of insanity through confused perception, the arousal of subconscious fears, dissociation and so forth. Vomit I do not however, and as suddenly as we fell into it, we are out of this plunging pull of water. Apparently the crossing is nearly always bad (this being the narrow and only sea channel between the large bodies of the east and west Mediterranean) but has been made far worse by the storms. Somehow the transition itself, to placidity, is unnoticed; there only comes a moment when it dawns on one that an agony has passed, that one is OK, that one is hungry. It is very difficult maintaining atheism at sea: I give thanks to God in abject, tearful fashion and polish off the ham and cheese rolls.

With fearsome bangs on doors, the stewards pass down the corridor saying pack up, we'll be in port within the hour. Night has fallen. On deck I face into a chill wind and discern by degrees an amber, fanlike glow in the black distance – the first hint of valiant Malta, a rocky riverless island which despite blockades and dreadful bombardments never surrendered to the Fascists during the War (in 1942 King George VI awarded the entire citizenry the George Cross, which emblem has been incorporated into the national flag).

The approach and entry to the Grand Harbour at Valletta is a marvel I have not been prepared for. With the wind dropping and the water calming at every stage, bastion upon bastion of the greatest fortress in the world, tier upon tier climbing from knuckles of rock and floodlit a coppery orange, unfold their crenellations and turrets in a slow, seemingly endless series of operatic tableaux on either side of the channel. Above the wavy curtains of these golden battlements, blue floodlight bathes baroque and neo-classical buildings among palm trees whose fronds show up like tiny green herringbones. Sea approaches are always magical – the finely graduated decoding of a mystery – and this approach to Valletta must be the most awe-inspiring in the Old World as that to Manhattan is in the New. Silently on smooth jet water, the ship advances, saluted everywhere by serrated magnificence.

Tucked on to a stone terrace is the Grand Harbour

Hotel, a much smaller establishment than it sounds. A young man of immense girth attends the night desk and his trusting affable demeanour is very conspicuous after one's period of living in Palermo tensions. He puts me in Room 67, tiny, with a view over luminous castled water. I sprawl on the bed, letting mental pictures sift themselves. Sleep comes slowly.

The Gozo boat is at lunchtime. Though spring this year has been unsettled, it is hot today, with a few detergent-white clouds in a flat blue sky. The run isn't long and extends north-west off the Maltese coast, chugging past miles of ugly cement buildings. The bare creamy rock of Comino Island is a natural relief, and then the eyes turn ahead to the distant lineaments of Gozo . . .

It isn't very green and is surprisingly built up, not out of a Conrad novel at all. And yet the buildings are mostly low, sporting mass-produced classical details. There is a sense of intimacy and coherence which is not crass. However, on the cliffs above the harbour several gothic revival churches look wildly inappropriate.

I take a taxi into Victoria and at a set of traffic lights on the harbour road the driver is obliged to stop. My attention is caught by a man. He is about thirty years old, heavily built with black curly hair, and standing on the kerb staring straight through the window at me. The face has finely balanced features, is slightly hard, but why its rather irascible expression should be directed at me I can't imagine. So at once on this island there is a sense of contact – and a sense of – not hostility, not at all, but of, well, disquiet.

The Duke of Edinburgh Hotel *is* out of a novel, if not by Conrad then by Graham Greene or Lawrence Durrell or Malcolm Lowry. I am captivated the moment its Italianate façade appears at the bottom of Victoria's main street. The foyer is dim and noiseless, spaciously cool with old brown furniture, and hung with yellowing testimonials from the

British Royal Family, the Governors of Malta, and Winston Churchill's private secretary. It has seen better days and is now absolutely abandoned – not a soul about – nothing – a few keys on hooks behind a dusty, dark wood reception desk are the only clue that this might be a place of accommodation. Like the man at the traffic lights, its interest verges on the creepy.

Eventually I track down in the bar a dreamy young woman who books me in. The bed and breakfast rate is of a cheapness which says that if you like you could stay here for ever, so at once I feel safe.

She hands me Key No.3, explaining that it is for Room No.2. An ancient and very, very tall housemaid with a few long teeth, Big Bertha, is persuaded to desert her slop buckets and show me upstairs. The staircase features haphazard photographs of the Royal Family and rises to a large, high-ceilinged landing where the floor is of floral tiles in muted colours and the furniture amounts to a faded gilt mirror, a rudimentary console table and a giant linen chest. It all strives towards an idea of grandeur whose charm lies not in the achievement but in the attempt.

My room is a suite. Heavy wooden double doors, once upon a time painted dark blue, open into a lobby which steps down into a bedroom with two beds, many primitive cupboards, and another pretty floral floor. Beyond is a bathroom with a tribe of ants scurrying round the bath as if in a white rollerdrome, and an overhanging water-heater which Bertha switches on with an air of pride, flicking at the ants with a cloth. Her English is not superb and when I say I'm from London she grunts and says 'Yes, garden', opening a door of frosted glass on to a south-facing balcony which overlooks the hotel's back garden and a small waterless swimming-pool. It will be possible to sit on the loo and stare through the open door at lemon and palm trees without feeling exposed. The balcony possesses a washing-line complete with wooden pegs and the afternoon sun streams on to it. Yes, one could live here for quite a while.

When Big Bertha has gone, half chuckling, half amazed, having strenuously tried to refuse my tip, I test the bed. Comfy. Linen sheets, cream woollen English blankets, worn but clean. High up on the ceiling is a fan which works. They tear out fans these days, lower the ceilings and instal air-conditioning, but thankfully not here. I am describing the place in some detail because it is a rare example of a type which has almost disappeared from the world. In how many tropical or quasi-tropical rooms like this have I slugged from a bottle or kissed a brown neck or dreamed? The Fonseca, Aurangzeb Road, New Delhi, now demolished – someone said there was a Holiday Inn on the site. The Constellation in Vientiane – God knows what's happened there. The Christina, Mexico City – more expensive now. These stylishly down-at-heel old-fashioned hotels with big, cheap, bare, decrepit rooms are so useful and becoming so scarce.

Victoria's main street, climbing in accelerating steepness to the small central square with its red telephone box and red pillar box, is lined with classical buildings of quality, including two enormous theatres, the Aurora and the Astra, each belonging to one of the island's two chief brass bands. At 9 pm it is cold and dark, the streets are empty, and there is not one restaurant open, just a couple of tacky bars lit by the heartless glare of strip lighting – a few gnarled peasants smoke and growl inside. From the citadel's breezy ramparts one sees perhaps as many as twenty great churches near and far, all picked out in lightbulbs because Easter is approaching, which for Christians is a sinister mixture of misery and exultation, horrible death and weird rebirth, but which usually affects me more directly, as the spring festival, joyous herald of the opening year.

Back at the hotel I have an excellent pizza – the pizzas, it seems, are what keep the whole establishment going –

and a bottle of red Gozitan wine (good colour, robust round taste with no trace of tartness or chemicals). So . . . here I am on the island with the wonderful four-letter name. But now that I'm here, what am I going to do?

I think I'm going to do nothing. In which case I'd better rent a car – in places like this you require a car if you are truly to wander aimlessly, lest you find yourself having to take buses to specific destinations. The bedroom is chilly; switch on heater. There are only two other guests in the hotel, a couple in the room next to mine (presumably put there for Big Bertha's convenience). The sounds of their love-making civilize the silence. No, I'm not jealous. I have all that back in Palermo – otherwise, yes, I should be jealous.

The agent who rents cars pooh-poohs any suggestion that I should pay a deposit. This is remarkable – as is the fact that the car is parked outside, unlocked, with the keys already in it. The gears are pretty wrecked – it takes some fishing about to find one – but driving on Gozo is sheer honky tonk pleasure. All roads fan out from Victoria and basically you move in the direction you wish to go and trust to instinct. You may be on the wrong road – but you cannot get lost.

I head between stone-walled fields for the principal sight of the island, the prehistoric Ggantija Temples, but they are closed today so I judder on to Ramla Bay. It is embraced by crumbly cliffs and green terraces of maize, and over-looked by Calypso's cave. This is the finest beach in a not very beachy archipelago and developers are always trying to destroy it but thus far the Government has resisted. Its orange sand is blank but for a couple of stragglers, a van selling snacks, and a man with long black hair leading a donkey. I scramble over low rocks, but looking down at my plimsolls, see that they are smeared with tar. Enormous clots of it cling to the bases of the rocks like a black death. So I climb to a higher track – but this one is waterlogged from recent rain. Some good way ahead a figure is walking towards me, so it must be possible to negotiate. Suddenly I realize this is the man with the fierce face at the traffic lights, and I sit on a boulder to await his arrival: he will know all about the condition of the path ahead. But strange to say, he never does arrive. The track curves in and out of one's line of vision and the man does not again emerge into view. I cannot see that it's possible for him to have gone in any other direction – so has the earth swallowed him up? This is very odd. And in an unsettling way, I feel connected to his disappearance, in that had I not been here, he surely would have passed by this boulder . . .

An onshore wind has whipped the waves into frothing lines, so I search for shelter among the low dunes and bushes at the back of the beach and chance upon a middle-aged man with trim white moustache, wearing a salmon pink polo-neck sweater and a large battered straw hat. He is reading but lays the volume aside and says 'Hullo'. His name is Gregory, an American painter and polymath, who has been living here since 1968.

'God, I bet you've seen some changes.'

'Oh, the centre of the island's almost filled up. I think they're running out of stone. Do you know, I was reading an article on Post-Modernism in architecture the other day, and the author said that Gozo is the only place where the production of the classical pillar has gone on uninterrupt-edly since ancient times. Have you been swimming?'

'Are you serious?'

'Rain or shine, winter or summer, I swim every day. But I don't sunbathe any longer. I had a touch of skin cancer which is now sorted out but that's why I'm done up like this.'

There is an exuberant noise above us. A shepherd boy is capering down the rocky hill in S-shaped descents, whoop-ing and laughing, leading his flock in a sort of Gadarene run. The sheep dart hither and thither in unison like a school of fish. I look at Gregory, thinking he might say something, but he is now gazing sublimely out to sea through translucent blue eyes, with the expression on his face of a stranded deity – thoroughly here, thoroughly not here, as though he has a great deal more space between his atoms than do most people.

'The atmosphere can sometimes be very clear,' he says eventually. 'Do you know, once or twice a year you can see Sicily from Ramla. And once in a decade you can see Aetna.'

'Do you go to Sicily much?'

'I don't go anywhere much. I have travelled. Widely. But now I can hardly get it together to go into Victoria to have my eyes tested.'

In a place like Victoria, with nothing to do at night, with no radio or television or company in my room, I rediscover the fantastic power of cinema. I hunger for every film at the Aurora or Astra, any piece of trash. At the Aurora I have just seen *Diamond Skulls*, about turpitude among the British upper classes. The auditorium was built on a lavish scale, refitted in the Festival of Britain style after a fire, and tonight there was a smell of rotting fish weaving about inside it. A mere two dozen customers partook of this giant space for the Saturday night show. Curiously there was an interval. They simply stopped the film halfway through. Nobody did anything; no girl came round with ice-creams; the film just ground to a halt, the lights came up for ten minutes, went down again, and the film flickered back into life.

But this wasn't all that happened, because when the lights came up, granting a break from murderous mayhem, I stood to stretch my legs, looked round the redly illumined hangar – and saw that man again, the traffic lights one. He was sitting about eight rows behind and over to the left. I didn't like to stare because his dark features were lost in the umbra and I'd be unable to determine his eye. But it was the Frowning One all right. So I decided to walk out to the foyer, and as I passed he held his eyes rigidly ahead, deliberately not looking at me. Therefore – I had been noticed too. When I came back in, I sat three rows behind and occupied the remaining interval in observing how the blood lamps reflected on his black curls, and when the film started again I was only partially reabsorbed by the unpleasant narrative. From time to time I checked out the head until – I don't know how it happened – it wasn't there any more. He'd gone. The man had gone. How could he have left without my noticing? He couldn't've done that. There was a quick flutter of panic. He couldn't've gone. But he had. I felt ridiculous. Who is he? And why is he playing these tricks on me?

Gozo is not fashionable. The last notables to live here were Nicholas Monsarrat who was writing to within a week of his death from cancer, and Anthony Burgess 'who complained,' said Gregory, 'that Maltese Government censorship was so severe he couldn't receive some of his own books!' The reason for its unfashionableness is the food, which if anything is even worse than on Malta. The food shops are full of rubbish and often dirty. But there's a small supermarket selling British and German tins and sadly (on those days when I can't face another Duke of Edinburgh pizza or afford the up-market Salvina's) I'm relying on these plus vitamin pills. The menu at the back of Ramla Bay's snack van reads: spaghetti & chips, hot dog, hamburger, fried egg, white bread & butter. I settle for a bottle of soda water and a packet of banana chewing-gum manufactured in South Korea.

Tonight (today being the Feast of Our Lady of Sorrows) a Madonna is paraded through the central square, supported by grim or giggling men, accompanied by rocking candles in red glasses. The effigy is followed at snail's pace by a baby Austin van inside which a big peasant priest, his knees forced under his chin, drones intonements through a crackly loudspeaker strapped to the roof. Around it and behind shuffles a throng of Gozitans muttering responses in dark clothes. Some German tourists, jazzily attired, are silenced by the spectacle, and look on motionlessly until one of them takes a snap, the spell is broken, and they disappear noisily down the hill. Overhead meanwhile, thousands of birds are screaming in the trees. Their multiple, overlapping chirrups grate violently on the ear-drums. The triple conjunction – shuffling Gozitans, jazzy Germans, screaming birds – makes me feel sick. Why this particular form of helplessness should strike, I don't know – but I'm not surprised by it – and decide to return to the refuge of the hotel and an evening with a book, 'Bacchus' wine (pretty label), and tins.

A Sicilian friend has a theory that the people of the sea are more intelligent than the people of the mountains because sea air confers some chemical advantage to the development of the brain. The Gozitans seem not to support this theory in that, though generally good-natured when you do get through to them, they are not great conversationalists or mentally agile. So in the bar tonight it takes persistence to extract from the owner's son that the hotel is over 100 years old and has always had the same name. For some reason he feels this is compatible with its being named after the Duke of Edinburgh, husband of Queen Elizabeth II. Such elementary failure of logic is what can shock you in the Gozitans.

In fact it must be named after the previous holder of the title, Prince Alfred, 'Affie', Victoria's fourth child, who married the daughter of Tsar Alexander II. (Subsequent research reveals that Affie was also Commander of the Mediterranean Fleet, a keen violinist, and a collector of stamps which he left to the British Museum on his death in 1900.) The hotel is very conveniently situated. All the amenities of toy-town – the bank, the post office, the English newspaper shop, the Rundle Gardens, the two theatres, the Telemalta overseas telephone service – are only a few steps from the front door. I must tell you – I was phoning from the Telemalta office yesterday and asked for a London directory. They didn't have one. They had very few directories. 'We have this,' said the pretty girl, keen to help, and handed me the directory for Costa Rica.

Good Friday. The Crucifixion of Our Lord. Why do they call it 'good'? It's like Sunday with knobs on – a floating gloom you could almost bottle and sell as a concentrated extract: extreme unction. Every flag is at half mast. The theatres have placed crosses over their entrances but from the balcony of the Aurora two loudspeakers broadcast tapes of the brass band blowing sedate Victorian and Italian marches and slow dance tunes from long ago, all in minor keys, with very lugubrious effect. The failure to hit notes adds an extra blighted touch and all is smeared into a whine by the poor quality of the sound system. A little boy and girl holding hands stare up perplexedly at the speakers as though trying to work out how the noise got up there.

Gozo's relative treelessness means that the salt air carries right across the island and when it isn't hot this makes the atmosphere noticeably clammy and chill. There is consequently a stickiness to the bedcover as I stretch out with a bunch of pillows at the head reading Pope's *The Rape of the Lock* and consider intermittently this solitary state ... There is nothing to worry about. Which can sometimes induce a free-fall panic because worries are the banisters of life. But at present, no: thoughts and impressions pass through me in leisurely, comprehensible sequences. And yet the very blankness of the worry sheet supplies a surface on which a fine seismic needle can now and again scratch that distant disquiet deriving from the Frowning One. In a busier world I'd not notice it – or him – but here ... Without disquiet there can be no sense of adventure. Disquiet is the awareness of possibility, that something might happen. Disquiet brings alertness – which means that Gozo is not bland.

But it is relaxing. The island still has something of what the Mediterranean had before tourism hit it, a self-sufficient character which is intimately connected to its drawbacks. Don't moan so much about the food. Good food demands a more aggressive, more callous sense of culture. And if British rule must take some responsibility for the awfulness of the food, perhaps it can also take some for the probity of the population, both features being untypical of the southern world. Gozo will do you no violence. Even the dogs are gentler than Sicilian dogs. I also feel here the calming power of religion, the embosoming glamour of tolling bells. It is now 10.45 pm and stepping on to the balcony I see a cross of golden lightbulbs on top of a nearby church, greeting me over the roof-tops of the town, including me, piercing the circumference of the self so that any lingering fretfulness leaks away and one flows in a larger, more benign rhythm. On this night I sleep very well.

Thus far the rain has held off but the Easter weather is not good. On Saturday fierce gales stream across the island from the direction of Greece and the sky is skidding lead.

'I'm sorry about the weather,' says Gregory in his carefully modulated Harvard voice, as if the climate is his personal responsibility.

'It's OK. It makes it like Cornwall. Will you swim?'

'This very second.'

He peels off his knitted salmon skin and totters down the sand into a heavy sea near rocks, a fragile but somehow invulnerable figure. Periodically his head becomes visible and the occasional flailing arm. Five minutes later he's staggering back up in a serpentine route, muttering 'Oh God . . . oh God . . .'

'Isn't it dangerous?'

'Yes. This sort of weather can generate a terrific current in the bay like a fast-flowing river. But I know where to go, along by those rocks.'

'I was reading *The Rape of the Lock*.'

'I love that bit at the end,' he says, 'about the birth of a comet.'

Over at Marsalform, Gozo's main and shabby tourist resort, the sea is in magnificent disarray. Waves crash across the short promenade and girls squeal with delight at these rocketing douches. Young spivs cruise slowly in dilapidated fuckmobiles and a large party of London schoolchildren, wearing dayglo sports clothes and sharp haircuts, gossip furiously in a café – their animation marks them out as not local.

At tea-time the rain arrives, sluicing the island without pause. A mothers' meeting is going on in the Duke of Edinburgh's bar among a caterwaul of babies and Big Bertha waves to me from the adjacent dining-room. She is doing her best to be a waitress but 'grace under pressure' is not a characteristic of hers. The owner's son is also here, babyfying, and I tell him how I've fallen in love with the hotel.

'Oh good,' he replies, 'and it will be even better soon.'

'What do you mean?'

'We will develop.'

I go cold.

'What do you mean?'

'The bank won't lend us money for improvements unless we become a four star hotel and the Government won't give us four star rating unless we have different type of rooms, air-conditioning, things like that – so to get the loan, we have to demolish it.'

I feel physically slapped. He must have noticed my expression because he adds. 'Oh, we'll keep the façade on to the street.'

'But the place is solid as a rock. It doesn't need demolition. It's a complete waste of money.'

'Write and tell the bank manager.'

'So what about the high ceilings and fans and flowered floors?'

'Bulldozer.'

'It's mad.'

'That's what my father says.'

'And Big Bertha?'

'Who?'

'Can I have a whisky?'

Certainly there is a case for doing the place up – it's not making the best use of itself. But really the 19th-century front half and the 1920s back half need only a clever, caring hand to turn this into a smart little operation. That's probably what's missing. The cleverness.

He shrugs his shoulders and says, 'If we don't demolish, the bank won't lend us money. So after the summer, the bulldozers arrive. September 1st.'

'Why not just demolish the 1920s bit? Keep the rest.'

'No. Demolish all.'

I return to my room in despair, wade through a packet of dates, and pop a vitamin pill while the rain pours down the window. This is the only hotel on Gozo with any history or personality – therefore it has to be demolished. Haven't they heard, in this wretched backwater of blinkered bank managers, that the name of the game these days is restoration? Character is *in*, mate! The fading royal photographs, the imperial plaudits from the Palace at Valletta, everything will be swept away except the name, that is to say, the façade.

The sense of loss is disorientating. Already I am mourning the hotel's death, seeing clearly that the room wherein I lie will be two rooms, maybe four rooms, the new floor slicing horizontally through my ribcage, the chemically conditioned air stinging the noise, the manmade fibres bringing out a cold sweat . . .

I pour a glass of red Bacchus. Suddenly the ghosts of the place are very strong, aroused by imminent obliteration – bits of talk about garden parties and someone's sister's adultery threaded by echoes of 1930s dance music – ah, the

English this way came – you can hear them laughing and sighing, drinking, ruling, playing tennis and gramophone records, being languidly noble and sardonically, ironically grand, controlling continents with a casual, throwaway gesture born of romance and rectitude and boredom and fun – cocktails and epaulettes, infidelity and justice, war and peace and pale blue eyes looking over a deep blue sea to beyond the horizon – nostalgia hisses into the room like a gas, as asphyxiating as a faceful of jasmin blossoms.

All at once the swoony sense of loss agitates then breaks through in a wave of upsetting power. Walls collapse. Wine gurgles in the brain. And out of the inner swamp, arises the hydra-headed monster of Death, dripping putrid weed and fanged with fire ... oh the death of many things, both relative and absolute ... the death of empire and of childhood ... death of the past ... death of dream ... and death of the Mediterranean, death of refuge ... death of beauty ... death of immortality itself ... and the waters of death and desolation, having churned, settle again, into a melancholy so rich, so profligate in associations, that it amounts to a kind of self-affirmation: any humour which moves so deeply and variously within us enlarges the map of our being. Nostalgia, loss, melancholy, are these not forms of love? Or are they forms of greed?

Actually I feel awful. More Bacchus. Yes, such a pretty label. I must take a few bottles away with me. Because I shall leave Gozo now – can't live here for ever after all. The clock which stopped is moving again. Time starts eating again, with a crunchy noise like that of the death-watch beetle.

Easter Sunday. I drive to Ramla to say good-bye to Gregory – he is, as always, there. And so is the Frowning One. In a small place such as Gozo I must have seen a number of strangers several times over, but because they have not attracted my attention these recurrences have passed unnoticed – have failed to be granted the accolade of 'synchronicity'. Today he is not frowning but playing on the sand with two toddlers, obviously his own, while a young woman, obviously his wife, looks quietly on. The weather is marginally better than yesterday's. Even so, the man is the only one on the beach who has taken off his shirt. Once in a while he stands hands on hips, looking round, displaying the T-shape of hair on his chest. The four of them potter for a further ten minutes, the man puts on his shirt, and they clamber into an old jalopy and drive off.

'I'm going tomorrow.'

'Come back again one day,' says Gregory.

For holiday-time, the beach is surprisingly deserted – a couple of people walking dogs, three schoolboys sitting on scooters near the snack van.

'They are going to demolish the Duke of Edinburgh Hotel.'

'Are they?' he replies. 'That's a shame. Here, let me give you this.' He forages in his bag under a bush and produces a small square painting, vaguely Islamic in manner, sort of golden letters appearing out of a cosmic whoosh, but subtle.

'It's very kind of you, Gregory. What do the letters say?'

'Don't worry about that. It's my own language.'

'Your own language?'

'Yes, I invented a language. And an alphabet to go with it. Oh look – the sun's come out.'

'Gregory, excuse me for a moment.'

I have seen the Frowning One. He is alone now and walking briskly round the rocky headland where I spied him once before. As I run across the sand he turns the bend out of sight but I keep following, climbing up beyond the tar line. The route grows more tortuous, the rocks ever more extravagantly varied, until I'm scrambling through a lunar landscape of mini-ravines and crags, tumbled boulders forming many small enclosed spaces. Here and there, stone has been worn flat by the diluvial lick – hidden sunbathing spots in the season but now as silent as the grave.

Pausing to catch my breath, I scan for indications. Maybe he found a short cut to wherever he's going, a secret passage through the maze of rocks. The terrain slopes sharply up from the shore and it looks as though in a couple of places there has been a recent landslip ... Then I register – not a noise exactly – perhaps a signal just beyond the range of the conscious senses – anyway a piece of information which causes me to climb carefully and peer between rocks.

Not far away, in a sheltered scoop, I see him. His clothes have been thrown off and lie in a jumbled heap. He is naked, with shaggy haunches pumping slowly against someone. The broad golden expanse of his back prevents the disclosure of who it is. Then he stops, twists his torso, turns his head and sees me ...

Blood rushes up through my whole body, tingling hotly into head and face. He turns further. There is a flash of white teeth – he's grinning! His erect penis bobs in the sunlight. Then he makes a gesture with his left arm and returns to the work in hand. The gesture was entirely ambiguous. It could have meant either go away, or join us. For several seconds I am held in heart-thumping fascination, then embarrassment drives me off, and I scurry quickly away over the rocks ... By the time the sand is reached, my body and mind have become fully alert and my whole being overtaken by a sense of profound dissatisfaction.

Back at the hotel Big Bertha is cleaning the bedroom – at 5 pm. I apologetically remove my tarry shoes. She says 'Tomorrow sun'. I say 'Tomorrow I leave' and give her money before she escapes. Again she tries to refuse it, as though suspicious of what it's for.

Lying on the bed, my eyelids close – and snap open. Nostalgia and melancholy – are they not forms of sleeping?

The sense of loss – enough of it! no more! Time boomerangs: the pull of the past is succeeded by the pull of the future. Sense of loss is replaced not by resignation – how boring resignation is – but by the sense of expectancy. And the death of immortality? What nonsense! It looked beautiful on the page but fails to convince as an idea. All single ideas fail to convince, because our world is embodied contradiction, our lives made possible only in the conflicts of reciprocity. And now it is the future's turn. So let the hydras of death be transformed into perpetual novelty! Besides, I've run out of books and there's not a proper bookshop on the island. If I stay I'll be forced, like Gregory, to invent my own language and 'a private language' is one paradox I don't go for. Hot water gushes into the bath and shampoo makes fragrant foam. Tomorrow – another boat, another destination.

Eliza Fewett

THE FAT LADY

The London summer of 1976 was very, very hot. A newly qualified doctor, keen as mustard, I was filled with idealism and wonder – yet to be exhausted, cynical, burnt out – so that when the squalling blast of the ambulance was heard, I raced out of casualty. The rear doors were thrown open and a sharp, keening sound startled us. The nurses, old hands, efficient at their business, impatiently pushed me aside. They were pulling, tugging and the strange noise became ever shriller, rising and falling rhythmically, a prim-eval sound. Bit by bit an enormous bulk became apparent, and then a human form, gigantic, swathed in red blankets. Atop was a tiny head, black hair clinging moistly to the skull, its mouth a round O from which now came dreadful shrieks.

A strange contraption was wheeled out from the hospital, two armless wheelchairs lashed together. There was a final enormous and concerted heave and a wail and the bundle was at last unloaded. The chariot, piled high with its human cargo, nurses and porters hanging on like flying outriders, whizzed through sterile corridors, its wheels screeching on corners. Shoe-horned into protesting lifts and then out again, it charged into the ward with a mad clatter of swinging double doors. A great bed had been made ready by tying two together in a corner room and with a whoop and a yell the fat lady was delivered.

We stood and marvelled. The scarlet swaddlings were unwound to reveal a truly enormous woman. She looked to be in her fifties – though not like any fifty-year-old woman I had ever seen – a pyramid of quivering fat, now quietly weeping. Tiny hands emerged from great bracelets of adiposity that concealed the wrists, with fingers like little bunches of chipolatas, tips vermilion-varnished. They dabbed at tear-streaked slits of cheek and brow, the eyes hidden. I looked for her toes: they too were painted red, peeping out from spiral folds of rococo fat that swagged her elephantine legs. Her belly was vast, moving, it seemed, of its own volition like a slow quicksand: pulled by decades of gravity, criss-crossed by lightning flashes of old stretch marks, it draped almost to her knees, hiding the pudenda.

Her distress was evident and terrible. Communication in English seemed impossible and no interpreter could be found. There was a spreading red stain on the sheets: she was bleeding heavily, probably vaginally. We argued as to how to proceed, disturbed and confused by her terror. Suddenly there was another loud bang, then weird howlings: her crying stopped and for the first time we glimpsed her eyes. She raised her head to listen as two very large, colourful and loud creatures burst into the room. They were the fat lady's offspring.

Whereas we had guessed that the mother might weigh fifty stone or so, the two daughters were lighter at perhaps thirty and forty stone respectively, with ages roughly to match. Gaudily made-up and perfumed, they vibrated with agitation like anxious fledglings, swooping and twittering about their poor grounded mother. Bangles clattering, earrings dancing, it was some time before they were coherent. They spoke poor and broken English and their story was sad. Ten years ago they had moved from a small fishing village in Cyprus. Their father had travelled to England a few times before and had returned with tales of sophistication and excitement. Husbands, he had promised, would abound. They had moved into cramped, cold rooms somewhere near Kensal Green, miles from the nearest

Greek speaking community, quite stranded. The father went away for ever longer periods and finally, after about a year, vanished completely. Money still sporadically arrived from somewhere in the North – here they gestured wildly – but no note or explanation. We wondered why they had not tried to find him, nor even tried to return to Cyprus, but they made us understand that they could only wait, hoping that he would return to pick up the slack reins of their lives. Marooned, without friends or language, they existed, practising the only skill they knew in this cold strange land: they cooked.

First of all the mother cooked, the two daughters going out foraging. The work was never ending and never beginning, never done but always in hand, and with the food they comforted themselves, awaiting their Ulysses' return. They never sat down to a meal but consumed it while preparing the next. From time to time they would rest a little to allow digestion to take place. The starch broke down into sugars and was absorbed into the blood and carried to the liver: fierce enzymes reduced the fats to a fine emulsion which was carried through the bowel wall into the lacteals, then to be released as milky chyle into the blood to make it creamy. Other molecular mechanisms strove to clear the ingested calories from the blood to fuel the basic metabolic functions and to provide the women with the energy to walk from bed to stove and back again. All excess was laid down as sumptuous deposits of yellow, rich and glistening fat.

The time came when the mother could no longer stand to work: the elder of the daughters took over her rôle while the relatively lithe, young sister expended more calories venturing quite far afield to search for specialist stores where she could speak Greek: her English improved but she feared the day when her sister would also be too fat to move. Then the mother had started to bleed. Her periods had stopped just before coming to England and at first the blood was greeted as the miraculous return of youth. The trickle turned to clots and then to frank haemorrhage and in a panic the younger daughter had dialled 999.

I attempted vaginal examination, but it was nearly impossible. The fat pressed back like rising dough. Lunges with a spatula were eventually rewarded with a specimen of sorts, and the suspected diagnosis confirmed. The lining of the womb, stimulated by excessive amount of oestrogen made in her vast factory of fat, had become malign, evil, cancerous. Endometrial carcinoma is a common disease in the obese. Cells crazed by intoxicating doses of the female hormone lose their ability to stop dividing: not only do they grow, but they migrate, setting up colonies of daughter tumours, and these are the lethal progeny that kill. But how to treat? No surgeon would dare crack open this immensely thick and waxy casing, like the rind of a monstrous tropical fruit, then burrow through the ripe yellow flesh to find the tiny human kernel nestling within. No available ray of ionizing radiation could penetrate to its core. We calculated that if we starved her completely, just replacing fluids and vitamins, it would take two years to render her fat down sufficiently for any treatment, by which time the cancer would have spread and killed her.

It was indeed an extraordinarily hot summer that year. The sun beat down on the new plate-glass hospital, the inadequate air conditioning laboured. Spheres, by minimizing the ratio of surface area to volume, are the most efficient retainers of heat. Man controls his *milieu intérieur* by the evaporation of sweat, relying on the cooling skin to lower the interal core temperature. Spherical humans, with little skin in proportion to bulk, overheat. The fat lady sweated and sweated on her extemporized double bed but still the temperature rose. Sometimes I fancied that she might quite melt away, like a blob of lard in a sizzling hot frying-pan, but every day she seemed the same size despite near starvation. She endured now in virtual silence.

Unfortunately 1976 was also a year of union unrest in hospitals, largely affecting portering and other ancillary staff: porters, alas, were constantly being needed for the fat lady was forever falling out of bed. Her immense abdomen would flow like molten lava, or like a Slinky, that metal toy spring that will climb of its own accord down stairs. When enough tissue had spilt over the edge of the bed, its weight captured by gravity, the rest would follow. With a clap of fat like summer lightning followed by a thunderous cry of pain, the fat lady would fall out of bed. The porters would then have to heave her back, cursing and swearing, threatening to sue. One day they refused to come any more. They struck.

Upon this final indignity the fat lady lost heart. Nurses, doctors, any available staff would sometimes take half a painful hour to lever her back into bed. She shut her eyes and sweltered. The sun rose yet hotter every day and beat through the blinds; any fan to be found was turned on to her, stirring her hair, causing the cardboard icons of the Virgin Mary that crowded the room to flutter to the floor. The nurses sponged her with cold water, her daughters with perfume. The sweet and sickly aroma of volatile breakdown products of dissolving fatty chains, ketones smelling of pear-drops, was borne on her starving breath and suffused the darkened room. Nevertheless her temperature rose: 37, 38, 39, 40 and then 40.5. The news flashed throughout the hospital – she had gone up to 41. And then – like an overworked engine, each part beginning to fail, thus overloading another dependent function until the biochemistry of the blood turned upside down and the muscles that drive chest expansion started to falter and the poisonous waste gases in the hot blood accumulated to toxic levels that started to damage the brain – with a final and great expiration of superheated air, the fat lady died.

The funeral arrangements were unthinkable. To this day I cannot imagine how the obsequies were performed. How could she be fitted into a coffin? Was the crematorium oven big enough, or was she buried in some immense pit, like a plague grave? I do know that we had to arrange an ambulance to take her to the funeral parlour, as she would fit no hearse. We persuaded the ambulancemen to drive over the public weighbridge both on the way there and on return. She turned the scales at 48 stone. I had bet on more and was disappointed because in the *Guinness Book of Records* were recorded two black American women well over the fifty stone mark.

Some years later I went to a Mediterranean island that they say is Circe's isle. Still today are found enormous megalithic temples, built in 3,500 BC, a thousand years before the pyramids and thought to be the oldest standing buildings in the world. They are dedicated to primitive female fertility goddesses, those that came to be called Astarte, Ashtoreth, Great Mother, Mary Queen of Heaven. Images of these divinities have been unearthed, varying from little clay figurines to huge stone statues that would dwarf any living man. Without exception, they are immensely and triumphantly fat. I was told that this neolithic culture had been widespread throughout the Mediterranean before the stern, bronze-wielding, law-giving patriarchs drove the fertility cults underground (though many would emerge again in strangely changed forms). I also knew that in lean times the fat were lauded. Nevertheless it was some time before I thought about the fat lady again. I was walking, not particularly thinking of anything at all, and whether it was a smell or the cry of a bird that triggered the memory, I do not know. I shivered. Into my mind's-eye she suddenly sprang, magisterially robed in white with blossom and bay woven into her hair. Her massive right arm rose, and I saw the finger-tips dipped in red pigment gripping the obsidian dagger as the hard sun struck sparks from the sacrificial blade.

Philip Gooden

TRADESMAN'S ENTRANCE

I hear them before I see them. There's a point near the top of the area steps where I can catch a glimpse of people arriving, but unless I'm quick – and speed is not one of my attributes – any visitor has stepped down and out of my line of sight by the time I reach the window. Then I just have to wait for the shapes to materialize behind the frosted glass of the lobby door.

There are two of them on this occasion, plus Mr Alasdair. Sometimes the visitors hold a small conference on the outside but now Mr Alasdair twists the mortise and opens up straightaway. As they enter he is peddling his usual line about the 'nice neighbourhood'. Not so nice in fact. Next door was burgled a couple of weeks ago by an old man wearing a baseball cap. I know this because before he broke into No.11 he limped down the area steps and crinkled his face against my window. He saw from outside what I see inside – bare walls, an uncarpeted floor, no furniture, no goodies – and turned away in quick disappointment.

Mr Alasdair ushers the couple in. A slight woman with a pointed nose and a young man who glances anxiously at her. They won't be interested, I think. They are hanging back while the agent presses forward, almost leaning into the living-room as if the lobby were the mouth of a treasure cave. But the cave is empty, the young couple understand that. They assess the atmosphere. The woman's nose twitches for something beyond or below the smell of damp. They pause at the stain on the wall. The woman nudges the anxious man. Mr Alasdair is expanding on the potential, the possibilities, until he notices the couple aren't listening.

'Oh those,' he says. 'Don't worry about *those*. That's not damp. It only needs a spot of paint.'

'How long's it been empty?' says the woman.

'Nine months about,' says Mr Alasdair.

Seven months and twelve days. Why does he always overestimate it?

'Feels ... dampish?' says the woman. Over the months I have heard several visitors, the women mostly, struggle to express exactly what it is about the place they find off-putting – unwelcoming – dampish. Something eludes them, they are never satisfied with their definitions.

Mr Alasdair is sounding off about damp courses. His office has the certificates, they have them on file in the office. Already he has lost his listeners. The couple (the woman's name is Katrin, I pick this up from the single remark I hear the anxious man make) go through the motions. They walk out of the living-room into the galley kitchen and then into the main bedroom. They peer into the second bedroom. The lavatory light clicks, the extractor creaks into action. Just inside the big bedroom is a flapping board which Mr Alasdair treads on as he struggles to keep up with his clients. I am able to track anybody down here by the noise. I listen out for the resonating patch of floor between bathroom and lavatory; I have learned to recognize the tiny click made by a coat button colliding with the hinged mahogany shelf outside the bathroom. People keep their coats on when they are being shown round. They seem to feel the, ah, damp.

Now Mr Alasdair, his sandy moustache looking rather dejected, huddles in the living-room with Katrin and her worried man. They stand there like guests who don't know how to make a graceful exit, enduring Mr Alasdair's spiel.

It's all right for them but I'm hearing it for the tenth time. That good neighbourhood again. Quiet, safe (the baseball cap squinting through the window the other night). Interesting period features (that useless mahogany shelf). Great potential. Right moment to consider your first purchase. But Katrin and her man are not buying any of it. They are looking for a way out. And on the way out, in the little lobby, Mr Alasdair begins to say something about the previous owner. I strain to hear but the front door is slammed and mortised over his remarks. Then there is the trudge of feet up the area steps and, presently, the sound of cars departing in opposite directions. I wonder what Mr Alasdair was saying, then remember he wouldn't have been talking about me but about Monica. Me he would never mention, for obvious reasons.

I return to the game. Last week it was 'transubstantiation'. This week it's 'metamorphosis'. The score: 241 so far. Last week's total was higher despite the presence of the 'e' in metamorphosis. It's a task keeping tabs on all those words but I have mastered the memory trick and fluently unscroll the two hundred and forty-one in my mind's eye.

My thoughts will drift though. Visitors invariably disturb. Maybe Mr Alasdair did mention me. I would like to have been mentioned. Even if he doesn't know my name he does know a thing or two. He knows about the dark stains on the wall. I saw him looking dubiously at them one day when he was measuring up the flat. He was alone. He stretched out a hand and brushed lightly at the stains, put his fingertips to his nostrils. Then he went to the bathroom and washed his hands.

I move effortfully to the window. Through the flecked, crusted panes I see: the top of the steps, a colourless valerian sprouting from a crack in the wall opposite, and random shapes where rendering has fallen from the wall to reveal brick beneath. I amuse myself by making new islands and continents in the sea of stucco. This is my world, my empire. My power blocs shift from day to day, so that the southern island which was yesterday leagued with the archipelago at the top of the wall is now allied with the star-shaped continent on the left. From time to time a fresh land-mass appears as more plaster flakes off.

This manoeuvring of imaginary power blocs is painful – but necessary for me. It is my thin link with the past. It is my telephone line to the other side. It reminds me of the period when I marched under the flag of Prudence Properties, and Goldcrop, and Kar Kass. Remember them? No? Well, there were a lot of us around during that decade, we mushroomed in the greedy cellars. I started a dozen or so property companies myself – and I was by no means a big time operator.

Prudence Properties was the most successful, the most elegant of my concerns. It was named after my wife, whom I loved steadily, unobtrusively, until she ran off with another man – whereupon my feelings towards her flared almost out of control. I managed one conversation with her, with Prudence, after that day when I returned to our shared penthouse (late – I'd been with Monica) and discovered the open letter attached to the fridge with a magnetic cucumber. She'd left a phone number. I recognized it as my brother's. My wife and I had one lunch conversation to wrap up thirteen years of marriage.

I had only one thing to say.

'Why?'

She shook her head, in irritation or as if to clear it. Her long rusty hair flowed across her shoulders. Her hair was her glory.

'Can you give me a single reason?'

'A single reason?'

'I'll give you a thousand pounds for every reason,' I said. It was a joke, but I was desperate to know.

'Oh dear, Alan.'

Dear Alan? But, after an instant, my brain corrected what my ears wanted to hear. All she was was sorry for me.

'You need help, Alan.'

'Possibly. But I want to know. Why you left.'

'A reason,' she repeated, as if reason were the most absurd thing in the world. 'All right. You thought you owned me.'

'You'll have to do better than that.'

'I don't have to do anything. But I will say I felt like one of your showhouses. Always on display. One of the show-houses on that estate of yours.'

'Mortcorp.' It was one of Prudence's affectations not to know the names of any of my companies. She even pretended to forget the one that was named after her.

'Whatever it's called,' she said. 'One of those shiny houses with shiny salespersons. I felt all decked out.'

I had noticed that she didn't look so decked out over the restaurant table as she used to. I was going to work round subtly to the money question (no more Glyndebourne for her, no more little trips to China) by impugning her new partner's earning powers. I started neutrally.

'How's Michael?'

Michael was my brother and the man Prudence had moved in with. He was company secretary of Goldcrop, one of my dozen interests. I took him on largely because his dull wife June pleaded with me. Sentiment is rotten business. Michael rewarded us by betraying me and abandoning her, and my little niece and nephew.

'Michael's fine,' said Prudence, that rusty hair catching the light as – years before – it made me catch my breath.

'I don't know what you see – ' I left the sentence unfinished.

'You're very alike in certain ways.'

'But . . .?'

'Plenty of buts,' said Prudence. 'You remember those

pictures as a kid when you had to spot the differences between two scenes that looked identical? It's the details that count. Don't do that.'

I had seized her wrist across the table, hoping that it would be interpreted as a spontaneous gesture. The initiative kept slipping from me.

'And how about you? How are you? And Monica?'

'Monica?' I flared up inside, then felt turned to glass. See-through.

'How did . . .'

'Does that matter?'

'Tell me. Did you use my money to hire a private detective? Was I paying to have myself followed?'

'Someone told me about your mistress maybe, or sent an anonymous letter. Who cares? You have plenty of enemies, Alan.'

'Nonsense,' I said, though what she said was true. Can I help it if people will not see things from my point of view, and then hold that against me? I tried to steer the conversation to money. I was getting desperate.

'Prudence, in a totally disinterested way, I ought to warn you that Michael's job mayn't be secure. I might be forced to restructure.'

Michael had remained as Goldcrop secretary. This kept him – and Prudence – in my debt. Proved I was civilized. (Showed he was a wimp.)

'If Michael loses his job I'll never speak to you again.'

'I thought you'd agreed to one meeting only,' I said, delighted. I had the initiative. But then I was dazzled by her hair. A bolt of late summer sun shafted through the restaurant window behind her and ignited her head. I said, 'It won't be me, Prudence, it'll be the market, if Michael goes. Let's hope it doesn't come to that – if only for the sake of his children. You look wonderful.'

Prudence, with her flaring hair and her knife and fork held childishly erect ever since I had issued my warning about Michael and his job, looked as wonderful as an avenging angel. I hoped she would threaten me, it would demonstrate I still mattered. She said nothing, so I prompted her, 'Do you know, for a moment there it looked as if you might want to kill me.'

'No, but I'll come to your funeral,' she said.

Did she? I don't know. I wasn't able to make it myself, for reasons that will shortly become clear.

Some months after the above lunch-time exchange with my wife I put the muzzle of my father's confiscated Luger between my teeth and fumbled at the trigger. There was a concussing noise, and a smell reminiscent of a dripping woolly sweater put too close to an electric fire.

Then a period of blankness.

It was dark when I woke up. My whereabouts eluded me. What day of the week was it? Eventually I recognized the outlines of Monica's basement flat. I felt oddly weight-less, as one does sometimes waking in the middle of the night. Then I remembered that it was Thursday night and that, prior to falling asleep (in Monica's sitting room?), I had attempted suicide. Obviously I'd failed.

Relief was succeeded by terror. What if my hand had wavered as I was pulling the trigger . . . and I had done no more than cripple myself? I felt nothing. I tried to shake a leg, flex a finger, raise an eyebrow. No go. Not dead then but incapacitated – paralysed – destined to live out my days on a life-support machine.

When the initial terror had subsided, I felt surprisingly tranquil and alert, as if I'd woken early on the first morning of a long holiday. To check my mental condition – because I'd have many hours to while away in an iron lung – I set out to see how many words of three or more letters could be extracted from 'metempsychosis'. During this process I must have wandered off. I was next conscious of my surroundings as light squeezed through the speckled win-dows. I made out a disagreeable mess on the wallpaper and, lying on the parquet beneath, a distorted shape. That wasn't there last night, I thought. After a time I realized what – or rather who – it was. I wanted to be sick but, of course, had nothing to be sick with, through or from. The postman had to do that for me. He was unable to force a parcel through so he rang and banged before pressing his face to the dirty window. I saw him looking at my remains on the floor, I heard him retching in the area outside.

Let me tell you that, after death, you can take it with you. Some of it. First the downside. There's no sense of taste and no smell. I can feel but only in a very distant way, as if I were swathed in a giant oven glove. There are no limbs to feel with, naturally, though from time to time I experience a phantom arm, a fugitive shoulder. Conversely nobody can feel me. People have cut me dead, walked not merely past me but through me. I am capable of impressing myself very marginally on my environment. I carry around the breath of a breath, which may be brushed aside by the careless human but which – nevertheless – makes itself known, as witness the 'damp' sensation enjoyed by my women visitors. And with this cold damp breath I achieve great things. Recently I shifted a half-full box of matches, carelessly left by Mr Alasdair, a few tenths of an inch along the mantelpiece.

On the positive side: I can hear, hear well in fact. Hear things I never heard before. I'm not certain but I suspect inanimate objects talk to each other all day long. The floor and ceiling of the living-room hold a stilted dialogue, while the walls have ears.

I see, but not in colour. Post-mortem sight is like television in the 1950s – it's in black and white and it's not very interesting. Imagine watching the potter's wheel inter-lude for eternity.

Oh, and I can report there's no great colony over here on the other side. I haven't chummed up with anyone, although it may be that they're shunning me because I used the tradesman's entrance. I'm a, you know, suicide, one of those.

I have an insect's freedom of movement, can haul my non-existent ears and black and white vision laboriously about the room in which I killed myself. I ponder the mystery of how I come to have some diminished sense of sight and enhanced sense of hearing *without* any apparent corporeal presence. I can hover by the window; near the door; next to the wall with those persistent and dark stains. Oh yes, I am free. All I am unable to do is make an exit.

When they took my body away, I naturally assumed that I – floating somewhere above the grisly scene, eyes averted – would accompany the corpse. Without wishing to escort it to the pathologist's slab or the crematorium oven, I did want to see my remains safely stowed. Once outside, on the pavement, I would come to a compromise with whatever breeze was blowing. Luckily it appeared to be a fine, mild morning. But, as I accompanied the mound on the stretcher out of the living-room and into the tiny lobby, I felt an increasing resistance in the air as we – my body and I – reached the front door. The corpse and the ambulance men slipped through to the great world but I, I was left on the threshold of a new life.

I panicked. I staggered like a fly in late summer around the room. They'd left the sash window slightly open. I launched myself at the gap and rebounded. I attempted to creep through the spaces in the front door, splintered by the police. Futile. I flew a thousand sorties at any hole or crevice. But there was – is – no way out. At every point of escape the air, miraculously, horribly, turns to transparent rubber.

Perhaps this is a macabre joke at the expense of us suicides, that we are condemned to mooch for all time in the very spot we tried to push the world off our shoulders.

If so, it's a joke that's wearing thin now . . . please.

My distractions down here: word-games; the play of light

on the walls; occasional visits by Mr Alasdair and his clients. I'd like someone to move in, I really would. I'm not possessive. It was Monica's place anyway. I set her up in it. Everything was in her name, she handled all the payments. To further the pretence she even used a building society, like ordinary people. After my castles crumbled I moved out of my penthouse and into my mistress's basement. She forgot to tell me that she was on the verge of being repossessed. The bitch skipped, leaving me her debts as well as my own.

I had warned Prudence about the market, told her that Michael's job wasn't secure. I was more farsighted than I knew. Prudence Properties and Mortcorp and Kar Kass and Goldcrop and a half dozen other interests boiled dry. There was a certain stench. To tell the truth, I had to sneak away from my penthouse.

In Monica's basement, but in her absence, I kept my head down. I contacted colleagues who didn't want to know. Every day I went to the Cypriot deli round the corner, despite the expense. I was reluctant to expose myself to the cheerful glare of the local supermarket. I returned alone in the dead corners of the day with tins of vegetable soup, steak and kidney pies wrapped in clingfilm. I wondered about Prudence. I hardly thought of Monica. We'd had some good times here, when I owned a body, in the main bedroom, in the bathroom, on the sofa that used to be in this room. But Monica was no Prudence. Funny, the thing that attracted me in the first place – that she was no Prudence – turned out to be her liability.

I wondered about Prudence. And Michael. My one consolation was that, with the collapse of Mortcorp etc., their straits would be nearly as dire as mine. They would have nothing (but each other).

When I was alive I fantasized about revenging myself on them but now I am dead those stronger feelings have been overtaken by a kind of wistfulness. A gentle grief on behalf of myself. I never paid much attention to my body when it was around. Abused it in an average way, I suppose. I'd quite like it back now. They used to bury suicides in unsanctified ground. We all go up in smoke these days. I can dream, though. I'd settle for parts of my body. The fingers only. I'd like to hold them under the waterfall of Prudence's rust red hair.

On the last afternoon of my life I returned to Monica's, my, basement with my canned supper and a copy of the *Standard*. On page 5 I read: 'Police have issued a warrant for the arrest of Alan Mason in connection with the collapse of his property empire. Serious Fraud Officers seized files and other records in a dawn swoop on Mortcorp's City offices today. Mr Michael Mason, brother of the chairman, denied any knowledge of his brother's whereabouts . . .'

Look at me, said Michael, jumping up and down. I'm a good boy, sir, I didn't know what was going on.

I went back to the Cypriot deli and bought a bottle of Famous Grouse. After I had drunk myself into nervelessness I retrieved my father's Luger from the desk drawer. I blessed the impulse that had prompted him to unfasten the holster of the dead German officer in the Ardennes seven days before Christmas, 1944. My father survived the war only to be knocked down by a bus on VJ day. I got his pistol. Michael, the favoured son, got almost everything else.

I almost gagged on the muzzle. My thumb skidded on the trigger.

I can commend suicide as a hangover cure. I'd consumed almost the complete bottle of whisky. I would not have been livable with the next morning. I can't recommend self-destruction in other respects – unless you fancy an eternity playing word games. It won't be an eternity, of course. Sometime the world will end, and what's going to happen to me then? What does a shade do when everybody's turned off the lights and gone home?

*

I can hear Mr Alasdair's ingratiating tones as he leads another hapless couple down the area steps. The figures harden on the other side of the frosted glass of the lobby door. The estate agent is first in, his sandy moustache a little prow. And behind him come – oh yes, I thought I recognized his shuffle, her swing – behind him come my brother and my wife. I am shocked but I am not surprised. It takes me only a moment to recover.

I'm happy to see them. Glad to note they're looking well, blooming in fact, although their presence in this basement is evidence of how their fortunes too have shrunk. They look constantly at each other, like a newly married pair.

Question and speculation tumble through my mind as Mr Alasdair shows them round. I know they are interested in the property. I identify their progress by sound: the creak of a board, the click of a light. How extraordinary that, in their arc from top to bottom, Prudence and Michael should end up in the flat of my departed mistress. And a departed husband/brother. They don't know that, do they? That I topped myself on the bottom floor? That would make their presence here ultra-ghoulish. Shockingly, it comes into my immaterial mind that Prudence and Michael may not even be aware of my death. Identification could have posed problems. My head was all over the place. The hands, though intact, were unfingerprinted. And repossessed Monica had skipped out of reach of the duns and the building societies. To her, to my wife, my brother, I may be just the latest in a long line of property developers who have relocated themselves in the sun.

They've returned to the living-room. They are huddled with Mr Alasdair. They are attentive, ask the right questions, don't mention those dark stains. In an aside my wife points out to my brother that the spare bedroom will be useful for putting up his little son and daughter when they come to stay. They are a little family, aren't they. But I mustn't carp. For the first time in my life (*life*? – old phrases die hard) I am pleased at the prospect of seeing my nephew and niece. There is much to look forward to.

They're bound to talk about me when they move in. In so many ways I am responsible for their being together, for their being here together. They will move in, of course, despite the fact that Prudence, like most women, seems conscious of a 'presence'. With good reason. She keeps glancing up at the fitted dresser (another of the period features made much of by Mr Alasdair), looking straight through her late husband a-hover. As for Michael . . . well, I might be regarding the shell of my old self. A balding, less successful version of me. What *does* she find in him?

Mr Alasdair is taking them back to his office to show off the damp certification. A mere formality. If I had bones I would feel in them the certainty of this: Prudence and Michael are destined to join me. Hearing Mr Alasdair mortise the front door, I glow with the knowledge. As the three glide up the area steps, I realize that a childhood fantasy will shortly be fulfilled.

I was small when my father was knocked down by the bus. I think he quite liked me, though I can't honestly remember. But there was no doubt that Michael was my mother's favourite. As he turns out to have been Prudence's. When they, Michael and my mother, had been particularly unpleasant towards me – spiteful – neglectful – I dreamed of dying in the night. Sometimes I wanted Michael to discover my little body first, sometimes my mother. What contrition there'd be! What hand-wringing self-excoriation! How they would hang over my bed, my corpse, regretting that malicious remark, that turned back, that Chinese burn. They'd be sorry. I would have happily made the swap: my life for their grief.

I am not so egotistical to imagine that Prudence and Michael will swathe themselves in grief for me now. They may not even know of my passing. But the moment will come – as Prudence slices onions in the galley kitchen, as Michael sits channel-hopping before the TV – when, together or singly, they understand I am never coming back. They'll talk of me, they might even be glancingly sorry. And that's enough.

As I hear the cars rev up outside, as Mr Alasdair is hastening to show his clients the damp course certificates, I have only one reason to feel sorry for myself: oh Prudence, Prudence, your hair! That waterfall – rusty or incandescent – is now, to my translated vision, just another shade of grey.

Kirsty Gunn

MUMMY

Mummy makes me show things, I don't want to. A bird I made from a feather that lives in a box with seed around it, matchstick animals, some clay dolls.

'Don't be shy, darling. Your little toys are so clever.' She smiles at her friends, they're gathered around her. 'Show Mrs Franklin your circus. Show her the trapeze man with his teeny weeny underpants . . .'

The ladies laugh, the brightness of the room crowds in. I wish Mummy wouldn't go into my room when I'm at school, go through my things. I wish Mummy would be peaceful.

Anyway, her friends are so pretty, they don't need to see what I've made. They wear dresses that look like cakes, pale pink, lemon, with icing on. Coloured buttons are sprinkled down their fronts like sweeties.

'Pass around the sandwiches, dear,' Mrs Edmonds whispers. 'Be a real help to your mother.'

That's something I practise at night, doing dishes, swabbing down the mess with wet cloths. When I wash glasses, I pretend the bubbles in them are champagne or another kind of fancy drink.

'Would you care for another?' I practise.

'Can I take that plate from you now?'

'Wear your black headband,' Mummy says. 'Then you'll look like a real waitress.'

She sits at her dressing table now, in the morning.

Sunlight comes through the window and makes a big yellow square on her bedroom floor. The thin sweetness of a grown-up scent marks the air.

'Shall I wear the blue eyeshadow or the grey? Or shall I not wear any eyeshadow at all?'

The face in the mirror, my own mother's, half painted is to me smooth and lovely. Her lips, without colour on, are raw as skin. 'Let me do it,' I say, I know how. 'I think blue would go best with the dress you're wearing.'

It's not lunch-time yet. It will be a long time before the ladies get here, the fluttering sound of them in the hall. Still, Mummy can't do her necklace, and she misses the holes in her ears with the tiny hooks so they make her bleed.

'Why don't you lie down?' I take her hand, stroke it. 'Go back to bed. I can fix the rest . . .'

When her friends arrive, she won't remember how clever I have been. Putting pâté on the little toasts, smoothing the hot sheets and covering them with the quilt so the visitors' coats can lie on her bed. I've picked flowers from the garden for a vase, the coffee grounds are spooned and measured into the china pot . . . So why does Mummy talk about me in front of the others like I'm just a little girl?

'She hides in her room making toys,' I hear her whisper to a lady. 'She has imaginary friends, she writes about them in a book . . .'

I pretend I don't hear. Besides, this tray is heavy and difficult to hold.

'Would you like a cup of coffee? Sugar?'

These are the things to think about now. The hand coming out, taking the cup, the jug of cream.

'What a helpful girl for Mummy.'

Liar, liar. How can I be a help to her when every day the house becomes dustier, it needs more cleaning. There are dishes by her bed with foods in them, rinds, tissues soaked in spilt drinks. From my room I hear her calling, 'Where are you? Where are you?'

The lunch party is finished, the sitting-room is dark. Only cigarette ends are there, curled up in the ashtrays like dead insects. In my room it's dark too. I sit on the windowsill, hear her calling. In my hands a tiny family, father, brother, sister, mother, I made them. Their clay faces, their bodies that can properly sit. Even their shoes I made to come on and off. 'Help me . . .' Up in her room, the sweet smell has come back. The bedclothes are messy again, she lies there in them.

'Look at me . . .' Her nightdress is half pulled down.

'Look what the doctors have done . . .'

In my own room, the family is silent. Their smiles are painted on.

'Don't cry now . . .' I whisper it. Mummy's dying.

'Everything will be all right, you'll see.'

Tobias Hill

A HONEYMOON IN LOS ANGELES

American Diary, first day. The taxi driver wore two wedding-rings. This is what he said:

'Hotel Angeline, of America's wonderful Second City. Now get the hell out of my cab, you fucking Nips.'

His shoulders were freckled like the skin of a salmon and red hair grew from his back. When he insulted our country, he didn't even turn his head. I think he was shamed by his own anger. I have never heard such an insult. Not even on TV.

I was crying when Shinzo helped me out of the car. He said nothing to the driver. A garbage truck, black and yellow like banana meat, was parked in front of the Hotel Angeline. In the tourist brochure there was no garbage truck and there were baby palms in European pots. Shinzo had to carry our luggage from the taxi by himself. He said nothing, not then and not later. We went and stood above the Pacific Coast Highway. Over the lanes of traffic we watched the ocean dance in its skin of sequins. After a short time Shinzo pointed to where Japan might be. We sat on the dirty rocks which are not like Malibu Lagoon and we waved until the hotel manager found us. He was wearing a silver suit and he looked unhappy. He took us into the Hotel Angeline, up to the Honeymoon Suite. The air-conditioner has baby angels painted on it.

I think perhaps Shinzo is a weak man.

*

American Diary, second day. My name is Yuko Aomori and I am the death of a family, an only daughter. My mother told me this when I was six, while she made miso soup. Over the pot she whispered, as if I were a shameful secret or a ghost, already dead. Now I am twenty-seven years old. My husband is Shinzo Nakayama but now he is Shinzo Aomori. His family will not die because he has two brothers. He is thirty-four and he is sales manager in my father's umbrella factory. My father says that he is good at selling umbrellas.

The Honeymoon Suite is pretty and clean. From the window I can see this:

Ocean. Palm-trees with swan-necks of white paint. Buildings made of mirrors and polarized glass, sharp as knives in the sun. An empty space between them where young black men are playing basketball. They are graceful as dancers, very dark against the bright shine of their sweat. Two beautiful girls watching them from a high window. A stall selling sunglasses for $3.99 and juice for a dollar. Bougainvillea flowers in the front of a restaurant and a thin dog chained in the back. Green hills in the middle-distance, and mountains up above them. Colorado Avenue and other roads where there are snakes of cars. Some have fins, some are the colour of champagne. Some are green as the chartreuse my mother drinks on Thursdays when she plays mah-jong. A dark haze in the low air which is the same colour as barley-dust at harvest: the breath of a great city. Is Los Angeles bigger than Tokyo?

Shinzo sleeps like a dead man. His hollow cheeks are painted with sweat. My husband, my father's heir. I am no longer the death of my family.

Last night we made love. My husband has the hands of a rice-field frog, soft and cold and moist. Under the skin, his desire is clumsy and cruel. It is blind like something wild trapped in a narrow cage. He hurts me. I have been his wife for three days and he was not my choice.

Soon I will order an American breakfast. Then I will wake Shinzo and he will miss the good smell of miso soup which I cook well. Then we will make love again, although I am still sore. Then the choices will be mine. We can go to Hollywood and Universal Studios, and then to Sunset Boulevard where I will spend my husband's money. He will be quite bored but he will say nothing, because he is a coward. It is my honeymoon and I will buy American clothes in the city of the angels.

American Diary, third day. My mother said that Los Angeles was not good for a honeymoon. She said to visit Europe. She said that there is no love in America now, only hate. It is a dying country, she told me. But I needed to make a choice very much.

This is what I saw today: Universal Studios and a young actress in a car with green wings. A movie in an American movie theatre. Beverly Hills where the streets are red with flowers and the houses are too large for real people – only temples should be so big. A Mexican skirt in Olvera Street. It has purple thongs and I bought it. Shinzo was not bored at all. He likes watching me, he watches the way I move. After shopping he took me to see a movie by Walt Disney. There were seats in the movie theatre – at home in Tosa there are no seats in the movie theatre – and outside was the actress and the beautiful car. In the movie theatre Shinzo stroked my hair, very gently. He is trying very hard.

No one walks in Los Angeles, only the street people. There are more kinds of cars than people and the air is sweet and grainy with their fatal perfume. There are cars from all over the world, and the sound of them is everywhere, like the song of red cicadas at home in the summertime.

When we came back to the Hotel Angeline I wanted to show my Mexican skirt to the hotel manager, but he was talking to a woman on the telephone. He was angry, and so his face was full of blood. He didn't greet us.

Now Shinzo is in the shower. He is singing an American song. He knows many American songs from his salaryman karaoke evenings. Sometimes he teaches me the words, which are strange and not English at all but American. He is kind and he has a good heart. But he is weak.

My father is a brave man. The Aomori family is old and respected on our island of Shikoku. When my father was young all the women in the Prefecture wanted to marry him. But when he was nineteen, he volunteered to fly a cherry-blossom plane in the war against America. He was the only son. The family would die to save the country.

And then the war ended so suddenly, so that they needed no more kamikaze pilots, only businessmen. Now my father is an old man, but his voice is still filled with strength. I love him very much. I would not let him be hurt. It was not planned that he should die so young; and it was planned that I should be born alone. An only girl-child. A shaming of my ancestors and the death of a name. My father deserved a son.

But now my father and mother have found Shinzo, who loves my body and who has taken my name. My death will not be shameful now. My father will die happy, and so I must be happy. I must try to be happy for everyone.

Now Shinzo is watching the TV news. His body is fish-white and thin but quite fine. On the TV a reporter is showing how American police kick black people in slow-motion. Do Japanese policemen kick people? I think my mother is wrong. America is full of death, but there must be love too. I will make love.

American Diary, fourth day. I must have a boy-child soon. I want my father to see it before he dies. I wish Shinzo was a stronger man. I am not sure I want him to be the father of my children. It is wrong to think this on our honeymoon.

Today the hotel manager gave us a surprise present – a free car for two days. The speed is measured in miles and the colour is pink. The hotel manager says this is because it is the Honeymoon Suite Car. Shinzo says it is primer paint. I think it is pretty. The hotel manager says we should go out to the desert, to Disneyland or further. I want to see Los Angeles. It excites me.

After the car, I telephoned my mother in Tosa. Her voice sounded dusty and tired. My own voice echoed like a stone in a well. She asked what Americans are like when they are in America. I told her that they are more emotional than Koreans. She asked me if I was being a good wife but I didn't smile at that. I know I am not a good wife. I only carry a name, like a parasite. Alive.

For lunch I had ice-cream. Shinzo had coffee and eggs, and there was a fight between two women. I didn't feel scared because women fight on TV all the time.

My ice-cream sundae had fudge syrup and cherries on top. Then there was English breakfast ice-cream, coffee wafers and lemon sorbet, and underneath it all there was coke. Between the wafers and the lemon sorbet a woman started screaming behind me. A small man with a beard jumped up next to Shinzo and hit the table with the heels of his hands.

The small man was grinning. 'Cat-fight, by God!' he shouted. Then everyone was clapping and whistling. I turned round and there were two waitresses. One had straight yellow hair like corn silk and she was kneeling on the floor and coughing. The other waitress had very dark skin and she was thin, but also strong, because she was holding the bigger woman up by the hair. The black woman was shouting. This is what I understood:

'Tell me again, you fucking white trash, was they just doing their job?' then, 'You want to call them? You want to? Why not? They're yours, ain't they? They're your stinking pigs.' Her brow was bleeding and she kicked at the woman on the floor. Then she let go of the blonde woman, and stood staring at nothing with her mouth sad, as if she was about to cry. Suddenly the blonde woman got up. There was a tall glass bottle of fudge syrup on the table with a silver nozzle on top. The blonde woman picked it up and hit the other waitress in the mouth with it. All her teeth broke. When she bent over the blood and syrup came out together, brown and red. Then we left.

Shinzo is quiet now. He thinks about the women's fight in a different way from me. It is more real to him. That is why he is so weak.

It is hot today. There is a man juggling outside the Universal News Agency and the sweat has made his clothes into a second skin, black and red and blue. No one gives him money today. None of the cars stop. America is full of death, it is a heavy smog, but we are Japanese. This afternoon we will drive and see the whole of Los Angeles.

American Diary, fourth or fifth day. We are going home now. A man from the Japanese Consulate found us aeroplane seats. It is midnight or later. From the window I can see stars and the wing, which is only an absence of stars. I can see the whole city below, drawn in light. Around it are the endless darknesses of the desert and the ocean.

There is a big fire in the West, where it is all factories, but most of the fires look small, now. There are no noises up here and the smells of burning are cut out, like in a movie, so it is quite pretty. When we were lost it was not pretty and the noise was frightening. It was worse than a typhoon or an earthquake because nothing was expected and there was no rhythm. A city breaking apart. Perhaps whole families have been killed, fathers and children.

Shinzo is asleep now. I have put a blanket over him. He is my husband and I must care for him.

First of all there were two explosions, but Shinzo said

they were car tyres melting in the heat. We were trying to find Olvera Street again and came out on to Colorado Avenue. Next to Tower Records was a pet-store with the alarm-bell ringing. Shinzo stopped the car.

The store was called Anything Except Aardvarks and there was a rabbit with long ears sitting in the doorway. The shop-window was smashed, and a boy was standing in it. He was black and there were patterns shaved in his hair like dog-teeth. He was watching us and saying something. Suddenly another boy came out by the door. He had black hair and tanned skin. He had a macaw parrot in his arms, cradled like a baby. He kicked the rabbit out of his way and both boys ran away. The rabbit sat in the gutter. A woman stopped and tried to catch it, but it ran away too. Someone said they would call the police, and so we left. We drove, and soon there were trunks of black smoke nearby to the North and West. People were running in packs, like dogs. There was a painting on a wall of Presley and Monroe. Then Shinzo got lost.

Now he is sleeping and I wish he would stay asleep, like a dead man. In the departure lounge I slept and dreamed of our families. They were giant creatures, bigger than whales, old and slow, without real faces but hungry to survive. Alive in the way that viruses live, or trees. They crushed against me and their skins were cold, like Shinzo's. I was drowning. They whispered the secret of breathing to me in a language I had forgotten. I woke, then, and watched Shinzo as he slept. He is the carrier of my name. He repulses me.

There was a beautiful car on fire on Colorado Avenue. It was a black Jaguar, very old, and someone had poured red paint on the roof and fired up the paint. There was a Korean, too. He was standing in front of his grocery store and asking people not to steal from him. His English was not very good and some girls were laughing at him, but nobody had broken into his store yet.

I was excited and not so scared because nobody noticed us. I asked Shinzo where we were going.

'We are going to the hotel and then we will leave this terrible country,' he said. His hands kept slipping around the steering-wheel because he was sweating so much. He turned South and bumped against a fire hydrant. Water burst out into the air and came down on the car with a slap. Shinzo whined quietly, like a child who does not want to be heard. He turned around and drove North down a side-street. When I told him we were going the wrong way, he commanded me to be quiet in very masculine Japanese. I wondered if we would be killed, but the thought did not frighten me.

The side-street was full of cheap hotels and small movie-theatres showing films about naked women. Outside them three girls were playing dodgeball in the road. There was nobody else.

'I will ask them the way,' said Shinzo. He pressed the car-horn softly so that the girls would notice us, but they only ran away. Then Shinzo became angry and he hit the car-horn much harder. It echoed between the buildings of mirrored glass with their sharp edges.

'A mad country!' he shouted. 'Foreigners are animals who kill for food. Why did we come here? We should have gone to Hawaii.' I told him that Los Angeles was my choice. He looked at me and became scared again. Then we heard shouting. The girl-children had returned with many people.

They were shouting 'Chinks! Hey, rich Nips!' There were many young black people, like the ones who were playing basketball days ago. They had lots of shopping-trolleys full of food. One boy picked up a pineapple and threw it at the Honeymoon Suite Car. It hit the roof with a bang, then rolled down the windscreen. Shinzo sighed, not disappointed but terrified. He tried to start the car and it stalled. Everyone laughed and now there were more people. An egg hit my window and I screamed. I told Shinzo to start the car, but it was dead. A fish hit the windscreen and left a trail of grey slime. Then all the people were chanting and throwing eggs and fruit. It went on for a long time. Shinzo tried to put his head between his knees, but his seatbelt held him up. He covered his face with his hands instead and wept. Something in me died then. I despised him. I knew I could not bear to love his child. Then a can of food hit the windscreen and it broke into a thousand diamonds.

I was leaning over Shinzo and trying to start the car when there was the noise of police cars and a megaphone. The crowd shouted louder and threw more cans. I had to hide under the seat. When I looked again, most of the people had gone, and the police were closer. There were four police cars, and a policewoman was knocking on Shinzo's door. She looked very worried. I think she had been there for a long time.

I wonder what it is in me that has died. Not my family, that passes away so quietly. What is there left? After my father dies, I will divorce Shinzo. Then there will need to be work, a shop assistant or a kindergarten teacher. I will play with the children and long for my own. It is the children in me that have died.

The paramedics gave Shinzo sleeping medicine. I asked them to take us to the hotel first, to pick up our luggage. The manager was gone. It was evening then. I went and stood over the endless roar of the Pacific Coast Highway while they searched for our possessions. From the bridge, the ocean was on fire all the way to Japan.

Jonathan Keates

THE GIFT OF FLIGHT

The cat, in terror, bounces through the room. She too, he is disappointed to perceive, is more than a little afraid. He has wanted her to know that he would come, has hoped that in some way or other a dream, a premonition, a nudge or two of fantasy, might cause her to long for his arrival. Not, you understand, because he is especially vain of the effects he can produce. These are always taken for granted. It is simply that he wants her to have something in the way of an imagination, and at this moment, his wings still beating in great slow sweeps as he circles for a perfect landing, he is dreadfully afraid that she possesses nothing of the kind.

The landing has to be perfect, though he fancies it would make little impression on her if he crashed clumsily to the ground and slithered a short way across the floor. Hovering yet, he takes mournful stock of the room, noting the hospital corners with which the bedcovers are tucked in, the careful arrangement of her slippers, the clean towel on the peg, and the small array of books on the shelf. He is quite sure, without looking at them, that they are not the sort of books which he would want to read.

She herself was reading when he flew in through the window. This was the act in which it was necessary for her to be caught. Of course he would have preferred to find her doing something more clandestine, sniffing an armpit perhaps, sliding an absent-minded finger up one nostril, scratching a spot and maybe cracking the scab between her teeth, but such things lack the kind of grace she is intended at this moment to express.

Circling for a last time, he notices the bowl of flowers standing precisely within the space where he had meant to touch ground. If he believed her capable of such deviousness, he would have supposed she had put it there on purpose. He doesn't know which irks him more, the vase itself, full of lilies, a plant he has always disliked for its brutal obviousness, or the disappointing realization that its presence in this spot on the floor is not deliberate.

Of course he knows why they have to be there, just as he knows why she pores over her book, and why, at this moment while his huge wings, which the room seems almost not to hold, make a final and, he has to admit, quite superfluous clap, she is turning away her head in a little wincing motion, her hands upraised, their palms turned outward, pressing against the air upon which, lightly, always lightly, he sinks to earth.

As if, in any case, he would touch her! It must spoil the impact his accomplishments have taught him to aim for. So he wants the hands upraised, yes, but in a different position, one which will say 'Goodness, that's wonderful!' or 'How cleverly you do it!' as his beautiful feet slide silently along the floor and his feathers rustle slightly before the wings settle into stillness. In short, he'd like her to envy him. Not everyone, he knows, can fly.

He has heard envy described as a tenth-rate emotion, something to be ashamed of, but he does not believe this. For him it offers another kind of fancy, an act of desire which, at its most intense, recreates those who feel it in the very essence of what they best long for. He has heard a story – and he'd tell it her, if only she would ask – of the man who, when he understood what he supposed to be love was actually envy, murdered his lover, flayed the skin from the body and wrapped himself within it.

She won't ask this, insistently, maddeningly won't want to know how he does what he does, how he launches himself into the air, how he flutters and swoops, his intrusive soaring integral to moments of salvation and epiphany. For an instant he wonders whether it was his beauty that frightened her, the whiteness of his skin, his thin fingers, the gleam of the reddish curls bouncing across his shoulders as he collects himself into the appropriate posture of reverence. He takes this inextinguishable radiance so much for granted that the effect it produces is now and then embarrassing. Things have happened in the past, in situations like this, which made him leave in a hurry.

But evidently it is not such effulgence which makes an impression. So why does she continue to turn away from him, in what looks suspiciously like humility? If there is one thing he can't stand, it is humility. He himself is a complete stranger to it, if only because it was left out – on purpose, he must assume – of the selective emotional kit with which he was originally furnished. A reliable measure of indifference to his own sublimity makes her abject cowering alien to him, almost nauseating.

Thinking about it later, when airborne and remote, he will blame this disgust for the subsequent banality to which he now falls in telling her not to be afraid. For fear, he starts to perceive, is what defines her. It is perhaps the closest she will ever come to the act of imagination so hugely absent in the *mise-en-scène*. She and the wretched skittering cat at the beginning are one creature – only the cat, he suspects, has more independence. Throwing back his beautiful curls with the merest little toss of impatience and contempt, and giving a light twitch to the tips of his wings, he lets his solemn glance travel round the room once again, reading a fear into each proof of neatness, the dreadful symmetry of those slippers, the way whereby the towel has been made to hang so that its corners match one another, the disposition of the books according to height, and the smooth, hard-edged bedclothes which, if he rapped his knuckles against them, might produce the dull ring of sheet metal. Order is a kind of fear, and he has always been above that sort of thing.

Almost wearily then, he begins his message to her, the form of words carefully rehearsed regardless of whether or not she is likely to pay any attention to its incidental stylish graces. Or rather, he hears himself deliver it, hears the words in disparate groups, over whose tone and colour he lingers with something suspiciously like impertinence, as though testing her reactions. 'Found favour', 'conceive', 'his name', 'unto him the throne', 'and of his kingdom'. She does not raise her head.

She does not raise her head, but she does venture a question, at the mere fact of which he is pardonably surprised. The good impression lasts only a moment, however, before an inherent sense of the commonplace sweeps everything else away, and he answers her as if he were talking to a child. The greatest intrinsic irony in the rôle he performs is that he himself should find innocence so unappealing. You'd have thought to detect, in the light he casts about him, in the sheen of his feathers and the deep luminosity of his large eyes (whose colour she will not remember, only think of as 'burning' or some such imprecise word) the image of a perfect candour, without shadow or ambiguity. Yet it is exactly this he has wanted all along to avoid. He piques himself on being able to inject, even into the simplest address, some humour of the quizzical, a note or two which will strike the hearer in such a way that after the air has settled again from the last clap of his wings, there will be things left riddling and unclear.

With her this is impossible. Possibility, indeed, lay at the root of that obtuse question she asked earlier, one he was obliged to answer with such condescending directness. Her failure – or the sense he has of it – to grasp anything but the absoluteness of a final reality suddenly makes him feel that she has no perspective, that the room behind her, the arched alcove with the bed in it, the bookshelf across one of whose sides the sunlight slopes, are all in some way flat, without dimension or tangible physicality. Perhaps it is merely that her dreadful acquiescence, insisting on nothing beyond what words and things vouchsafe in the form of immediately comprehensible meaning, has created a new system of space and proportion, one in which his gift of flight can no longer hold its place.

We believe, though we cannot be sure, that this was why he lied to her. It counts as lying, though some may view it as a sympathetic omission. For there is another part to his message – more strictly speaking, it is two parts connected to each other – which at this point somehow gets lost, like those additional layers of significance which are always said to disappear in the course of a translation.

He was going to talk to her, you see, about death, was going to share with her everything he had imagined regarding it, this particular special dying, an agony he has experienced vicariously, not through the medium of compassion, but by virtue – if only she were able to understand this – of the extraordinary skill he has in flying. In the beating of his wings he has seen that death, the skin seamed with sweat, the blood-matted hair, the ruthless incompetence with which the feet have been spiked together, and the attempt someone makes at delivering a *coup-de-grâce* (in charity or in anger? he isn't yet clear on this point) through a deep wound to one side of the torso.

He has tried to feel these things for himself as he flies, the passion and energy which went into their deliberate creation, as if the body had been a subject for discriminations in colour, texture and arrangement, a matter for art which he, beyond everyone else, would understand. In a manner he has watched over the completeness of her misery, her bewilderment of loss, the terrible resignation with which she has stood, another beside her, while the dying man hangs there talking to her, the almost automatic fashion in which she and her companions prepare the body for burial and the way whereby, after this moment, she appears to be forgotten, none of the texts making any significant mention of her in their anxiety to communicate the very curious nature of what happened next.

His profound sense of decorum has entered so far into the spirit of the whole occasion, with its storm and darkness contributing touches of the pathetic fallacy, that he feels as if entitled to a share in her emotions. He will not go so far as to shed tears – nature denies him that specific reaction – but he might claim, hand on heart, that he knows how she feels. On her behalf his mouth has opened in those soundless cries that rage against absence. Mimicking what he fancies she ought to say, he has had various of those dismal phantom conversations which assume the presence of somebody else to whom alone the chosen words could have been addressed. In flying, he has noticed, for her sake, details scattered here and there, like the stones and branches gathered into a mysterious referential order by savage magicians, half their meaning lost now because one of the two people who could interpret them properly has died. And when the other dies, we shall be left either with the mere sticks and stones or else with the apparatus of a garbled rhetoric from which issues a holiness imperfectly understood.

She looks at him now, her eyes full of that same acquiescence which sickened him earlier. At this moment, however, a different feeling altogether steals upon him, a sudden wave of longing, accountable only in terms of something he is eager to add to his collection, not necessarily for the thing itself but for the satisfaction of possessing it. He longs, in this instant, absolutely to be her. He wants to know, with his particular species of devouring curiosity, how it is possible to exist within the limits set by a complete ignorance of what follows. The burden of vicarious pain he has carried, the whole laborious episodic death, the smell of it, the untidiness, the sense, as with every death, of a lingering irritation on the part of the dead themselves because there was something they still had left to do and were peremptorily interrupted in the process of doing it, these things are so conspicuously not there in the glance she raises, however furtively, to meet his unpitying eyes. And it is that very ignorance he feels he must master, as part of his rhetoric of borrowed and imagined emotion, because he never knew its power until now.

Consumed with this new desire, he scarcely listens to her final submissive acceptance of his message – of that fragment, at least, which he has deigned to convey. His wings flutter with a renewed peevishness to depart, and taking care not to upset the lily vase, he mounts to the window, too preoccupied even to carry out the little circuit of the room which good manners, under ordinary circumstances, require him to perform as an earnest of his special nature. How can she? How can she fail to see, fastened within this promise he has given, never again to be made or hoped for, the truth of an ineluctable mortality? Perhaps it is because, as he tells himself with epigrammatic smugness, all imagination prefigures death.

Brooding still, he mingles with the blaze of morning. Only when aloft and serenely airborne does he recall the other part of his message purposely kept from her, the part which he had originally so looked forward to delivering as an ironic denouement, an and-now-for-my-last-trick turning tragedy into tragicomedy. He might have done it as he made ready to fly out of the room, in the purest expression of *esprit d'escalier*, if he hadn't been so captivated by that radiant obtuseness of hers. For it was rather a case of 'tarry a little, there is something else'. He was going to tell her, had he only remembered, about what happened at the very end, about the way in which the body disappeared, then came back alive – the oddest thing! – and spoke to people and let them touch it, in an ultimate trouncing of death. Something in the nature of a gift. A bit like flying.

Irma Kurtz

THE LAST TABOO

Rhoda, my oldest friend, was taken in the first culling of our generation. Before that, death had been haphazard: a playmate gone in childhood to leukemia, another drowned. But the fact is, children are practically interchangeable except to their parents, and in no time we others re-grouped around the spaces. When Rhoda and I were at Columbia University, there were two suicides after the first year. We were shocked by them, outraged: what kind of fools threw away such interesting times as we were starting to have? After the suicides not many of us died for a long time, and those who did, died unsystematically after aneur-ysms, or car crashes, and several men in battle. It must have been five or six years after graduation I heard that a girl from our year had been murdered by her husband. We remembered her as a pedantic swot; Rhoda said he prob-ably killed her in self-defence, before she corrected him to death.

And then Rhoda upped and died. Died seriously. It was 1979 in London, where we had both been living for some time, no longer the great chums we had been. (All opinionated, mostly childless, women used to quarrel in those days. A dinner party was not over until one of us was crying.) When Rhoda rang after a long silence, I knew something was wrong, but I never dreamed she was dying. Her birthday was six weeks before my own. We didn't die. Not seriously. Not yet. But Rhoda did; Rhoda seriously died after much suffering: the way grown-ups die. It was a very bad death.

I took it more or less in turns with a Buddhist friend of hers to sit beside her bed in hospital. Her physical pain was controlled with drugs but her dread was savage and unbiddable. She moaned constantly and sometimes cried out for her mother who had died long before, also by cancer. It was not a ward for terminal patients, nobody else was as bad as Rhoda. When she screamed 'I'm so scared of dying!', men visiting at the other beds shrank into themselves; the women busily passed around grapes; neighbouring patients pretended to sleep; nurses averted their eyes, and not a doctor was to be seen. One day when I arrived and took my place beside Rho, she stirred, lifted her head and fixed me hard with her eyes. They were the same deep reddish brown her hair had been before chemotherapy.

'Who needs you?' she said, and fell back on her pillow.

They were her last words to me.

Next time I saw Rhoda, she was comatose. Her lips were white and scaly, like badly weathered paint, and around her was a fungoid, dirty smell of death and also of some unthinkable version of life. I steeled myself to touch her hand; it lay grey and weightless as a shadow on the ugly coverlet.

'You've done well, Rho,' I said, feeling silly, as if I had been caught talking to myself in a public place.

That night, an hour before dawn of what would have been Rhoda's forty-fourth birthday, she died.

'My oldest friend died last night,' I told my agent, who happened to ring the next morning.

'Sorry to hear it,' she said. 'How about a book on death and dying? The last taboo.'

So, I donned a white coat and strolled the cancer wards. I visited mortuaries, crematoria, cemeteries. I pulled strings to sit in on an autopsy, too. Why not? I took, as they say, copious notes. I knew about hospices, of course, we had tried to book a place in one for Rhoda, but by the time it came free, she was gone. When a friendly doctor suggested to the Medical Director of a hospice in her bailiwick that they let me visit, he agreed, but only if I came as a nurse's aide, not an observer. By that time I'd read a lot of bumph by terminal caretakers; often as not they came across as smug and self-congratulatory that in the struggle between light and eternal darkness, they had backed the winner. Viva death! En bas, the living! In the land of the dying, to be even just half-alive can make anyone a big shot, and there are quite a few pious hypocrites in terminal care, some relishing martyrdom, others facing down private terrors; I had come across one self-appointed Queen of the Underworld, who tolerated no dissent in her dominion, not even from the dying themselves, if their opinion of death's carrion function challenged her expectations of an epiphany. Clearly, I anticipated giving offence to my colleagues in the hospice. Furthermore, terminal nursing is much involved with human waste products, and I wasn't sure I had the stomach for it.

The hospice buildings were serene behind walls of local stone. In the dayroom, big windows gave on to a splendid garden being tended by local volunteers. Jugs of cabbage roses and vases of mixed flowers were on every flat surface, even atop the cold grate, blackened by winter wood-burning fires. In accord with the belief encountered widely in terminal care that imminent death makes us simple-minded, only uplifting tracts from the 'let us be joyful' schools of religion were in the bookcase. But a cosy smell of frying bacon came from down the hall; the sofas were worn and comfortable; I did not yet know that the pretty little carriage house off to one side under swags of mature wisteria was where bodies were held for collection; all told, it could have been the kind of unpretentious country hotel where retired couples on fixed incomes turn up year after year for their holidays.

Matron hurried in at last. She was robust and sensible, a million miles from the evangelical raptures I'd feared. She hurried me up to the nurses' dressing-room where a uniform was waiting and a badge already printed with my name. A few minutes later, downstairs, in the room shared by the three women patients resident at the time, there stood I in starched primrose cotton, feeling myself to be a perfect hoax, and wondering what on earth a hospice nurse's aide was supposed to do. All matron had said to me before she hurried away was to be ready to prepare a special snack whenever any patient wanted one. But the breakfast trays had just been cleared away and nobody was hungry. One patient, Rosie, was dozing. A busy young nurse told me in passing that Rachel, whose bed under the window was empty, was in the garden or the sunroom. 'She likes to be on her own, does Rachel.' And in the bed nearest the door, Mary was dying.

I recognized the final coma. It has a unique concentration about it. Consciousness and recollection and will, and all Mary's living dreams, had passed forever beyond the body's distractions or recall, and were united on the trail of one utterly bright idea. Her husband sat beside her bed. He looked weary, shut out and confused, not in the pink himself. I'd just got up my nerve to offer him tea, when a fair young nurse, her badge said 'Heather', told me to draw the curtains around the bed of the dying woman.

'We're just going to make Mary a little more comfortable,' she said.

The man kept his gaze fixed on the flowered curtain as I closed it between him and the bed. Scared half to death myself, I slid my arms under the dying woman. Her skin was chill and dry, and when Heather gave me the nod, as if we'd come across a helpless sea creature on the beach and were returning it to its own element, we briskly and expertly rolled the carcass over.

'Let me get you a cup of tea now,' I said to Mary's husband as soon as the curtain was opened, and when he nodded, I felt it to be my second triumph of the morning.

Dying generally happens during the small hours. (So, incidentally, does birthing.)

'We lost Mary,' said the night nurse handing over to day staff on my second morning.

There was a pause, no longer than it takes to say 'ouch'. 'And Charlie got into a bit of a flap last night, I'm afraid. He was poorly.'

'Ah Charlie! He's a lad, isn't he?' said Heather.

She pushed away the plate of chocolate biscuits we were having with coffee. Heather was cute as a button, but she had to watch her weight.

'He was that distressed,' the night nurse said, 'but when I went in to him, didn't he look right up at me and say he'd tell my hubby if I didn't behave?'

A stranger hearing the indulgent laughter would have assumed Charlie was an adolescent boy bruised in rough-and-tumble, not a sixty-three-year-old labourer dying of lung cancer.

'Trev tried again to move his bowels. It's there, but so high up, we'll have to try something else. And Rosie could be roused, but only just.'

'Aaaaaah, ooooooh, dear Rosie,' all six nurses murmured in unison.

Rosie was close to ninety-five years old and fading so gently, it was more like drying than dying. So sweetly extravagant were Rosie's thanks for even the smallest attention, I had a hunch she must have been in service once upon a time.

'Come on, Rosie, my poppet, my pet, have another

spoonful. That's my good girl.' Barely a day gone by, and already I was cooing baby talk to a woman twice my age. Furthermore, although I had intended earlier to read Rosie's case notes as soon as I had a chance, I'd ceased to care a fig where her malignancy was lodged. Least of all did I care that she was dying. Absolutely all that mattered to me at that moment was that the old darling loved vanilla ice-cream and was waiting for another spoonful, her mouth open like a baby bird's. The dying appetite is fanciful but capacity is diminished, and the portion of ice-cream I was feeding Rosie was hardly more than a child would offer a doll. A few days later, when Rosie became comatose, I helped another nurse turn her. There was little flesh left on Rosie, she was all bones covered in papery skin; we had placed blocks to raise the sheets and keep them from chafing her. The old woman's pelvis was hairless, spread like a pale moth. Within the coma, her memory was busy at its terminal inventory; she had been born before the beginning of this century, and the medical case notes I never did get around to reading in the end, albeit the only document Rosie was going to leave behind, were less than a postscript to the library she was taking to her grave.

Life departing inflicts countless discomforts and frustrations, and easing them is the essence of terminal care. Replacing soiled bedsheets courteously and fast, pouring tea, bathing patients, shaving an old man whose beard comes away as dust, chatting, listening – especially listening – after the big guns have surrendered, these small services become urgent: patients' care at the geriatric end remains pretty much women's work. 'Nobody without faith can work with the dying,' I overheard Matron say once. She was a sterling woman, but in this case, she was wrong. Humility, humanity, humour and common sense are of infinitely more value at the deathbed than any supernal virtues, and there is no reason on earth an atheist cannot work with the dying, if that is what she feels herself called to do. Priests of all denominations were on tap at our hospice, but prayer was pretty much by choice, peripheral to the daily routine. The only religious to turn up regularly was a nursing nun who doled out tea and diamorphine with penitential solemnity. Pain and fear were controlled among our patients by an extremely precise, supervised use of drugs, but no further aggressive measures were taken against death itself, and doctors in general were neither seen, nor much needed, in the hospice. Even our Medical Director was an infrequent visitor to the nursing floor, rarely visible outside his weekly meeting with the staff.

The morning round of baths and cleaning was heavy work. Patients able to walk needed to be helped into the free-standing baths, otherwise we had to hoist them in on pulleys that made the smallest of us able to lift a man dying in full flesh. It did not embarrass me or seem immodest to bathe the naked men, though not my ordinary occupation. Nor did I give a second thought to changing the bedsheets for Trev when his bowels opened at last. It was hardly more distasteful than changing a baby's nappy and even more quickly done. Once while a teenaged student nurse was helping me and one of the older nurses give Charlie a blanket bath, he insisted on wearing his briefs.

'You two old girls I don't mind,' he said, 'but she's too young to know how a man is put together. And if she does know, then she ought to be ashamed of herself.'

'You have eight children, haven't you, Charlie?' the older nurse said. As she passed the flannel rapidly from his armpit to his wrist, her smile was of a woman's ancient satisfaction when she corners a lusty old troublemaker at last. 'You must be a Roman Catholic.'

'Are you a believer then, Charlie?' I asked him.

'Me! A believer! God, no. I'm no believer. I'm an alcoholic,' he said, and winked at the student nurse.

Visitors to a hospice can come and go at any hour, and

among Charlie's devoted regulars were the barmaids from his local pubs. Gaudy and highly scented, they collected around his bed whenever they could for a gossip and to laugh. Later, when Charlie's toes had turned the colour of aubergines and he was taken very bad, they used to slip away into the corridor two by two and weep in each other's arms.

Death hadn't made a eunuch of Charlie as it had of Trev, for example, sitting all day like a peevish Buddha, frowning at the rills of his belly. Then one day we removed Trev's pyjama top to give him a wash, and for the first time I saw a tattooed dragon writhing around the biceps of his left arm, its tail in the crook of his elbow and its head spitting flames towards the heavens. Our Trev, whose chest sagged like a matron's and who grunted with annoyance whenever we interrupted his sullen reverie, in his day he must have been quite a lad to choose so alien and salty a familiar. I swear I would not have been surprised if the dragon had unwound itself from its dying host to pass the spark in life's defiant relay and take up residence on the arm of the pretty nurse who was at its scales with a soapy flannel.

Bill was brought in on my third morning. He was a fine-boned man whom death was making beautiful, and whom it had also unhinged. Mandarins of the death-bed write that the dying want to talk about what is happening to them, if only we, the craven living, would let them. But it seemed to me the dying people I met had not become philosophers or theologians on short time; right to the last they preferred to talk about hobbies, families, memories, and all the small perplexities of everyday life. Bill's black depression lifted only for flowers. And whenever he broke his dark silence to tell me about the cultivation of day lilies, say, or the best soil for roses, I had a glimmer of how a doctor must feel when treatment works, and for a moment death stumbles back against the ropes. Fortunately, we always had plenty of flowers at the hospice.

'Look, Bill. Aren't they beautiful!' Bill's wife exclaimed when I put a bowl of carnations on his bedside table.

'They are donated,' I said.

I did not show her the tiny punctures under the blossoms where they had been pinned to a funeral wreath. Wreaths were passed on to us all the time to be disassembled for our vases.

Rachel kept herself apart from the others and it was a few days before I met her. I'd wandered into the sunroom to see what needed doing. At first, I took her for a visitor. It was only when I saw her carpet slippers I realized the woman of about my own age, meticulously dressed for town, must be our elusive Rachel. To sit talking with a patient is not to be seen doing nothing; on the contrary, it is one of the most important hospice services. The dainty singsong of Rachel's speech was not an accent but a symptom of her fatal disorder. Sometimes, she broke off to search for a word and often the one she found was the opposite of what she'd meant to say, though she did not appear to notice.

'A year ago, I think, it must have been less because the chrysanthemums were out. Or the day after. I was at home. I was going to cook a chicken. I'm a widow, you know. But I have a suitor.' For a moment she looked younger than a student nurse, and the fuzz on her face, a by-product of medical treatment, was quite peachy. 'He does like his meat, the way men do. I was feeling well, just about to . . . what did I say? Knitting. I'm always knitting. The telephone rang. I got up to answer it. It was, you know, one of those tables for telephones. 'Six-oh-two' I was saying, the way I always do. And . . . that was when . . . suddenly, you know . . . everything went away from me.'

After that, Rachel said, were more blackouts, and then came the tying of her tongue, and words that jumped away. Recently, however, she had been feeling much more her old self.

'The doctors say I can go home soon. I am grateful even if my hair hasn't grown back as soft as it used to be. But please, I told them, I don't want any more, you know . . .' She frowned, searching. 'No more experiments.'

Only when she stood to move to a chair in the shade was it clear how feeble she was; she shuffled, and leaned heavily on my arm.

'Irma,' she said, and I was charmed by her trust, 'Irma, would you get me a bowl of my . . .' she shook her head, smiled. 'My strawberries.'

In fact, they were blackberries. They were in a jar labelled with her name at the bottom of the fridge. Heather was in the kitchen, too, scrambling an egg under the critical eye of the cook, a warrior-woman called Maggie.

'Rachel says she's going home,' I said to Heather.

'Our people go home sometimes, when their pain is under control, and if their families can cope. Rachel has a brain tumour. She'll go home. And she'll be back.'

Heather looked away, frowning. At last I understood the disquiet Rachel's name seemed always to provoke in the staff: she believed one day when she was better she'd marry her suitor and live happily ever after. Her doctors, or someone, had funked: she was the only one in the hospice who did not know the case was terminal.

Patients were not taken to one side to die. Death rolled in on wheels muffled by morphine and there was no reason to separate those *in extremis*; as a matter of fact, the quiet of their passings offered consolation to others waiting their turn, and to us all. On my final day in the hospice Charlie started to die in earnest. Because he so clearly loved his wits and consciousness, he was by his own request on a relatively low dosage of painkillers. Next to him on the edge of the bed was his dumpling wife; handsome sons stood to attention at his feet, and daughters sat between him and Trev who was locked into his usual ponderous meditation. Only a few days earlier the nurses and the barmaids had been talking about taking Charlie out for a last drink in his favourite pub. But now it was evident he was never going to lift another glass. He fought the sedation, dozed, woke, then sat up and coughed.

'Oh Jesus!' he said. 'This is murder.'

The youngest of his daughters went white, and the little gold crosses in her earlobes began to shake like telegraph poles in an earthquake.

'Is there anything you want, Charlie?' I asked him, when he'd fallen back, blue and sweating.

He drew one more breath against the iron in his chest.

'I can have anything I want. And I know that,' he said. 'Except ...' He gestured towards the window and the garden. 'I'll never see Dublin again.'

His hand dropped back on the blanket, his wife reached for it tenderly.

'Ah, what the blazes,' Charlie whispered. 'For I never did care that much about the place.'

An hour later, towards the end of the afternoon, Charlie's wife and the others left to fetch more relatives from the station. Only his youngest daughter stayed. She had regained her calm and her colour. We sat on either side of Charlie's bed, each holding one of his hands, she his left and I his right, watching him, not speaking but busy and companionable, like a pair of women at the spinning. From time to time, Charlie lifted himself off the pillows, coughed, thrashed restlessly, dazed and annoyed to be roused, then gave in again to the encroaching sleep. At last it dawned on me his breathing had stopped. And if there can properly be degrees of stillness, the features of his face had suddenly become more still. I reached for the bellpush that would sound an alarm and light the red bulb outside our door, but before my hand closed on it, Charlie's body tensed and air rasped like sandpaper through his lungs. There were more gasps, the pauses between increasing so

I counted to ten, fifteen, eighteen, before there was another jagged, juddering breath. It was like timing birth contractions, only in reverse. My eyes were on Charlie but I sensed his daughter watching me, waiting for me to do something professional. After I had counted a dead silence of twenty-five, I pushed the button to ring the alarm, and the moment I did, Charlie sat straight up in his bed. That was when I knew I was never going to write a book about death – to hell with death – when Charlie looked around and said, 'Who rang that bloody bell?'

James Loader

FLIGHT

Tonight you are distracted. You sit opposite me, staring at nothing, and I do not know whether you are pondering what I have just said to you or letting it drift past, bored, or simply unaware of what I am trying to tell you. You pause often before speaking, repeat yourself, go off the subject at a tangent; you are by turns dogmatic or full of complaints – how I have let you do all the cooking, or been in a bad temper, made you drink alcohol when I know very well that you are trying to do without it, drunk the last of the tea; in short, I have not shown you enough sympathy. I am being cruel.

We have been driving around Connecticut; it is very beautiful. We have a long walk along a river, into woods, near a place called Gaylordsville, where I will catch the bus back to New York City. New York: that is where I want to be at present, not here, not with you, only I do not know how to say so. The trees, the clouds and sky are picturesque; so are the houses. What is it you are saying, about blue-collar workers made good, the sort of people who live around here? It could be England. I want to say to you, I do not like it very much. I have not come all this way to be in the English countryside again, God knows, I wanted the city, I wanted New York, with its soaring horizons, its possibilities for renewal and escape, the streets that lead to the sea, the glimpse of water at the end of its canyons. Why do you make me stay here?

Today I have my camera with me and I take snapshots, everywhere we go; the centre of a small town; a pretty church; the shore of a lake, directly into the sunset, and you tell me that this will not come out. You are wrong, but I do not fight you on this one. You do not like me taking pictures, you never have liked me taking pictures, you think it is somehow common, as people think it is common to prefer milk chocolate to plain or to take sugar in tea. Furthermore, you worry all the time that I will take your photograph, and, in fact, I manage a covert shot of you, facing away from the camera, a hand on your hip, the hem of your shirt lop-sided. So now you are fixed as a sturdy blue figure against a background of trees and river, as you stand on a jetty, looking at the water. Always. You will not like to be remembered in this new, heavy body, but that is how I have recorded you.

A more poignant image, not on film: you in a cemetery, a gentle green slope with stones set flat into the grass. I think of Harper's Ferry, wonder why American cemeteries are so much more beautiful than ours, the legends on the stone somehow more evocative, even the names. *Verlinda Stipes. Gazaway Cross. Priscilla Alice: Thirty-one months only did she exist on this earth, but shall live an angel forever on high* . . . That sort of thing.

I wait apart from you as you stand at your mother's grave. The suicide. You have sorted out her picture from the pile of photographs in your loft in New York. She looks young and frightened, and beautiful; even so . . . to do that to herself. To do that to you.

I have my ghosts too, and it was in a restaurant in New York that you asked me how I coped as a child with my own mother's death. You seemed to want to know. But then as I started to reply you broke into my sentence, you changed the subject. (I have not known you bored like this before. Your distraction is a symptom of this summer, new.)

Today, as we walk back from the river you talk about

being ill. This time you really talk about being ill, the state of being ill: not about the contingent details, the women in the hospital ward, the friends who slept on your sofa to be with you while you were in chemotherapy (an implied rebuke to the friends who were not there), the fortune teller who said you would marry and have many children, after they had taken out your ovaries. Now you try to tell me what it was like to be ill, feeling a lump, for the first time, inside you, as you were lying on your stomach, exercising. And how you got fat. You do not find the words yet to describe the chemotherapy.

This sort of talk upsets you and somehow your anger is deflected on to me. You seem very restless and I wonder if the peace of the cemetery has reached you at all. Later you tell me about the dying woman who talked to you about God; you tell me you believe in reincarnation. But you do not want to explain these ideas. You are apart from me, as you were in the cemetery, when you stood at your mother's grave and I waited over the brow of the hill, out of sight.

The house is like a doll's house, square, weatherboarded, pretty. And there are dolls in it, sitting almost everywhere a doll can be sat. They are all girls. Most of them are on a long windowsill, facing a wall of books. Nineteenth-century dolls, with simpering china faces, little white teeth. Some more modern: here's a piccaninny, and a Raggedy Ann. And, at the end of the line, a horrible one, a magic one, made of bones. Of course they are all sinister and inappropriate, as dolls always are in a home without children. What have adults to do with dolls? But what child might ever have played with that little figure made of bones, animal bones off which the meat has been chewed?

There is a son to this house, but he is no longer a child. We do not see him; he is staying somewhere else, while you have been offered the house for a holiday. Yesterday we moved the mattress off his bed, so we could watch videos (there are no seats in the room with the television, which is upstairs, small and chilly). There are pornographic magazines under the mattress. But you have also found a magazine, not under the mattress, not pornographic, in which your name is mentioned. A rock-star says he would take your novels to a desert island with him. This amuses us as much as the girlie magazines.

We watch *The Fly*; *Aliens*; *Scum*; *Alphabet City*; *The Man Who Would Be King*. You are annoyed that I am not more moved by the latter. As Sean Connery goes singing to his death there are tears in your eyes. I am amused by the scene in *Aliens*, when the heroine is protecting the little girl against the egg-laying monster: Keep away from her, you bitch. The film is saying something about motherhood, after all. Strange how expendable the male characters seem.

Downstairs, as well as the dolls, there are birds. It is my job to feed them. On the table in the window there is a canary, bright yellow, sleek. Hanging from the ceiling is a cage of fancy finches, darting little birds; one of them is white. Two love-birds are near the piano.

The piano is quite a good one, a Bechstein upright, modern. You would like me to play it. I search the wall of books opposite the dolls but can find no music; there is none upstairs, none in the boy's bedroom (of course) with its stripped bed and girlie magazines. I wonder what sort of person owns an expensive piano and has no music to play. I cannot improvise, but I like the feeling of the keys under my fingers, I like working the pedals, and I divert myself in this way until you call out to me to stop.

During the day, when it is very hot, you sit inside working, while I lie out in the sun, reading a novel. I am covered with sun-tan lotion; it is necessary. The novel is by a friend of ours. Every morning you tell me not to get grease on the pages. When you come out into the garden to ask me to do something, you look down at the pages, look at my arms glistening in the sun, and tell me to wipe the lotion off before I spoil the book. You do not notice that I have no lotion below my elbows, and that the book is spotless. It takes me three days to finish the novel and every day we go through all this at least twice.

Then there are your commands; at odd moments of the day, for example, the birds will need water, something has to be carried in from the car. Or I will have to listen to one of the sentences you have written, and judge between two words. Sometimes you want something to drink. At other times you simply want to check there are no grease-prints on your friend's novel. The rising inflection of your voice, when you call my name, a minor third up the chromatic scale, becomes infuriating. I will never be able to forget this.

It is so very hot, and the garden is so very secluded (I have found a little lawn behind a patch of tall vegetables) that I have taken to basking in the nude. My main hope, however, is that this will keep you at bay, and I am right. Next time you come out with some command you are plainly embarrassed by me, sitting up with my towel pulled round me, inadequately and too late. There is some sort of a taboo here, your composure is lost, and it is disturbing. I do not know why I should feel sorry for you, as you retreat to your work, but I do. You do not trouble me again. Later when I go into the house through the studio, I see you lying out half-naked on another lawn. That part of the garden slopes steeply and I can see you clearly from the high windows of the studio. You too are reading.

You have already finished a book about the female nude in art and tomorrow, during the day, I read the manuscript. There is no nonsense about sun-tan oil this time; I sit in the shadowy room, the ranks of dolls watching me, the birds twittering. I read the chapters on Bonnard and Maillol, on Picasso. Your book is very good, but long; I will leave here before I finish it.

We notice something odd about the little white finch. It looks untidy and spends most of the time sitting on the floor of the cage. The others, brightly coloured, fly about over its head, with shrill squeaks. They seem all right to me.

Outside, at the side of the lawn where you sunbathe half-nude, is a dilapidated barn. I take a photograph of it, because you have told me, perhaps wrongly, that it is the barn where a painter went to kill himself. This was his house. He walked out through the garden, into the barn and killed himself, you say. I wonder what it was like inside when he lived here; presumably he used the studio. Was the hammock in the garden there, as well as the boulders set into the grass? What did he place on the long shelf where the dolls now sit?

The house is made of wood and looks flimsy; we lock the door carefully at night, but, as you point out, anyone could smash his way in if he wanted, and this is the country, far away from any neighbours who might hear us scream. So you will not allow me to leave you. I spend part of an afternoon on the telephone to one of my ex-students; his family are anxious to entertain me, and they only live a few miles away. But they want me to spend the night with them, and you will not countenance this. You are scared, and besides, the videos give you bad dreams. Just inside the front door we find a hatchet. That would not be there if it were not needed, you reason. So I miss my dinner party. My ex-student is offended; I sense this, over the phone. I shall not see him again.

I long to be back in New York. I think of the galleries, the bars, my friends there, the beautiful loft you live in, and where I could be now. I would live on virtually nothing, eating in the cheap bars around the South Street Port, chatting to strangers and watching the world outside me. I would be separate, peaceful. But you cannot bear for me to be there and you here; you even, at one point, suggest I postpone my flight to London. Strange; you do not enjoy my company, you say it inhibits your work. You just do not want to be left.

One day we have an argument. We are both depressed, it should be easy enough to understand each other, to have sympathy. We're both, to be honest, having love trouble. Sex trouble. I think you know you may not see your lover again. I know it is all over with mine. And yours ... he won't come out here, anyway, not with me here. You try to describe him, but all that you convey to me is his white Irish skin. I take it on trust that he is attractive. He is ten years younger than you and has a girlfriend.

Despite this, you tell me, despite this, and your having lost your figure, your looks going also, you tell me that you have never known such sexual happiness. Never felt yourself to be so desired. You tell me that happiness is there to be grasped. 'Be a Mensch,' you say. 'Join the dance of life.'

(In the two years or so following I will often want to ring you and fling these words back at you, as I cannot apply them to myself; I can see no truth in them. But I will continually get your answerphone, and one cannot put this in a letter. And then, the time when such things can be said at all will have gone.)

At night it is very hot. I cannot sleep, and wander out into the garden. The dance of life is elsewhere. I lie in the hammock in the moonlight, looking at the house, thinking of the hatchet by the front door, the piano with no music, the caged birds, the doll which is bones with the meat gnawed off, the disgusting prettiness of it all. The pretension and the horror. I walk around naked on the lawns and I hate being here.

But you are creating, this week, and every evening you show me what you have written. You write eight to ten pages a day, I suppose, and it is always good. Every evening you start me at page one again; you say I have to read from the beginning, to judge the continuity. Then you ask me what I think. We do this again and again.

It is about your mother ...

Sometimes, usually, all I think is that it is good and that

I want to go on reading. But you want more than this; every evening, you want a critique, you pay close attention to what I say. Sometimes I do not notice that you have made changes in the first few pages; you will always want to know which is better, the earlier or later version. You do not like either praise or criticism, it seems to me.

One day the woman who owns the house rings up, to check how we are. There are photographs of her in the bathroom I use; she is with other dancers, in leotards. We do not tell her about the pornography but we are worried about the birds. The little white one is losing its feathers; it now has noticeable bald patches. We are afraid that it is ill. She tells us that it is very old, there is nothing we need do. It doesn't matter. It will probably die soon.

One day after we have argued and made up you try, illogically, to make me stay longer, when I have been trying to tell you that I miss New York. I try to make you understand that I want to be alone, that I have waited all year for the summer, so that I could be alone. You are sympathetic. You tell me about Maine; you can get us a house there, you think, we could go there, it will be beautiful. You will leave me to myself . . . I like the idea of being in Maine with you, but it is so clearly impossible, it is all impossible . . .

The morning after the woman telephoned I see one of the little green finches swoop down on the white bird and stab it with its sharp beak.

The son comes in, briefly, while we are out shopping, to collect something. When we return the mattress is still in front of the television, but the girlie magazines have vanished. We are embarrassed for him; the magazines were very mild.

This is my last day here. The bald patches on the little white finch are suddenly much larger and I can see scabs of blood on it as well.

Finally, late in the afternoon I catch the bus at Gaylordsville. We sit in a hotel by the river, having a drink until the bus comes. Conversation is awkward; we are bored with one another, it has been too long, this time together in Connecticut. The bus is very late, or it may have been very early and already gone; you suggest that I leave tomorrow morning, and suddenly this is a necessity for you. But I am invited out to dinner in New York, and I prefer to go now. I feel, suddenly, that if I don't leave you now I never will. I need to escape you, I need to escape. You don't like me to take the keys of your loft; you make difficulties, suddenly, about how I should return them to you, although it is perfectly simple, I shall give them to a friend in New York, he will give them to you when you return. But you do not want to be alone tonight.

So I am relieved to leave you, relieved to be in the bus. New York is beautiful as we come in, at dusk. There is a patch of green under a flyover, and a man lives there, alone, in a shack he has made himself. He has a chair and a table out on the grass, and you have told me that he will see any intruder off his patch with a gun. Then in Harlem people are sitting out on the sidewalk, the colours are all soft browns, everyone looks relaxed; it is warm in the evening in New York City.

It is not till tomorrow, in Manhattan, as I am crossing the street to post a letter, that a sense of your unhappiness will come crashing down on me, it will at last be as though you are with me, and in the road, in the traffic, a desolation will overwhelm me, which is both yours and mine. I will hurry back to your loft and as I close the door behind me the telephone will be ringing and it will be you; you unhappy, alone and lost.

John Saul

SMALL CHANGES
IN GERMANY

The chair factory

The chair factory is now dust but is being revived in the
consciousness of local people. It was blown up with dynamite. Here I'm going back a hundred years or more.
Dynamite was not necessary for a one-storey building
barely more robust than a theatre set. But the owner,
Carstens, had read nitroglycerine mixed with sawdust
(nitroglycerine + sawdust = dynamite), properly managed,
would bring down the walls in one pleasing moment. He
was (1) curious and (2) had plenty of sawdust. The factory
stone had been pink so he got pink dust.

Moritz and Jutta

Whenever Moritz and Jutta (pronounced Yutta) meet in
public they kiss full on the lips. Take their time. Stroking
the other's neck or cheek. Moritz is dark and grey and
curly. Jutta is gold and bright blue and sad-dog looking. (As
a couple they would dance rock 'n' roll well together.)
Despite being sad-dog looking Jutta is in fact cheery and
interested, a good talker. Moritz, less of a talker, is full of
ideas. He has a major idea, about something, anything,
roughly once a week. (In fact he has many more but has discovered that the receiving world cannot hold them all.) This
may be a reason Jutta is so readily affectionate with him.

Why do people fall in love; stay in love; and what do
they want from it?

Anyway the lovers' greeting is genuine, quite sweet, touching. People freeze in what they're doing until Moritz and Jutta are through. But they freeze also because it can be a little disconcerting. Very disconcerting. Feel the lumpy throats; see the halting smiles. Lumps and smiles of people with a lot of aching to have an equivalent Moritz or Jutta in their lives.

The grey dust of the lot

The grey dust of the lot lies next to the pink dust of the lot and now it's simply one lot, pink and grey, empty, derelict, weeds, rusty scrap, piles of rubble, the object of plans and speculation. Billboards run along one side, down another is the front of a department store (abandoned). The grey dust is the fine remains of buildings already ball-broken and bulldozed. Under the dry impacted mass of buildings/dust are three hundred years of bones and head-stones, the latter also now beneath the ground. Some of these gravestones were laid flat and covered with two feet of earth so a café might be built over them. That meant small talk and coffee spilling, just three feet above where Josef Cohn lay. Then came a shoe shop. A bakery. Finally the department store, its foundations deviously sunken, Isaak Levi holding a pillar of the ironmongery department in the crook of an arm.
(Read Bertolt Brecht)

Now here comes one of Moritz's ideas

Two buckets of orange paint. Two paint rollers tied to poles. Old clothes. Organize a ladder, two ladders, enlist helpers. Go in broad daylight to the department store wall on the edge of the lot and paint the message: this building is full of asbestos. It may contain asbestos, it may not. No one knows. Well I think this is a good idea of Moritz's, says

Jutta to the gathering. (A gathering indoors, of about a dozen people.) Moritz holds back his ideas for the video, the questionnaire of local people, the book for the district archives, the series of books for the district archives, the day for planting shrubs and flowers on the lot, the protest postcards, the leaflets, the press statement, the public information stand and the fifteen-minute disruption of the city hall. Jutta crosses the room and kisses him. He strokes her thigh, her backside. She ruffles his hair lightly.

All the while the meeting has held its collective breath. Jutta has an idea too, said Moritz. She returned to her seat. Yes, said Jutta, I've been studying the local archives as we agreed the other week, and I discovered there used to be a chair factory beside the cemetery. I've heard there was too, said Moritz. (The effect of their display of tenderness: the floor stays theirs.) Then by chance, said Jutta, last week in the street I came across an artist who balanced ten chairs on his chin. How did he do that, asked the young man next to Moritz. Jutta spread her arms upwards: he locked the chairs together into a sort of wedge shape. He said they weighed a lot, said Moritz, but in fact they'd been hollowed out; by the way, love, did you come on your bike here? Yes, she called back. Why? Because I need the pump. Have you got a flat again? Moritz nodded, then yawned suddenly. Jutta cleared her throat. My idea is for us to employ this artist, *artiste*, to draw people, then hit them with our information. In saying this she smacked her fist into her palm.

(Moritz had never seen her do this. He felt shock. She's spunky but she's gentle, he often told himself; or was it more than spunk? He felt the urge to revise she's spunky but she's gentle. He found he wanted the meeting to end so he could think about this undisturbed.)

Logic

When something develops organically logic has no say, no place. Logic cannot connect the chair factory to the cemetery or to local opposition to developers' plans. The chair factory was not erected over the cemetery. No one alive can remember more than the barest mention of it. Allegedly, Carstens had a dog he walked on Sundays. He made only chairs. The chair factory is apparently of no relevance to anything. However it is possible to see how interest in it has surfaced. For once the lot was cleared it became possible to contemplate the whole sequence, the layers of building known to have stood there. Thanks to the open space an interest in history had been sparked.

The developers have no interest in history though

$DM. In Germany, as anywhere, building a shopping centre over a Jewish cemetery is more expensive in the long run if digging is not authorized. Then the car park has to be on the roof. However a shopping centre with a roof car park in this area may still pay more than a centre in another, even adjacent area. But does it pay better than leaving the land idle and selling later? Study of the money markets suggests building is currently about as worthwhile as not building. So the best option is to reopen negotiations on digging down. What is the cost of compensation compared to the returns. And what is the likely result of the next city elections.

Jews from here, there, and almost everywhere

One job international Jewry has had to take on is protecting cemeteries. 'A grave must stay as long as the wind blows or a cock crows.' Cemeteries have been saved all over the world. (This is not necessary with plots named Schulz and

Müller.) At the same time the life of an international protester is hard, hard, and often thankless. For one hundred Jews from the USA, Europe and elsewhere came to save this cemetery, vehemently protesting, climbing the north-east fence in their best clothes; but unlike the local speculators they some time had to go back where they came from. Moritz and Jutta's group, meanwhile, are less concerned about the cemetery, it's the shopping mall idea* they hate. As Jutta once quoted from the aforementioned archives, 'a cemetery was important for the community to establish or consolidate itself, but today fewer than one person in a thousand here is a Jew.'

Yet the very faintness of this presence is itself a most transparent signal. The question now is one of respect.

In the way, that possibly German handicap: the inability to put yourself in someone else's shoes.

* Once I heard the writer Ian McEwan speak in public. In answer to a question about whether a character of his was not rather a delicate flower he replied: Well I think we are all delicate flowers. This sounds right; but should not detract from what is uppermost in a person's character, from that which most impinges on the world about. A property developer who slashes housing and drives out people is: a thug.
(More on thuggery shortly.)

A small change befell Moritz and Jutta

Shortly after Jutta had smacked her fist into her palm a small change befell Moritz and Jutta. When they met in public they kissed full on the lips but all the accompanying, tender gestures vanished. Moritz noted this change right away and though he didn't exactly pounce upon it (ah, and Moritz can be so exciting, so attractive when he pounces) he saw fit to ask Jutta if she still loved him. ('It's all right to hesitate if you then go ahead.' – B. Brecht.) Jutta thought it most brave of Moritz to ask this, and whether or not she had still loved him before then, she knew she loved him now for this. Of course I love you, she said, loving him. (They have been together thirteen weeks and five days.) In the short meantime of these few seconds Moritz had realized anyway she loved him and wondered why he'd asked. The question had taken him down a wrong track somehow and he lay back in bed a minute, feeling stupidly and messily entangled in knots, all his own work. The other oddity was just when he could have done with a brainwave, a major idea on how to cut through this tangle and throw away the Sellotape, Scotch tape, stringy bits of it, his mind was a complete blank. I've a question too, said Jutta suddenly: Do you have ghosts of other people when we're making love?

Take a relationship and its difficulties, our childhood trauma now a weighty part of us, do we none the less find the nature of our true selves when making love?

I don't, said Moritz. But his mind was already turning to the action with the paint, planned for 11 am. There's just me then, Jutta harped. Now Moritz understood very well about the empty space of the lot ('. . . it became possible to contemplate the whole sequence, the layers of building known to have stood there'); and, conversely: that the presence of a building obliterates all conjecture on what preceded it. When you're there you're everything, said Moritz, in strict accordance with this idea. I couldn't even begin to think of someone else. I also suspect, he said, this is in the nature of love. (Moritz, twenty-three years old.)

Thuggery and the German language

An English THUG is a German SCHLÄGERTYP.

Of particular comfort . . . no, let me call it interest; of particular interest to the English-speaking reader:

It is sometimes said the German language tends to brutalize. One reason for this notion may be: it's true.

Take the root of the above word, SCHLAG.

SCHLAG = blow, punch, smack, slap, kick, etc.

German	English
SCHLÄGER	racket, bat
SCHLÄGERKARTEI	police file
SCHLAGBALL	baseball
SCHLAGFERTIG	quick-witted
SCHLAGSAHNE	cream
SCHLAGWORT	catchword
SCHLAGZEILE	headline
SCHLAGZEUG	drums

The innocuous English and their language. But Schläger-typ still lacks the resonance of THUG.

Up the ladders

The scene: A pedestrian shopping street, benches under trees; an immigrant boy tormenting an accordion keyboard and passers-by with aimless finger runs; trestle tables and rugs on the ground, with desperate people offering desperate wares: old raincoats and trousers, chipped oil-lamps and cracked crockery, old clocks, old boots, old ashtrays, old radios, old calculators, old purses, sunglasses, typewriters, barometers and televisions (and methadone, heroin, cocaine). In the midst of this, new white café chairs and tables; to the sides, a flower stall and a booth with trays of warmed-up pizza.

They stood about conspiratorially, hesitant, each waiting for the other to say the word. Finally Moritz said it and it was Moritz straight up the ladder (he's a physical monkey) with his bucket and roller at the end of a pole. An instant later he was describing an orange A. On the street Jutta held out leaflets. She looked particularly sad-dog that morning. Why? Weariness over the issue itself, perhaps. The lot had been a field of dust for five years. And she had been remiss: quite forgotten to find her performer with the chairs. At this point she started daydreaming, forgetting she was to look out for the first sign of the police. She visualized the *artiste*'s blue and silver glitter costume, then the chest hair up to his collar bone. Dark curly, Latin, foreign hair. (But what was his name?) Moritz was on an E already. Moritz. Moritz would manage all right. Moritz loved her. He said he loved her. Damn it what was his name? She might remember by going back over his performance. Now his chairs had been white with gold stars, very circusy. Then: somebody nearby was shouting. She wondered if the police had been alerted yet. There were dozens of onlookers. Moritz was on his final S, having trouble. She willed him to concentrate. He concentrated. They would get away with this if he hurried. When he asked down for more paint she felt suddenly closer, protective towards him. Come down Mori, that'll do. That's just fine. Come down while you're safe, my love.

Why might things none the less be cooling between Moritz and Jutta?

1. *The most physical reason.*
   No one can kiss twenty-four hours non-stop. Or make love every night for ever and ever and ever. It just doesn't work.
2. *The most common reason.*
   Jutta or Moritz (or both) sense a difficulty between them. Or a telling difference. A difference in what they want or need. They may well resolve this but for the moment it's a hairy, troubling thing.
3. *The most obvious reason.*

Jutta is a bit bored listening to Moritz's endless flow of ideas. Or she finds he frequently makes love faster than she likes to. He her vice versa. She does yoga and he has always found yoga so goddamn stupid. A brain-softened vegetarian sympathizer sits down to the dinner table next to a rapacious carnivore.

4. *The deepest reason.*

Moritz finds Jutta is like his mother/father and Jutta Moritz her father/mother and actually they discover they are involved in a six-person relationship.

In vain Moritz looks for the physical bird

Isaak Levi hugs the sunken pillar close. Moritz and Jutta are asleep in bed. Jutta dreamt she came across a picture of a chair factory in the Paris Orangerie, painted by the Douanier Rousseau. It was a *fabrique de chaises* and out in the country, by a canal; not beside a cemetery, not dynamited, not pink. The factory sign said not Carstens but CHESNOY. In her dream she rode round it three times on her bike and blew it up by pumping on her pump. After a long hush hollow parts of wooden chairs with golden stars clunked down in struts and moulded legs around her. Na, she murmured, a word that bridged her physical sleeping self and her dream.

Beside her too Moritz stirs occasionally, tugging for the bedclothes. Moritz dreams politics. Scandals rack the city council; fresh elections threaten. Destroying/carting off/ asphalting the remains of dead Jews is OK. As at the last elections, real life elections, it's not a major party issue. (It would have been orthodox Nazi policy.)

Out in the night the paint is dry. The glistening orange has been quenched by the porous stone and now by darkness; the message is none the less bold and clear. Already someone with a spray-can has added two black skull-and-crossbones. Over the street from this a great speckled owl, waylaid trekking over continents, a dark something in its claws, settles and stops on a window-ledge. So huge, it effaces half the window. (A creature on the morrow in the papers and talked about in schools.)

What a night it is. The low moon; the trees and buildings making faint-hued silhouettes. Now Moritz can't sleep. He walks round looking for his t-shirt before finding it in the living-room. He then looks out at the silhouettes, swears he hears an owl. Well. Does Jutta love him? What does love him mean? That time he heard one. In vain he looks for the physical bird; then simply stares, trying to make rough, chunky guesses at pieces of the future. He has to peer, shield his eyes, as the floodlights on the back of the abandoned store flicker on. They sap the grey and pink out of the dust down on the lot. Eventually his eyes become accustomed to the lights, and he locks his stare at the dark green creeper covering the high west wall. It makes a surreal sight, one which Jutta says charges her with awe.

Moritz senses the temperature outside is dropping rapidly. He has no reason for thinking this, no evidence. At this hour the animal in him is taking over: all reflection halts. He looks and listens. The night feels long. By now he's kneeling on the floor, with his elbows on the windowsill.

Elisa Segrave

HAMSTER

Dear Mrs Sanderson,
   I have been asked to write an obituary of your
husband. You said a few days ago he was very ill. I hope
you don't think this is terribly tactless, but I thought
you might want to add something.

Richard was worried about putting this note under his
neighbour's door. He asked Inma, his Spanish cleaning
lady, who also worked for Mrs Sanderson, if she thought it
would be all right. Inma said she had just seen Mrs
Sanderson come out of her house, looking very cheerful
and wearing a pink dress. Richard therefore put the note
under the front door. It was 10.30 am.

Two hours later he was packing the car to go to the
cottage for the weekend. He carefully put his son's hamster, in its new cage, on to the back seat, fastening the cage
with a seat-belt. As he turned he saw Mrs Sanderson at her
kitchen window in the pink dress.

He had just loaded the final item, artichokes from the
Portobello Market, when the door opened and Mrs Sanderson, a small woman with a squashed face like a pekinese,
came out. She touched him on the arm.

'Richard, my husband died this morning at 10.30. I'm a
bit shocked.'

Richard said how sorry he was and she went back into her
house. He started the car and set off for his son's school.

What a fool he was to have left that note! It was exactly the time poor old Sanderson had died. At least Mrs Sanderson hadn't taken offence. At least she'd had the kindness to come out and tell him. He felt shocked himself. A few weeks ago Tim Sanderson had been walking his cocker spaniel up and down the road every day to the public library – last month he'd even come in with a key to bleed Richard's radiators; he was a damned good neighbour. Now he had died, of cancer, earlier than expected.

As Richard drove slowly down his street a man sweeping leaves waved at him. The man was there every Friday. He was thin as a hare, with a gap between his front teeth, and seemed a bit simple. The Friday before he had been sweeping leaves outside the house while Richard loaded the car. He had asked a question about the hamster, thinking it was a guinea-pig.

Today, Richard just nodded at the man and drove on past him. The ordinariness of seeing him in the same place again at the same time made Sanderson's death seem even more unbelievable. He almost expected to see him coming up the hill with his cocker spaniel.

Richard stopped at the library to collect Sanderson's autobiography, which he'd reserved on the telephone that morning. He'd planned to read it over the weekend and do the obit on Monday or Tuesday. Now he'd have to do it tonight.

Whenever he stopped at traffic lights, Richard glanced back at the hamster to see that it was all right in its new cage. The Friday before it had been in a tiny travelling cage, formerly used to house a Middle Eastern cockroach bought for £3 in a Brighton pet shop. On that Friday, when Richard had left the car for a few minutes to post a letter, he had returned to find the cage open and the hamster gone. It must have pushed the door open with its little paws. He had been sick with anxiety. Then he had luckily found it crouched under the front seat of the car.

His son had given the pet the odd name of Ranald, after 'Ranald' Reagan. Richard, whose wife Diana was in America for two weeks, had bought Ranald the new, bigger cage the day she had left for New York, thinking their son would be pleased.

However, when Peter returned from school he had shouted that his father had paid far too much for the cage – he thought it cost £100 – and that he hated Ranald, calling him 'that skeleton'. He said 'The cage makes my flesh creep' and paid no attention when his father said that it cost £25, not £100. He threw the cage downstairs and tried to climb inside it. Two days later he had got used to it.

Richard found himself growing fond of the hamster. While his wife was away he had to supervise its supplies of food and water and bedding. It was a plucky little thing, determinedly amusing itself in the ways it knew, i.e. going round and round on its wheel in the evening and desperately biting at the bars of its cage to keep its teeth down, instead of using the circular bit of wood the pet shop had provided. It loved fruit and Richard sometimes popped a grape or bit of apple through the bars. Sometimes when he was alone with it in the evening after Peter was asleep he thought it looked like a rat, particularly when it gnawed its wire cage so ferociously. At other times, when it sat on the palm of his hand, it seemed as light as a bit of thistledown and he was moved by the thought of its pathetically short life, only two or three years.

When Richard was a child he had had two guinea-pigs. When he was seven they were killed by a fox. His mother had found them 'dead in their cage'. He still remembered her awful words. Out of some instinct of self-preservation, he had not gone to the garden with his mother, but had stayed with his baby brother Frank. His sister Joanna, two years younger than him, had insisted on going to have a look. She had come back sobbing.

A year later Joanna found Frank in the barn. The little boy had fallen from the hay bales and broken his neck. On her twenty-first birthday Joanna died of an overdose. His surviving brother Julian had emigrated to Australia and Richard, now forty-seven, hardly ever saw him.

He had found it difficult to explain these family tragedies to his son. He had hardly taken them in himself. When people asked him how many brothers and sisters he had, he was never sure what to answer. If he said one, meaning Julian, it seemed dishonest. He was not one of two brothers, but had been the eldest of a family of four. But if he said that, he felt obliged to add that two out of the four were dead. Sometimes he stated the facts coldly, like someone rehearsing lines in a play. He was afraid of being thought melodramatic. He felt as if, by having both a brother and sister who had died unnaturally, he had done something shameful.

He remembered the first time he told his wife Diana about his brother and sister. They had been in a restaurant. Across the table he had been surprised to see that Diana's eyes filled with tears. He had thought, 'She's crying for me. Because I can't cry.' Soon after that he asked her to marry him.

Now he wished he had bought another type of pet for his son, one with a longer life.

He was worried about breaking the news to his son about their neighbour. Peter was already too preoccupied with death. Richard was afraid that his son had been affected by the deaths of Frank and Joanna, even though they had occurred before he was born.

When he was five Peter had been interviewed for a new school. Afterwards the head-teacher had asked for a short meeting with Richard and Diana on their own. She explained that she had shown Peter a series of pictures and asked him to tell a story about each. One picture was of a boy climbing a ladder up a high building. Peter had provided two endings to this story, she said. The first ending – she quoted Peter's words – was: 'The boy fell and no one would save him.' The second ending Peter provided was that the boy fell but was rescued. She said these alternative endings were to do with Peter's needing help and feeling that he might or might not get it.

When Richard heard 'The boy fell and no one would save him,' he had been stunned. He had suffered a familiar sense of paralysis, and shame, that his family's past was being dredged up, albeit unconsciously, by his son. He could not possibly have mentioned Frank's tragic accident to the teacher, a stranger, even if to reveal it would have cast light on his son's difficulties. Richard's own feelings about his little brother's death, and that of his sister, remained buried deep within him.

Outside the school he saw his son standing on the edge of a group of children. He looked skinny and awkward. His hair hadn't been brushed and the collar of his jacket was rucked up.

As soon as he got into the car Peter opened the hamster's cage and took it out. Richard turned round, nearly hitting a car in front.

'That's crazy! You must never take him out in the car. What happens if he escapes under the seat and gets into the boot? Please put him back.'

Peter put Ranald back deliberately slowly. Richard thought his son was intentionally taking risks with the animal. He knew he had the power of life or death over it and was exercising this. He guessed that his son was terrified of losing Ranald and, by taking these risks, was perhaps getting himself used to the idea, so it wouldn't be so awful when it happened. The morning after they had bought Ranald Peter had come into Richard's study and announced: 'The hamster's asleep and won't open its eyes.'

For a second Richard had been terrified, then had said: 'You're trying to frighten me into thinking he's dead.'

However, in that split second when he had believed Peter, he realized that he dreaded Ranald's death almost as much as his son did.

'Mr Sanderson's died,' said Richard, trying to sound casual, as they drove over Chelsea Bridge.

'What? What? That makes three. Betty is still in extensive care and Granny's dog died last holiday.'

Peter took the news of death or injury almost as a personal insult, his father observed. Yet he hated the thought of things or people having longer lives than him, even inanimate objects. In the cottage in the country, Richard had an old toy, a bulldog, which barked realistically when you pulled its chain. He had hidden it in the attic when his son was small because it had frightened him.

'Granny's dog will die and the dog in the attic won't,' Peter had commented.

Now Betty, their neighbour in the country, had been kicked by a horse and was still unconscious after two months. Also Richard's mother's dog had died that summer. Peter, on their last visit to his grandmother, had rushed to the end of the garden and poked about in the dog's grave with a stick, trying to dig up the earth. He had shouted that he hated Granny for preferring the dog to him. Was his behaviour at the grave morbid, or was his curiosity about what happened to the body after death natural? Richard wasn't sure. A few days later his son made a model of the dog out of paper. He took some raw mince from the fridge to use for its insides. When his mother remonstrated with him he replied: 'That's what's inside people and animals, meat.' He added: 'That's what's inside my head. Meat and blood, a lot of blood.'

The next time they went over to his grandmother's, Peter asked Richard if they would see the dog again.

'No, because he's died.'

Peter had again gone into the garden on his own. When he came back he announced:

'I found Ben lying on the long green grass – then I threw him into the air and he was alive!'

Richard found this vision of the dog's resurrection so powerful that he wanted to believe his son. He remembered a dream he had had as a child, soon after his brother had died, or was it a wish-fulfilment fantasy? He had wished, or dreamed, so powerfully that Frank was still alive, that they were still a happy family, that it had seemed almost true. Then, recently, he had dreamed about Joanna. He had heard her voice clearly, sounding very normal:

'I've just come to help Mum.'

Unfortunately, while his sister was still talking, the doorbell had rung, waking him abruptly. Would Joanna have gone on talking if the postman hadn't rung? What else might she have said?

'When I first got Ranald I wanted to open him up and see what was inside him but then I thought he was so sweet that I didn't,' Peter told him now from the back of the car.

'Oh good, I'm glad you've decided against that; yes, he is sweet,' said Richard. 'You must never be cruel to an animal, particularly anything smaller than you,' he added.

During the drive they listened to a tape of Handel's *Messiah*. Peter seemed to settle down. Ranald was asleep in his little plastic house.

Later Peter said: 'Mrs Heath had a dachshund. It died in her arms then she threw it in the bin.'

'Good God, are you sure?' said Richard.

A few minutes later Peter asked, 'Do you know why Mrs Heath's dachshund couldn't be buried?'

'No.'

'Because he was squashed flat by a car.'

'But you said a few minutes ago he died in her arms.'

Peter ignored this.

He told Richard that Mrs Heath had another dachshund, which had died in a crate on a plane from Australia.

'They opened him up and discovered he'd died of heat.'

Richard couldn't always tell if his son was lying. He often discussed this with his wife. Sometimes she was furious with Peter for telling lies, saying he was making a fool of people; at other times she seemed to find his vivid imagination amusing. She had pointed out that in one of the obituaries of Fellini someone wrote that the great film-maker had lied until the last, giving different versions of his age and birthplace. Richard said his son's tall stories did not necessarily mean that he was another Fellini, although he secretly hoped he was.

While he was driving Richard started composing Tim Sanderson's obituary. When he had to stop behind another vehicle or at lights, he flicked through the autobiography lying on the seat beside him. In the early 50s Sanderson, a columnist on one of the tabloids, had been writing four columns at once. In the year of the Coronation his name had been on buses all over the West End. Sanderson wrote disarmingly: 'Most of my columns were shallow as a puddle.' Although he had lived next door for seven years, Sanderson had hardly ever spoken about his past working life. Most of the time he had simply behaved as an exemplary neighbour. There were few specific dates in the book, which would make the obituary more difficult to do in a hurry. It was annoying.

'After you die, can you become another person at will?' Peter asked.

'I don't know,' said Richard. He could not answer his

son's next question either; after you die, can you go back to the past?

They were driving under arches of copper beech trees. They were near the house of Richard's mother's oldest friend, Angela, a place he had loved visiting as a child, because Angela was so full of life, always occupied with something – bringing up a baby fox, looking for rare birds in the wood, planting bulbs, or cooking delicious things from her garden. She was the daughter of the vicar and had spent most of her life in that village. On an impulse, Richard turned right up a small hill and stopped outside her church.

He and Peter walked up a little path and through the graveyard where an elderly man was gardening. A Jack Russell dog was tied to his wheelbarrow. Peter seemed awed by the inside of the church with its stained glass window and vases of orange and white chrysanthemums. In a side chapel were some stone statues of children of a local family, some holding skulls. Richard guessed that the ones holding skulls had died young, but did not tell his son this.

However Peter asked: 'Are those the people who are with God?'

He then said he wanted to pretend to be a priest. He got into the pulpit and mumbled a few words. He asked his father to sing a hymn. Richard sang a few lines of 'Abide with me'. It made him feel lonely.

When they got back in the car Peter asked: 'Will you be with me for many days and many weeks? Will you die?'

When Richard was silent, his son went on: 'An extraordinary thing happened last week. I woke up in the night and saw a boy from school, Bob Pizanelli, in my bedroom. It may have been a dream-vision. When I told my teacher she said Bob Pizanelli had died that weekend in hospital. He'd died without any pain. Isn't that extraordinary? I was so shocked. The next night I cried in bed.'

Richard thought it unlikely that a child at the school had died without any of the parents being told. But when he calmly said that he must ask the teacher about it, Peter didn't seem at all worried.

Meanwhile the hamster, which had been sleeping in its little house, woke up and started maniacally going round and round on its green plastic wheel. It was the poor little thing's only form of exercise, Richard realized. However he couldn't help finding the squeaking noise of the wheel extremely irritating.

'My teacher said cats were just snakes with fur,' Peter said. 'Ranald is just a spider with fur. That's all a hamster is. A spider with fur. When Ranald dies, will you get me another hamster?'

He asked Richard to play a game with him in which Ranald's death was formally announced. They took turns to say the appropriate lines of dialogue. When Peter asked: 'Will you get me another hamster?' Richard took the opportunity to say: 'I will make sure you really want one and will look after it properly.'

When Peter asked him to play it for the fourth time he refused, thinking it was getting too macabre.

That night when Peter was in bed Richard sat up late writing the obituary. He telephoned a couple of Tim's colleagues, retired journalists, and also the publisher, on holiday in Spain, who had commissioned the autobiography.

'Make sure you put in that he masterminded the Cortini elopement scandal,' said the publisher. 'That was Tim's biggest coup. The other papers were hot for the story but Tim kept them guessing. He was with the couple for three weeks in hotels all over the Continent. The story finally only broke when he wanted it to. His paper ran an exclusive full-page spread.'

*

It was two in the morning. Richard sat staring at the word-processor. He had finished. He was sure he had put everything in, but wasn't satisfied with himself. Why?

He thought about his son, with his deep brown eyes, which often wouldn't look at him, and his searching questions, which Richard couldn't answer. Compared with his son, he was cowardly and inadequate. All his life he had tried to keep death at one remove. Writing the obituary was a journalistic exercise. It was part of his job, but it was also a way of keeping at bay his feelings about the sudden death of a man he had liked. His son, however, with his unsettling and disturbing remarks, was genuinely trying to confront and understand death.

Richard watched the hamster climbing sideways up the bars of its cage. Its stomach looked like a tiny pure white rug. He thought back to his own guinea-pigs and to his dead brother and sister. He did not remember ever crying about them, or the guinea-pigs, for that matter.

What had poor Joanna felt just before she died – that everyone, including him, her favourite brother, had abandoned her?

Now he thought about Frank. He remembered how, a few days after his little brother's death, he and his sister had been sent to the children's Christmas service in the village church. He and Joanna had held hands, as they followed the other children up the aisle to receive their present from Angela's father, the vicar. He was eight, and Joanna was six. They were two little children whose brother had just died.   How sad it was! For the first time, he pitied himself. He a father, and a man of forty-seven, had never learned how to mourn, had never even seen the dead body of someone, or something, that he loved. Perhaps his son would show him the way.

Lynne Tillman

LUST FOR LOSS

'*What gives value to travel is fear ... this is the most obvious benefit of travel.*'

ALBERT CAMUS[1]

Though she didn't really like to travel, Madame Realism often wanted to be someplace other than home. Travel caters to the uncanny, to impulse and serendipity, and Madame Realism took chances. She gambled away some of the time allotted to her in life, and defiantly, almost wantonly, acknowledged and nurtured a craving to wreck her own schedule and daily routine. I am my own home-wrecker; it is one of my freedoms, she told herself.

To Madame Realism the self-inflicted habits of a typical day were no comfort. She disliked the idea of a typical day. Though habits afford a reliable sanity, Madame Realism resented her own customs. She even resisted them, as if they were the amorous advances of a former lover. Easy, but who needs it, she thought. I'd rather be sitting on a crowded train, next to smokers, living dangerously.

Tainted by wanderlust, resigned to a permanent tourism, Madame Realism plotted journeys she might take. She indulged a fantasy, like envisioning a movie she longed to see, then set it into motion, which was akin to that movie appearing on the screen. First there was a desired setting and then there was an outcome, a reality – a hotel, a museum, an avenue, a beach, a café – all of which she'd conjured before. After all, Madame Realism mused, when you're watching a movie, it's your reality.

But she suffered the pangs of most thrill-seekers – she hated departures. After one particularly lugubrious leave-taking, she observed that train stations and airports were, like graveyards, watering holes for the sentimental. Or the mournful. She suspected that people who hung around might be waiting for no one or nothing but a good cry. There were always reasons to cry, she knew, but not as many places to cry as reasons.

I like it when I don't know where I am, or why, but it also terrifies me, she admitted to herself. Madame Realism was taking off, running away, going on a vacation or just roaming. Her destination was the coast of Normandy. She was curious about World War II – she was definitely a postwar character – and had, if not a valid reason to be there, a valid passport. With it and money, she could get out of town. But just as she was suspicious of the reasons for following a routine, she was suspicious of the reasons for disrupting it.

Unsettled by her own vagueness, Madame Realism threw a bottle of aspirin into a bag. She tossed in another pair of underpants, too. The black silk underpants were an afterthought, a last-minute decision. Maybe all my decisions are, she worried, then closed her suitcase. She hummed an ancient tune: 'Pack up your troubles in your old kit bag ...' And do something. But she couldn't remember the lyrics. And what is a kit bag? She hesitated and cast last-minute glances about the room.

Madame Realism couldn't know what lurked around the corner, at home or abroad. From reading travel books and maps, from studying histories of particular locations, she could plan a course of action. But actually she yearned to be out of control in a place where she didn't know a soul. It's better to be a cliché, a reprehensible image, than not to venture forth, not to take a risk, she contended as she walked out of her apartment. Madame Realism might be both Sancho Panza and Don Quixote. She might also be the horse.

After having been asked by an airline representative if anyone had packed for her, if she was carrying a gift from a stranger, if she had left her suitcase unattended, Madame Realism boarded the plane, settled into a seat, and nervously considered, as the jet shot into the sky, what a first-minute decision might be. A decision of the first order. A crucial, life and death decision, which would certainly be made during war. That's why I'm going to Normandy, she concluded. To be alive in a place haunted by death and by great decisions. If that was true, if that was her motivation, Madame Realism felt even more peculiar and unreasonable.

> *'What explains this mass mania*
> *To leave Pennsylvania?'*
> NOËL COWARD[2]

In a hotel not far from the beach, Madame Realism was standing on a small balcony. She was gazing out at the sea. Large, white cumulus clouds dotted the blue sky. The Channel changed from rough to smooth in a matter of hours. She found herself watching the rise and fall of the waves, the rush and reluctance of the tides, with fascination or dread. Or concern. Which characterization was most true she was not sure. Truth was so difficult to be told, small and big truths, she could never tell it completely. Much as she might try, she couldn't even adequately define the weird anguish she experienced at the sight of the placid stretch of beach that touched the sea. The five beaches of Operation Overlord – Juno, Omaha, Sword, Gold, Utah. She had memorized their wartime names. The code names intrigued her, codes always did.

The light blue water – maybe it was more green than

blue – grew progressively darker as it left the shore. The
sea was always mysterious, ever more so with depth.
Unfathomable, she reminded herself, the way the past is as
it becomes more distant and unreadable with every day,
every day a day further away from the present or the past,
depending upon the direction from which one is thinking.
But is something that is regularly described as a mystery,
like the ocean, like history, mysterious?

Puzzled, Madame Realism was never less contemporary
than when she traveled. Each journey was the fulfillment
of a desire, and desire is always an old story. Like everyone
else's, Madame Realism's desires were born and bred in an
intransigent past. Even if she imagined herself untethered
as she flew away, she was tied. When she journeyed to an
historic site especially, she kept a date with history. And
when she trafficked in history, she was an antique. At least
she became her age or recognized herself in an age.

Spread on the bed were histories and tourist brochures
of the region. Military strategy appealed to her; secretly she
would have liked to have been privy to the goings on in
one of the D-Day war rooms. But there hadn't been any
women in them. I'd have to rent a war room of my own,
she laughed, and then recollected, in a rapid series of
images, the war movies she'd consumed all her life –
Waterloo Bridge, *The Best Years of Our Lives*, *The Longest Day*,
The Dirty Dozen. Celluloid women waited and worried about
men. They were nurses, wives, secretaries. Sometimes they
drove ambulances, sometimes they spied. They grieved,
they loved. Madame Realism learned from a TV program
that the first woman to land on the Normandy beachhead
at Omaha was an American named Mabel Stover, of the
Women's Army Corps. Mabel Stover, earnest and robust,
appeared on the program, exhorting World War II veterans
to contribute money to a US memorial, a 'Wall of Liberty.'
'Your name belongs on this wall,' she exclaimed. 'It's your
wall. Go for it, guys and gals.'

'You receive unforgettable impressions of a world in which there is not a square centimetre of soil that has not been torn up by grenades and advertisements.'

KARL KRAUS[3]

Early the next morning, restless and sleepless, Madame Realism left the hotel and went for a walk on the beach. There was hardly anyone around. The sea was choppy. With each barefoot step on the sand – the tide was out – Madame Realism concocted a battle story: Here a man had fallen. He broke his leg, he struggled, and a soldier he never saw before helped him, then he was shot. Both were shot, but both lived, somehow. Or, here someone died. But without pain, a bullet to the brain. Or, here a soldier was brave and sacrificed himself for another, but lived. They both lived. Or, here a man found cover and threw a grenade that knocked out an enemy position. Or, here someone was terrified, sick with fear, and could not go on.

At the phrase 'sick with fear,' Madame Realism kicked her foot in the sand and uncovered a cigarette butt. She wondered how long it had been buried. It was trivial to contemplate in a place like this, even absurd. But I can't always control what I think, she thought.

Madame Realism jarred herself with vivid images of thousands of soldiers rushing forward on the beach. She thought about the men who had been horribly seasick in the boats that carried them to shore. On D-Day, years ago, the weather was bad and the sea was rough. Madame Realism looked again at the water and toward the horizon. Imagine being sick to your guts and being part of the greatest armada in history, imagine being aware that you were making history in the moment it was happening, imagine having the kind of anonymous enemy who is determined to kill you – or being a terrifying enemy yourself. In the next moment she scolded herself: If you're throwing up over the side of a boat or scared to death, you're not thinking about history. You're just trying to stay alive.

At the horizon the sea was severed from sky, or it met the sky and drew a line. As she did when she was a child, Madame Realism speculated about what she could not see, could never see, beyond that line, that severe border. She squinted her eyes and stood on her toes, hoping to see farther. It was impossible to know how far she actually saw. Still, she lingered and meditated upon the uncanny meeting of water and air, how it was and wasn't a meeting, how the touch of the air on the sea wasn't like the touch of a hand to a brow, or a mouth to a breast. It wasn't a touch at all. Just another pathetic fallacy. The sky doesn't kiss the sea. Jimi Hendrix must have been wildly in love or high when he wrote that line, ''Scuse me while I kiss the sky.'

Madame Realism licked her lips and tasted the salt on them. She loved that. She always felt very much alive near the ocean. She breathed in deeply. It was strange to be alive, always, but stranger to feel invigorated and happy in a place where there had been a battle, a life and death struggle. Maybe it wasn't weird, she consoled herself. Maybe it's like wanting to have wild sex right after someone dies.

Life wants to live, a friend once told her. Especially, Madame Realism thought, digging her toes into the sand, in a place where it was sacrificed. Death wasn't defeated here, but victory transformed it. That was the hope anyway. Hope disconcerted Madame Realism. It was just the other side, the sweet side, of despair.

The soldiers landing, the planes dropping bombs, the guns shooting, the chaos, the soldiers scrambling for safety – she could envision it. But an awful gap split her comprehension in half, much like the sea was divided from the sky. It split then from now, actuality from memory, witnesses from visitors.

From time to time, Madame Realism forgot herself, but

she was also conscious of being in the present. She was aware that time was passing as she reflected on time past. But even if she had not lived through it, the war lived through her. She was one of its beneficiaries; it was incontrovertible, and this was her war as much or even more than Vietnam.

Of course, she told herself, it's odd to be here. The past doesn't exist as a file in a computer, easy to call up, manage and engage. We can't lose it, though we are, in a sense, lost to it or lost in it. But was WWII being lost every day? she wondered. Everything was changing and had changed. The former Yugoslavia, the former Soviet Union, a reunified Germany. She recalled Kohl and Reagan's bitter visit to Bitburg. Was the end of the Cold War a return to the beginning of the century and an undoing of both world wars? It wasn't cold now, but Madame Realism trembled. Once history holds your hand, it never lets go. But it has an anxious grip and takes you places you couldn't expect.

> 'And the wall of old corpses,
> I love them,
> I love them like history.'
> SYLVIA PLATH[4]

Suddenly Madame Realism realized that there were many people around her, speaking many different languages. Tourists, just like her. She shrugged and marched on. I go looking for loss and I always find it, she muttered to herself, a little lonely in the crowd. She reached Omaha beach and the enormous US cemetery. The rows and rows of grave-stones were rebukes to the living. That's precisely what entered her mind – rebukes to the living. She shook her head to dislodge the idea. Now, instead of rebuke, a substitute image, sense or sensation – all the graves were reassurances, and the cemetery was a gigantic savings bank with thousands of tombstone-like savings cards. Everyone who died had paid in to the system and those who visited were assured they'd received their money's worth. That's really crazy, she chastised herself. Over seven thousand US soldiers were buried in this cemetery, and Madame Realism knew not a soul. But what if the tombstones were debts, claims against the living?

'I'd rather be,' W.C. Fields had carved on to his tombstone, 'living in Philadelphia.' Sacrilegious to the end, Fields was outrageous in death. And surrounded by thousands of white tombstones, Madame Realism was overwhelmed by the outrageousness of death itself. But since she was only a visitor to it, death was eerily, gravely, reassuring. Madame Realism looked at the dumb blue sky and away from the aching slabs of marble. But when she reluctantly faced them again, they had become, for her, monuments that wanted to talk. They wanted to speak to her of small events of devotion, fearlessness, selflessness, sacrifice.

Markers of absence, of consequence, of heartbreak, of loss, each was whispering, each had a story to tell and a silenced narrator. Madame Realism was astonished to be in a ghost story, spirited by dead men. But it was a common tale.

Everyone hopes the dead will speak. It's not an unusual fantasy, and perfect for this site, even site specific, in a way. Though maybe, Madame Realism contemplated, they choose to be silent. Maybe in life they didn't have much to say or didn't like talking. Maybe they had already been silenced. What if they don't want to start talking now? That was a more fearsome, terrible fantasy. In an instant, the tombstones stopped whispering.

More people joined her, to constitute, she guessed, a counterphobic movement, a civilian army fighting against everyday fears. During the Second World War, President Roosevelt had advised her nation: 'There is nothing to fear but fear itself.' War is hell, she intoned mutely, silent as a grave.

Haunted and ghosted, Madame Realism stared at the tombstones. The sun was shining on them, and they glared back at her. They glowered unhappily. And she had a curious desire. She wanted to sing a song, though she didn't have much of a voice. She wanted to sing a song and raise the dead. She wanted to dance with them. She wanted to undo death and damage. Even if it was a cliché, or she was, she gave herself to it. All desires are, after all, common, she reflected, and closed her eyes in ecstasy.

At last Madame Realism was spinning out of control in a place where she didn't know a soul. Maybe she was discovering what it meant to be transgressive. She wasn't sure, because that happened only when you couldn't know it. For a moment or two she dizzily abandoned herself to a god that was not a god, to a logic that was not logical. She imagined she'd lost something, if not someone. She had not lost herself, not so that she couldn't find herself again once she returned home. But she felt foolish or turned around, turned inside out or upside down. I'm just a fool to the past, she hummed off key, as the past warbled its siren song. And in a duet, and unrehearsed, Madame Realism answered its lusty call.

[1] Camus, Albert. *Notebooks 1935–1942*. Paragon House, New York, 1991, p.13.
[2] Coward, Noël. From 'The Wrong People'.
[3] Kraus, Karl. 'Promotional Trips to Hell', in *In These Times*, Carcanet, 1984, p. 93.
[4] Plath, Sylvia. 'Letter in November', *Ariel*, 1961.

William Trevor

ASSIA

The sixties in London had the flavour of a dream. After the drabness of the previous decade, in which nothing more exciting happened than Ban-the-Bomb marches, the Suez fiasco and a dog propelled into space, all of a sudden there was the razzmatazz of Carnaby Street and the E-type Jag, and smart Mary Quant bringing fashion they could afford to shopgirls and typists. Flower people ran barefoot in the park, James Bond pushed aside the fuddy-duddy heroes who still trailed a Bulldog Drummond sense of decency and a stiff upper lip. Cannabis was in, LSD if you were daring. Sex set up its stall. *Jesus Christ is alive and well*, the graffiti said, *and working on a less ambitious project*.

Fantasy arrived in London in the 1960s. 'It's fantastic!' was the cry as wives were swapped at parties and there was dancing without steps. Fans ruled London's football terraces, tuneful with 'Here we go!' More fans than ever before mobbed the entertainment idols. Popular music acquired significance, and the record companies a very great deal of money. Going topless was all the rage.

So were rude words on chat shows, doing your own thing, and youth. Jack Kennedy, ikon of the young at heart, became President of the United States. Suave Dr Stephen Ward, osteopath and sexual provider, amassed a stable of nubile lovelies for the delectation of the powerful and the good.

In 1962 a young man in a lounge bar won a wager of a

shilling by kissing on the lips a girl who was a stranger to him: she'd have slapped his face in the nineteen fifties, and taken him to court in the nineties. But in the sixties – mid-century breathing space between the World Wars and AIDS – everybody laughed and anything went. 'Yeah! Yeah! Yeah!' sang the Beatles, and all over London there were poets – barrow poets and Putney poets and Hampstead poets, poets in movements and in groups, poets homing in from the antipodes and from Africa, from India and Ireland and Wales and Scotland, beat poets, obscure poets, sober poets, drunken poets, good, bad and indifferent poets. All of them were reading aloud, sonorously or quietly, in drill-halls or cold upper rooms.

With one of them came Assia, tall and beautiful, her features reminiscent of Sophia Loren in a tranquil moment. When she spoke it was huskily, her tone aristocratic, its perfect English modulations belying a background of muddled nationality. Of Russian extraction – though reports of this from Assia herself varied – she had arrived in England via Israel and Canada. Her poet was David Wevill, a newly acquired husband with a look of the young Gary Cooper and sounding like him too – a whispering Canadian drawl reluctantly emerging from the poetic reverie that seemed always to possess him. Charming, attractive, unobtrusive, they were Scott Fitzgerald people sixties-style, their innocence brushed over with sophistication, their devotion to one another taken for granted.

Telling the story of their meeting, and their subsequent marriage, Assia's recollection of detail varied also: the encounter on an ocean voyage was sometimes an encounter on a train or in a café. But discrepancies never mattered much: what was consistent was that two strangers fell in love, that the wedding was romantically impulsive, that film-star lookalikes can belong together as totally as other people.

Assia liked getting married, but was vague about how many times she actually had been. Once, walking past

Moyses Stevens the flower shop, then in Berkeley Square, she said: 'Let's try this,' and a moment later was introducing herself as someone's secretary – which she was not – and ordering flowers in his name.

Glancing over the vast array of delphiniums and freesias and carnations, she arranged for a dozen and a half red roses to be dispatched immediately to her declared employer's wife. Her sudden inspiration pleased her enormously. On the pavement outside, among hurrying mini-skirts and warm-complexioned executives jostling for after-lunch taxis, she said:

'The poor woman's pregnant.'

Sending roses, or anything that might bring comfort, to a pregnant wife was, apparently, not this husband's style, a man you had to nudge if you were after some modest courtesy.

'In error I married him once,' Assia said.

But if Assia made mistakes she also had vision. You couldn't buy a decent ice-cream in London, she rightly pointed out, and suggested that a simple co-operative venture would rectify the situation and solve the acute pecuniary problems currently experienced by most of the people she knew. All that was necessary were a refrigerator, which could be purchased in a junk yard, an old bread van, various ingredients, an Italian recipe book, and a little practice. The produce would be conveyed about the suburbs of Primrose Hill and Hampstead Heath on warm Saturday afternoons, welcomed by the local children. She herself would dispense the largesse at economical prices, requiring only a wooden spoon and a supply of cones. She saw herself splendid in white, her Saturday arrival in the suburbs a cause for celebration among delighted children. But no one knew of a junk yard with abandoned refrigerators for sale, or where an ice-cream recipe book might be obtained, and no one possessed an old bread van. 'We'd have made our fortune,' Assia declared sadly but philosophically.

In much the same way, while strolling about the lunch-time streets or ensconced in the corner of a bar, she would outline the complicated plot of a novel that someone else might care to write. What she related never sounded quite like fiction, more a sleight of hand involving real people and the real world. Relating her plots, fantasy and fact flowed over one another, confusing the convoluted story she was attempting to communicate, but enriching the actuality of Assia herself. In all this she managed never to sound dotty, well aware that dotty girls are not attractive. Being attractive was important to her.

She smoked but did not drink. Coca-Cola was what she asked for, and always with an apologetic smile. Some people distrusted that smile, were made uneasy by this big-limbed girl with the *femme fatale* voice and elegant dress sense. Yet Assia seemed less a predator than a notably happy wife: in one another's company, both she and David Wevill continued to exude the good fortune that had brought them together. When their sudden break-up came it sounded like news misreported, a fate that belonged to two other people. And ironically, as related by Assia herself, the news was not without inaccuracies.

She reported that she and her husband, advertising in the *Evening Standard* a table for sale, met – through their efforts to sell it – David Wevill's fellow-poets Ted Hughes and Sylvia Plath, who were at that time man and wife. According to one at least of Sylvia Plath's biographers, what was advertised was a flat. But a table formed a more interesting heart to the story Assia told, the fingers of the poets passing lightly over its surface as value and age were assessed. The biographer's version of this encounter is no doubt the correct one: tables, in 1962, were rarely adver-tised in the *Evening Standard*.

'Heavens, the coincidence of it!' Assia exclaimed in genuine wonderment. 'All three of them being poets!'

Her tone of voice made her the outsider: she had no

lines to offer in that charmed poetic circle. One day she might have the right to be there, but for the moment she possessed little more than beauty and an imagination she could not properly make work for her. As with the rich, she was fond of saying, when you were beautiful you never knew why people liked you. Being loved for herself alone was what she hoped for when she tried to sell ice-cream.

'We were invited for the weekend,' she reported, and then there was a description of the train journey, the landscape, the tranquillity of a Devon farmhouse. The occasion of this fateful weekend was recalled in Grosvenor Square, on a warm June afternoon. Office workers chewed their sandwiches or just lay about. Perched on a huge Dennis lawnmower, a man was cutting the grass.

'On the Saturday evening I made a salad in their kitchen,' Assia said, and described a scene in which her host had found her doing so, and how they'd talked, and how she'd been attracted by him.

'I think I'll send him this.' As she spoke, she bent down and picked up a blade of newly chopped grass. She held it delicately between a patiently manicured thumb and forefinger. She said:

'Just by itself.'

'D'you think that's a good idea?'

'Not really.'

Later she addressed an envelope, and dropped into it her blade of grass. It didn't seem like a brazen action, more like a bid to enter that charmed circle by playing with fire for the sake of it. Within three days, I was told – since I was now the confidant in all this – that an envelope had come back: beside the scrap of London grass lay one from Devon. I wasn't shown it; I didn't know if what was claimed was true. It sounded unlikely, a romantic novelist's device clumsily deployed to stoke up the plot. But some weeks later Assia confided:

'We met for tea.'

The Beatles might have made a song of it: tired waitresses among the aspidistras while a beautiful woman searched yet again for marital perfection. That she had already found it, as everyone thought, was too ordinary and old-fashioned for the bright new sixties, in which doing your own thing was still what mattered most. But the times were changing even as they occurred. When Lee Harvey Oswald did his thing it wasn't so good. Nor when Brady and Hindley did theirs. Stephen Ward's loveliest lovely was in gaol, the osteopath himself was dead. Tut-tutting over bad taste in some Northern schoolroom, Mrs Mary Whitehouse was planning to clean up those parts of the permissive society that showed. As London boasted of being the fashion centre of the world, the feminists were grimly burning their bras. The seeds of Europe's Vietnam were germinating in Belfast and Derry. With half the decade to go yet, the fun fair was sleazy at the edges.

'Tea!' Assia said. 'Imagine it!'

Since the whole episode – the table for sale, the salad preparation, the eccentric love tokens – was already imbued with the wild instability of a dream, nothing now seemed impossible. Whether the recollected minutiae of the tea-time rendezvous were exact, or tinted with a personal emphasis, was irrelevant. Liars lie in order to obscure; Assia exaggerated only in the interests of what she saw as a greater veracity and, as her voice continued, doubts slipped away. Clearly, some part of this was not invented, but how the truth and the liberties taken with it were arranged I did not then know.

All that was luminously apparent was that Assia already saw herself as the Other Woman, and already she spoke of Sylvia Plath as an Other Woman might be expected to: 'a brisk, hard, magazine-editor kind of American'. This assessment was considerably at odds with the opinions of those who knew Sylvia Plath well, but in making the statement Assia spoke from the rôle she had allocated to herself, her judgement swamped by prejudice and the fear of being considered hard herself. Then, unexpectedly, reality called everyone to attention: for reasons that were mysterious and have remained so since, Sylvia Plath killed herself.

A long time later, after Assia's only child was born, she telephoned me and we met in the lounge of a bar near Waterloo. Chain-smoking and still drinking only Coca-Cola, she continued the history of her life: in the interim since last we'd conversed she had been, as she put it, 'far out into the night'. Her marriage to David Wevill was over. She was alone with her child in a flat in Primrose Hill. Bleakly shadowed by the extravagance and vigour of her past, this mundane existence did not sound tranquil.

'What would you say if I got married again?' she suggested.

'Nothing very encouraging, Assia.'

She mentioned the Heather Jenner agency, a well known marriage bureau in Bond Street, fashionable at the time. Quite seriously, she suggested filling in various forms and ending up with a widower in the country somewhere. She'd had enough of poets. With her eyes half closed against the stream of smoke from her cigarette, she even referred to a cottage garden, with lupins and fuchsia, and wistaria round the porch. She gave the impression that she meant every word of it.

'It's not a good idea, Assia.'

'I want to take my child away from Primrose Hill.'

'There are less complicated ways of doing that.'

'I think I might make a farmer happy.'

There was the lavish smile. The freckles on the bridge of her nose were disturbed by a wrinkle that came and went. Nowhere in her features was there any sign that she felt sorry for herself. Her eyes were full of yet another Alice-in-Wonderland future: an elderly, kindly man in gaiters, touches of white in his hair, she herself stirring milk in a saucepan, her child in its cot by an open fire. She had no doubt she could make it happen.

She went on talking about that with increased conviction. For the first time she called herself a displaced person, tumbled about by circumstances, and war; for the first time she confessed she had created the woman she seemed to be, teaching herself an upper-class English voice and making the most of her looks, using them as a stepping stone whenever the chance offered. She spoke of her Russian blood, of childhood in Israel, and then being shipped away to Canada and the first of her marriages. The hours she talked through that night near Waterloo Station were like hours spent in a cinema. Images were left vividly behind, flights of fancy mingled with undecorated verities. Outside, on a cold night, she turned up the collar of a smart tweed coat and for a single instant seemed weary, as though she'd talked too long and said too much. Defeat, suddenly there, faintly distorted her features, dragging at the corners of her mouth.

'Actually I'm afraid,' she murmured, before she smiled again and went away.

A month or so later Assia killed her child and then herself.

Elizabeth Young

MOTHER CAN TAKE IT

A memoir

L's JOURNAL

First time I smoked H was in the lavatory at the China Fleet Club, in Wanchai, Hong Kong.

I'd been trying to score some weed and, after making the smoke sign to a rickshaw driver, I bought a HK10$ wrap of H. He showed me how to smoke it.

Pinch the end of a Camel filter until some tobacco fell out, empty half the wrap in, twist up the paper again, tap it to settle the grey powder down into the cigarette.

In the loo I sucked greedily, holding down the smoke. Thick grey coils of it, talcum scented, writhed away from the tip of the cigarette.

Back in the bar I nursed a half pint of San Miguel which I'd suddenly got no use for.

My experience of drugs at that time was limited to grass in South Africa and Mombasa, and Rangoon Red in Singapore.

Feeling a sudden urge to be out of the bar I left my drink and took a rickshaw to the Peak Tramway. I caught the ascending car with seconds to spare.

L was still a teenager when he first took smack in China. He wrote about it in his notebook, not long before his death. He'd been trying to remember things.

All I have left now is two plastic bags. One contains his

notebooks and letters, address-books and sketch-pads. The other is full of photographs. The pictures he took are obsessive, repetitive. Many of them are townscapes, showing what is obviously a Northern city; dull, rain-streaked, old-fashioned. Narrow streets, hills of tumbledown terrace houses, net curtains, puddles in the road.

The other photos are of young boys with soft hair and wary eyes. They look uneasily into the camera, uncertain as to whether to smile. They hold syringes in the air, needle up, flicking the barrel, trying to settle the bubbles. Some of them are unconcernedly naked, apart from a leather belt wound tightly round the upper arm, making the veins stand out in relief.

('He's got pipes on him like the Pompidou Centre!' L boasts one evening in a London pub, rolling up the boy's sleeve to show me. The boy is bashful, unresisting. He looks at L and smiles lovingly. L is getting old. His teeth are almost gone. He has started wearing a soft-brimmed grey hat. His cheekbones stand out like adzes. It is a summer night. Other teenage boys drift up gently, wearing heavy, unseasonal overcoats. One of them has a piebald mongrel on a string. 'That one works double-shifts. They always throw more cash if you've got a pup along.' They start producing bags of stolen goods, stowing them under the wooden table. Sirloin steak and candy kisses from Marks and Spencer, piles of shining books from Foyles and Zwemmers. 'Hmm, well,' says L. 'Don't just stand there, our Mark. Get a drink. Mek yerself at home. And one for the lady. What would you like m'dear?')

L always had this Fagin aspect. I remember reading somewhere that Fagin was the real hero of *Oliver Twist* because he took all those children off the street and gave them a purpose.

The town in the photographs lies west of the Pennine Hills. Peter – L – was born there in 1947. That was his home and he always returned to it. He went back there to die. He left London just a few days before the end, in the deepest part of winter, as 1991 became 1992. We spoke on the telephone every day after he'd gone but soon he didn't know who I was.

L's parents were well into middle age when he was born.

'You were never wanted, you know.' That was what his next door neighbour, Mrs MacDonagh, told him one day.

'After that,' L said, 'everything seemed to fall into place.'

His parents had each served about twenty years in the Army before they met. His mother's pregnancy – and probably the conception too – was entirely accidental. His Scottish maternal grandparents, shamed and horrified, forced the reluctant couple into marriage. They retired from the Army and L's father built a small, grim house for them.

'They were that cruel,' said Loz, shortly before he died. 'I could never understand it.'

L wrote of a cold house, run on military lines. Carbolic soap, Bronco lavatory paper, thick skin on tepid milk at bedtime. They wondered aloud, he said, how they could ever have bred 'such a wee shit-bag.' His mother had one of those forties fox-furs that were worn draped over the shoulders. It had the traditional shiny boot-button eyes and sharp little yellow teeth. As a child L was terrified of it. One afternoon his mother brought it down from the bedroom and chased him with it till the little boy was near crazy with fear.

'They just wanted to make trouble for somebody they hadn't encouraged to be alive at all. Ian and Myra – what a fucking pair.'

L was largely brought up by Mrs MacDonagh-next-door. He loved her. Her husband was part-owner of one of the town's chemists, MacDonagh and Ellis. After he grew up it was the one local chemist that L would never rob. He sent his best mate to do it instead.

He would usually pop in to see her in the mornings. 'Oh Peter,' she'd say. 'Them vandals have been back. We've bin cleaned out.'

'Oh aye Mrs Mac? That's terrible.'

'This town's a changed place.'

He didn't feel good about it but there was no point muddying the different streams of your life. You'd only end up with shrinks and counselling and detox groups, all the crap they go in for now and he couldn't be doing with any of that.

There is a photograph of L smiling – too knowing to look ironic – beneath one of those large, tin advertisements that used to hang on city walls. It says YOUR CHEMIST IS ROUND THE CORNER. A helpful, pointing hand indicates the direction, just above the address.

When L was five or six his mother died. His father married a woman L always called 'that slag' and they moved westwards, to the sea. As soon as he reached school-leaving age, that slag enlisted him in the Royal Navy. He was sent away at the age of sixteen.

By the time L returned to the North in 1970 everything had changed. The dreary, brown uncut moquette carpet of the 1950s had been rolled up and put away in an attic. The town was full of kids in t-shirts and bell-bottoms hanging around the cobbled courtyards of the pubs in the sun and frightening the old folk. 'Time' had been called for the traditional North of clogs and lamplighters. The last cotton mills closed down and although the docks, the river and the canal looked the same there was less and less work to be had on them. The Northern teenagers who'd come of age in Wilson's candy-floss Britain had no time for all the hippy-dippy shite that was dizzying the rest of the world. They fastened on the heart of the matter – the drugs

– with all the wolfish intensity of a generation released forever from a lifetime's drudgery in factory and
mill.

L returned with a fixed sexual identity and a lot of
tattoos – he even had one on his belly-button, a squiggly
thing somewhere between a comma and a sperm – and
became notorious. He was shooting speed which made him
pernickety and he looked after his flat – a basement in a
crumbling wedding-cake of a house surrounded by a jungle
garden – with a combination of amphetamine obsession
and Navy-trained meticulousness. He shared the flat with
Billy, a headless man-sized dummy with stuffing shooting
out his neck. Billy had huge muscles, emphasized with
strokes of paint. His legs too were painted brown, to
simulate sunburn. Once he had been part of an open air
tableau under an umbrella at Happy Mount Park,
Morecambe.

L was constantly planning trips to Morecambe to sell
drugs, or to Wigan for Northern Soul Night, but usually he
stayed at home and shot more speed, sometimes dripping
blood neatly on to the spotless tiles. He kept his works
taped tidily to what was probably a syringa bush in the
garden.

The local – hastily formed – Drugs Squad knew L well.

Dear Sir,
    I refer to your letter dated 15th June, concerning
property taken from your room at 43, Moon Street, -----.
    I wish to inform you that this property is stored at
Drug Squad Office, Heysham and if you contact the
office on your release the property will be returned to
you against signature. Yours faithfully, (scrawl) Chief
Superintendent.

A lot of people died in those years and a lot of people went
mad.

L'S JOURNAL

*To my surprise the lock clicked off and I slipped inside.
It was a long, narrow lavatory and he sat, like an unstrung
puppet, blond hair hanging over his face, his trousers
pushed down exposing his groin, legs apart as far as the
trousers and width of the loo would allow, probing away at
the vein in his groin with a syringe full of vivid pink
liquid.*

*Between his legs lay bloodied tissues, needles, swabs, and
two foil squares.*

*I knew I had to move quickly to get a taste. I shouted his
name over and over and finally he looked up and shaking the
hair away from his face gasped and gulped. 'How the fucking
hell did you get in here?'*

*'Can I have some, eh? C'mon,' I pleaded and to my
surprise he indicated the remaining tablets.*

'How many?'

'Tek 'em, tek 'em.'

*I took 'em. I knew I'd still got to move fast, so did a
hurried crunch of two of the three and a half I'd got, shook the
powder up in a works and banged it in, wheezing as the wave
of prickling hit my lungs.*

*I used to think it was the silicon base of the pills blocking the
fine blood vessels of my lungs but a friend with a Double First
in Chemistry and a raging habit told me the effect was 'purely
pharmacological'.*

The Northern kids seemed to run at night, in packs. From
disco to dive to late licence, to offie. The girls werethrough
their dyke phase with their cropped heads and fistfights.
Their big boots clattered over the cobbles, the dawn chorus
of another century. The Pendle Witches still walk the
barren land outside town. There were babies buried all
over the moors. Everyone knew. The boys tried to outdo
one another in pharmacological psychosis. Sex was mainly

dancing. Otherwise it dwindled before the crazed clash of gender politics in the pub or a sudden scream and crash of ampoules shattering on a floor. Think on.

'Oh what a night – late September back in . . .'

L'S JOURNAL

His torso and his arms were an appliqué of nick tattooing, knife scars and burnt patches like raffia mats. When I returned my books had been torn asunder and scattered round the room.

'I sucked my little brother off but he didn't come in my mouth,' he shrieked.

'Why not?'

'Cos he wasn't OLD ENOUGH!!!'

I was glad to laugh, believe me, the atmosphere was electric. He raved off into the night. Later I heard he'd been put away. It was happening all the time, people burnt up on re-entry.

I met L when I was passing through the North in 1975. He heard I had a first edition of Kenneth Anger's recently published *Hollywood Babylon* and came round to look at it. I lent it to him and never saw it again. L was as extreme a bibliophile as you could find. At the time we grew up an unhappy childhood was not a public thing, a focus for therapy and discussion and social workers, but a private agony, often alleviated by a desperate amount of reading. Later, reading had taken L around the world where he'd seen little but the greasy interiors of industrial vessels or a brutality to which he occasionally alluded. It doesn't take much imagination to enlarge a voracious consumption of books into one of drugs. The two experiences are very similar. Especially smack – Tin Tack, Plastic Mack – which makes the world go away in a very similar manner. L was never mercenary enough to be a real drug dealer so his life was always a precarious spider's web of small-time theft, fucked-up Giros arriving late, tide-over loans and minus-cule drug haggling – 'Two of them for one of these, go on, mek it three.'

L and his friends were always in and out of nick – 'It's amazing how being inside can give you an entrée isn't it? Especially the circles we move in,' he wrote. Stupid, small-time charges – possession of drugs, possession of stolen goods – which meant that those most vulnerable were always being swept up, uselessly, pointlessly in other raids, like the wretched dolphin in tuna nets. Very soon I was visiting him in Preston Gaol, a blackened, archaic Victorian workhouse, tastefully situated beside a new motorway where the north winds spun down the lanes to rage and tear at the prison. 'What a fucking hole. Like Siberia in winter and so lonely.'

Actually he always adjusted well to institutional life, particularly as the prisons, like everywhere else, responded to Western policies of drug prohibition by becoming increasingly saturated with them. He worked as librarian. 'The first few days I were here,' he said, 'I just couldn't understand it. There was one cell that no one went near. No one spoke to the inmate. He didn't dare come out to eat. It was like he was on Rule 43 only he weren't. The screws had to shove his meals through his door. No one ever saw him. I were dead puzzled and eventually I ask the Senior Librarian what's up wi' the guy. Is he some sort of fuckin' leper or owt? "Oh no," says the Librarian. "That's the Preston Cat Strangler."'

By the end of his life L was up on his forty-seventh book stealing charge. This one made *The Times*.

THIEF WAS OBSESSED BY SMELL OF BOOKS

A trainee bookbinder with an obsession for books was put on probation for two years yester-day after giving an undertaking in the Central

Criminal Court that he would stay away from
bookshops.

P – L – , aged 44 of Stepney, East London, who
admitted stealing three astrology books from a
central London bookshop in March, said he
could keep out of trouble if he was not tempted
by the smell of books. 'I don't miss them as long
as I don't get a whiff of them,' he said. 'If I
could go into a library that would suffice.'

Astrology? For re-sale only. By this time, of course, L had
AIDS so they weren't going to put him in prison. Too
expensive.

During the 1980s L spent more time in London. Eventually
he was given a council bedsit round Royal Mint Street in
the Minories, at night little changed in its blackness and
silence from a century earlier when Jack had whispered to
the whores. It was a big, airy room, overlooking the railway,
and once Billy the headless torso was installed and the
books and compilation tapes placed in their neat piles, it
looked very like his previous flat, as neat and fastidious as
ever. Did he really only have two homes in nearly half a
century? Yes. Otherwise it was always squats and friends
and burned-out houses.

At the beginning of the 1980s I hired L to come and
paint my new council flat. I would pay him in cocaine. My
boyfriend dealt it. L rarely saw coke, it being so expensive.
The decor ended up beguilingly spontaneous, tastefully *au
courant* in its stripped-down minimalist look, garnished by
the sprays of blood on the walls. We just sat on the stairs
and shot all the coke, this being before the days of the AIDS
panic in needle park. He later undertook to be my house-
keeper, tutting like an old maid as he scratched his initials
into the gunk on the cooker. 'The glory that was grease!
You could do a Bolero on this fuckin' floor too. To the ice

m'dear! And over and back . . . and again!' He laughs, starts coughing and spits into the sink. 'I'll mek us a cuppa.'

But, accustomed to popping round to see people in the North, he hated to use the telephone and so would just turn up. And then he would push you. For a bath, to borrow a book, for money, for another cup of tea, to have a fix – I'd given up needles so we'd start arguing. It always ended in screaming rows and L's lacerating insults. He did this to all his friends, tested them and tested them as if he had to know how much they could take. And most took it and never held a grudge. L had to live entirely without safety nets and it is hard for most people to imagine this. No heating. The plumbing goes. The kitchen window gets punched out. Who pays the plumber? Who pays the glazier? But no one put up with him out of pity. They did so because they loved him. He made them laugh. That was it. (But think what it's like in this cold, tight-arsed country for the drifter bereft of charm. Dennis Nilsen's cooking pot?) The loyalty and devotion of his friends – and there were many closer than myself – make a nonsense of all those theorists, their mouths clogged with shit, who insist that there can be nothing but betrayal and selfishness among criminals and drug-users.

L grew older. He lost his hair, took to wearing the hat and acquired that ghostly, seamed, old junkie look. His boy-friends stayed the same though, always Northern teenagers, fluttering around him like little drunken butterflies, hustling, scrounging, ducking and diving. L became less sexual and more avuncular, although there were still days when 'There was so much dried come lying around this morning I could have gone to a Fancy Dress Ball as a GLAZED DOUGHNUT!' He had only had one great, shattering love-affair in his early life, with a beautiful, intelligent redhead – long gone – but he was very loving towards his boys, all of whom had nicknames – The Shadow, The Fledgeling,

The Kitten, Donkey Wanger ('Drum my upraised face with your meat truncheon'). He liked them sulky. He liked them sultry. He liked big dicks. There was the inevitable shrinking from judgement – from thought – on the morality of L involving these kids in his life. The inexorable diffidence of deviance. Throw stones? Who gets stoned first? Then you can laugh again. One friend could in a couple of hours make contradictory assertions on the subject, if he bothered to: 'L has a great capacity for corruption'; 'L has a strict working-class morality.' It is safe to say that all the little chickens had shown a marked disinterest in the straight and narrow long before they ran into L, otherwise they would never have done so. He showed them great concern, writing endlessly and exhorting them to treat the more dangerous drugs with care: 'Be sensible for your old Uncle Fester – he who loves you dearly. Please, Caution! EAT THE FUCKERS!'

L was killed not by sex or by drugs but by insane legislation. Although he liked speed he was primarily a junkie. Since 1968 heroin has been almost completely unobtainable legally for addicts in Britain. The American system of methadone maintenance was adopted. L, like most junkies, hated methadone and turned to the black market, to the streets, to the crime and the dirty needles and the disease to get the drugs he wanted. This enforced lifestyle created the conditions wherein AIDS was passed on between drug-users. If L had been able to get clean heroin on prescription when he needed it, his life – and probably his death – might have been different. L *was* a sufficiently extreme case to get heroin prescribed for a while (Diamorphine Injection 30 mg. Two to be administered daily) but the doctor ministering unto him was tracked down by a television crew and his life made difficult by those who have an economic interest (clinics, counsellors, doctors, shrinks, high-level corruption in industry, finance and God

knows where) in keeping the methadone madness under-
way and the junk on the streets. As he aged, in common
with many lifetime junkies, L could no longer summon the
resources to acquire heroin, which is expensive. If it were
available legally, people might not find themselves burnt-
out and exhausted in mid-life from hustling for their drug,
with no employment record – only a criminal one – and no
future prospects just at the point when many of them start
to 'age out' and lose interest in the drug anyway. I don't
mean that L would have had a straightforward and conventional life, just that things would have been a lot easier if
drugs had not outlawed him. He was no big-time criminal.
He just wanted to get by, in his way. As heroin became
more inaccessible he started shooting instead the very
much cheaper and more lethal tranquillizer benzodiazepine
which he used in the form of sleeping pills named Tema-
zepam. He called them 'eggs', for their shiny, gelatinous
look and the way you could suck the liquid out of the
capsule with a spike. 15 mg. ones were bright yellow and
looked like egg yolks. 30 mg. ones – he called them
'double-yolkers' – were dark green. He also started drinking more, again a common reaction as junkies get too old to
hustle for their drugs – and that didn't help.

L's deterioration was very sudden. AIDS, one year from
diagnosis to death. He knew he'd probably got it but had
put off having a test. Drugs were his first love and by this
time I don't think he was capable of endangering other
people sexually nor would he have wished to. He was not
lethal. But, in the spinning months before the diagnosis, as
he coughed more and became even more gaunt, the
needles were around. Always.

He had nearly completed his HND in bookbinding around
the time of diagnosis. Although as he pointed out to me –
more than once – there were no jobs whatsoever in the field
so what then? 'I never thought I'd make old bones,' he said.

*

The first time I went to see him in the London Hospital, they had, with characteristic sensitivity, put him in a ward of men with leg injuries, largely cab-drivers. L made no secret of his condition and these burly men, hair sprouting like rain forests along their shoulders beneath their string vests, were all of a twitter at having L in their midst. I arrived to hear him screaming at one of them, 'If you don't turn that flamin' telly off this fuckin' instant I'll be *straight* over into yer bed and I'll have my tongue *right* down that gorgeous gullet!'

L never lacked courage. He was not self-pitying. During that year he became increasingly skeletal and the sores on his feet and legs made it hard to walk. He struggled to college nearly every day. Only occasionally in letters did he allude to the nightmares they inflicted on him – 'Screaming nerves – change of medicine from AZT to DDI which *didn't* agree with me at all. So I took the whole coffin-sized box back to the clinic and said, "Forget it – if you'll poison me with this why won't you give me the smack? What a performance a girl has to go through."' Even then they withheld the morphine and heroin until it was too late to matter. He never did like doctors – 'Those stuck-up middle-class cunts working off their guilt on us.'

L did speak kindly of some of the hospices he was in – although he left one when a visit from Princess Di was imminent. L had never been a morbid or ghoulish person and descriptions of suffering were rare: 'Abscesses, thrombosis, phlebitis. It took two nurses two hours from 9.30 pm to 11.30 pm to find a vein suitable for a cannula (a thick, flexible needle with another one which slips inside it) and get it in and the blood flowing. I was shagged out completely (so were they!) and covered in plasters.' Generally he preferred to talk or write about happier things. 'Fuck the pressure. Still, Mother can take it – it's great to be tucked up in bed, a supply of eggs, a spoon of Tin Tack, the odd can of Tennants, Radio 4 and the World Service, a good book or three. A blessed comfort.' He could still manage a J. Arthur, he said.

L needed very little to make him happy – he wasn't greedy – and it seems cruel that so much of it was withheld or made so hard for him. As he said, 'I've lived off fuck-all so long.'

L didn't want to die any more than anyone else once he knew he was going to. He'd never been suicidal or even depressive but like many people whose life gets fumbled in the first half he was careless with it. But some of his friends who were not yet under sentence seemed to care far far less than he had ever done. They really didn't seem to mind whether they lived or died or more probably they never thought about it but just went on and on, grinning blindly into the steady, relentless slap and suck of the media tide. Rubbers, shame, shock, horror, HIV, ARC, syndrome, euphemism, synonym, antonym – it all seemed to ebb away from them just as the sea withdrew further every year – in horror or indifference – from their North-West coast.

The beginning of the end blew in from the North. L knew he was sick. He had a good idea of what it was but he hadn't been to see a doctor yet. He always went up North for Christmas and this year was spending it with a man he'd known for some time. Too long perhaps. This guy was a veterinarian who liked to do operations on his penis. Or best of all he liked his young, stoned boyfriends to do the ops. He lived with his current boyfriend Al in a sort of Quonset hut somewhere on the Yorkshire side of the Pennine way. The first night they had their friends in – L described it as 'the speeding of the five thousand' – but the rest of Christmas was to be given up to arcane delights with L as spectator. 'You wouldn't believe the state of this house,' L wrote. 'The veg racks are *crammed* with capsicum, tomatoes, lettuce, carrots, *everything*, all well rotten – as if Howard Hughes had done the shopping.'

L wrote the rest down in his notebook, sporadically. The vet had to explain the procedure to him.

L's JOURNAL

He indicated a plate in an old medical book which lay open on the table between us.

'I've already been through all this with Al. Tomorrow, when we go down to the surgery, this is what I hope to be able to do.'

The picture was of a prick, cut away to show the components. His eyes twinkled over the tops of his half-moon shaped glasses as his finger pointed out and named them, the Latin flowing easily. 'Now this body of tissue here is the corpus spongeosi as you can see from this cross section. It's surrounded by three kinds of tissue and they keep everything together.'

He chuckled to himself happily. He was looking forward to the operation he'd been promised as a Christmas treat. Across the room, his boyfriend, swinging a joint from his fingertips to shake the tobacco down, winked at me and flashed a quick smile.

'What's happened is that on the last operation I had done, afterwards two of the outer sleeves grew together, so when I get a hard on now my willy bends to the right and up which is all right for what Al and I get up to but if I ever put it in a woman again I might damage her internally.'

'What were the other operations?'

He needed no prompting. In seconds he was standing over me, jeans pulled down, underwear ditto, with his bunch in his left hand, his right being used to pull his large though still soft prick until the extent of the scarring and cicatrizing could be seen. It looked like a cumberland sausage.

'This is the one that Al did last year. THAT one has been fine, haven't had any trouble there, but look, here's where it's grown together, this lumpy bit here.'

Even the most cursory inspection revealed that all was not well. For although still soft, under the ridged and lumpy surface you could feel an area the size of a ten pence piece which was obviously two if not three of the 'inner tube' sleeves he'd described earlier, fused together into one dick-distorting knot.

'What's this patch here?' I said, indicating what at first seemed to be an area of surface veins but on closer inspection with fingertip was found to be a kidney-shaped area of puckered and hairy skin.

'Ah now, that's where I had to have a skin graft when another operation went wrong. I didn't do this one myself. That skin was taken from my scrotum, that's why it's hairy, you can see the similarity. Look!'

He took up a couple of fingerfuls of scrotum. He'd had some of his balls grafted on to his prick!

'Are you using gas tomorrow?'

'No. Local. And we'll want some sandwiches, pork pies, meat pies, cans of lager, there's tea and coffee at the surgery, better take some milk. I'll get the video camera down.'

So off they went. L and Al liberally sample the medicine cabinet at the surgery. The video is set up and Al, the boyfriend, begins hacking away. L feels sick. He has a terrible cold, slowly sinking towards a deadly pneumonia. He goes off to make a cup of tea and returns to discover Al—

L's JOURNAL

Sitting behind the bathroom door, naked except for a towelling robe, his cock a gruesome spectrum of bruised and varicosed meat from where he'd been hitting the dorsal vein. 'Can't seem to get a hit anywhere else.' The shells of double yolkers littered the floor about him, mostly 'blown'. After washing the sore on his prick thoroughly with a can of Fosters, Al went back to carry on the operation.

L felt wretched and forlorn. The great spotlights in the surgery were making his head ache. He didn't want to watch so he kept making cups of tea. He couldn't get a picture of the vet's tool box out of his head. It was a chrome box with a hinged lid filled with what seemed to be craft knives but *as I quickly realized on closer scrutiny, peering close down into the clear reddish fluid in which they lay, they were scalpels*. He had to struggle not to think – about his sickness, about their sickness. *Later they put my single bed next to their double bed so I wouldn't feel lonely*. When he got home to London L went to the hospital and had the AIDS test.

I never thought I would miss someone so much. L had an ill-deserved reputation for misogyny and it was true if you objected to hearing women described as 'Little miss smelly fishbag whore' or 'A rancid-snatched shag cow' you had better stay out of his way. Or if you were squeamish about a vivid, graphic way of expressing a horror of menstruation. This was someone with a mouth so foul he managed to get fired from a radical bookshop for his language. But L chose his friends regardless of sex. What he didn't like was femininity – not the external femininity of clothes and scent and make-up on either men or women, although he was by nature butch in appearance, but the internal femininity that convinced a woman that she was different, special and probably morally superior. He hated self-righteous feminists. He liked non-political dykes. L's indifference to politics kept him away from much that happened in the years of post-war gay politics but he always felt that his own homosexual state was not only natural but superior and that most men, however straight they seemed, must really be homosexual. He was out all his life. He never backed down, never apologized and never compromised his integrity on the subject. He wrote to young boyfriends telling them about gay history, gay writers and artists. He writes to his young lover, Jay, 'Oh my pretty pretty' and tells him that 'Red Indian gays were revered as special people in touch with their gods – they dressed in women's clothing and looked after the young and were respected' – conducting a gentle epistolary education between the screeds of pornographic illustrations. Teeth and pricks and dogs and bums and more teeth.

I have a photograph of him hitching North way back in the seventies, holding up a sign saying 'Honk If You're Gay.' I hope he scored for the ultimate ride. The car slicing northwards like a knife, celebratory pink and golden ribbons whipping in the slipstream like the unravelled DNA of all possible possibilities, as bright and brave and unforgettable as that first sure touch upon the knee.

'Do you still use that pig's grease on your nipples, Liz?' someone roars from behind me in a long Christmas queue at Marks and Spencer. L carries on as the queue inches forward, blenching, to enumerate my (bestial) sexual tastes, ending, 'We should never have got married, you slag – all that stuff's too gross for me!' He's waiting round the corner with a steak and some oranges beneath his black leather jacket.

'Bet that made their Christmas.'

'Mmm. It's my local branch actually.'

'Well I nevah! It's my No Cash 'n' Carry ectualleh.'

'What you got? Protein for once, I see.'

'Build me up. Not that I need it. Well, not all of me. Heh! I allus told you it were a whopper. Remember the time – Missed yer chance dintch'a?! Buy us a drink then. Buy us a Guinness.'

Down Camden High Street. Into the autumn, into the dusk.

L went back North a few days before his death. His last – and longest – affair was with another teenage angel-face, Jay, a skinny child doll with soft red curls. Jay stayed till the very end, crying, laughing, crying, holding L's hand, whispering how much he loved him. He died with the old year, in the deepest, darkest part of winter. I have never been to his grave. The bereavement counsellors and all the rest say you should do stuff like that to face up to the reality of death but I won't. I don't want to. As it is, I know he's in a cemetery but when I picture it I just seem to hear L's words: 'All human life is there. And the rest of it.'

With deepest thanks to
Howard Downes and Tony Carricker.

ABOUT THE AUTHORS

Paul Bailey has been twice short-listed for the Booker Prize, and has been the recipient of the E. M. Forster Award, the Somerset Maugham Award, an Arts Council Award, a George Orwell Memorial Prize and a Bicentennial fellowship. He is also the author of *At the Jerusalem, Trespasses, Peter Smart's Confessions, Old Soldiers, An Immaculate Mistake, Gabriel's Lament* and *Sugar Cane*.

Jan Brokken is one of Holland's leading travel writers, besides being a novelist and short story writer. He has written books about Africa and about Jean Rhys and Dominica, and has published several highly acclaimed collections of short stories, one of which, *De zee van vroeger*, was awarded de Lucy B. en C.W. van der Hoogtprijs. His novel *De Provincie* has been filmed, and in autumn 1995 his novel *De blinde passagiers* (*The Blind Passengers*) was published.

Simon Burt was born in Wiltshire in 1947 and educated at Downside and Trinity College, Dublin. He worked for some years as a teacher in South London, and now lives in North Kensington. He has written a book of short stories, *Floral Street*, and two novels, *The Summer of the White Peacock* and *Just Like Eddie*.

A. S. Byatt's *Possession* won the Booker Prize and the *Irish Times*/Aer Lingus International Fiction Prize in 1990. Her other fiction includes *The Shadow of the Sun, The Game, The Virgin in the Garden, Still Life, Sugar and Other Stories* and *Angels and Insects*. She was educated in York and at Newnham College, Cambridge, and taught at the Central School of Art before becoming a full-time writer. She was made CBE in 1990.

Michael Carson taught English as a foreign language around the world for fifteen years, but now lives in Powys. He has published

ABOUT THE AUTHORS

many successful novels, including *Sucking Sherbert Lemons* and *The Knight of the Flaming Heart*, and a book of short stories, *Serving Suggestions*.

Clare Colvin was born in London and has lived in Southern Africa, the Lebanon and India. A regular contributor to Constable's *Winter's Tales*, she has recently completed a collection of short stories and a novel. She has worked as a journalist and critic for a number of national newspapers, including the *Times* and *Sunday Times*, and is currently the Literary Editor of the *Sunday Express*.

Slavenka Drakulić is a Croatian writer who lives in Zagreb and Vienna. Her books include *How We Survived Communism and Even Laughed*, *The Balkan Express*, *Marble Skin* and *Holograms of Fear*.

Elizabeth Evans lives in London. She was a bookseller and is still involved in work with books. She has been writing short stories for years, nine of which have been broadcast by the BBC. She has no wish to write a novel, preferring the shape and constraint of the short story.

Duncan Fallowell is the author of novels, travel books, profiles and the libretto of the opera *Gormenghast*. 'Sailing to Gozo' is an extract from his forthcoming book, *Mysterious People*.

Eliza Fewett is a consultant oncologist. She has written for the *Spectator*, *New Society* and the *Evening Standard* as well as various medical publications, and has broadcast on radio and television.

Philip Gooden lives and works in Bath.

Kirsty Gunn's stories have appeared in *First Fictions: Introduction 11*, *Slow Dancer* magazine and the Serpent's Tail anthologies *Border Lines* and *The Junky's Christmas*. Her first novel, *Rain*, was published in 1994. She lives in London.

Tobias Hill lives in Japan and is associate editor of *Trafika International Review*. In 1993 he was joint winner of the LAB/Serpent's Tail Short Story Competition and in 1994 he won the Sheffield Thursday Prize. Hill is primarily a poet, having won sixteen poetry prizes and thirty-two commendations in the last two years. His first collection of poetry is due to be published by the national Poetry Foundation in 1995/6.

Jonathan Keates is the author of a recent biography of Stendhal.

His collection of short stories *Allegro Postillions* won the Hawthornden and James Tait Black prizes. He teaches at the City of London School.

Irma Kurtz's books include *The Great American Bus Ride* and *Jinx*. She is the Agony Aunt for *Cosmopolitan*, (UK, USA, South Africa and Australia). Her latest book, *Irma Kurtz's 10 Point Plan for an Untroubled Life* was published in 1995. She lives in Soho.

James Loader is the Head of English at a Grammar School in Kent. He has travelled extensively and has taught in Central India. He is currently collaborating on an anthology of poetry and is working on a travel book.

John Saul's short fiction has appeared widely in the UK as well as in France, Italy and Germany, finding its way into the *Best of the Fiction Magazine*, the Serpent's Tail anthologies *Sex and the City* and *Border Lines*, and in *New Writing 4*. He has published a novel *Heron and Quin*. He now lives in Hamburg, where he works for Greenpeace.

Elisa Segrave's stories and articles have appeared in other Serpent's Tail anthologies and in various newspapers and magazines. Her book *The Diary of a Breast* was published in April 1995.

Lynne Tillman is the author of *Haunted Houses*, *Absence Makes the Heart*, *Motion Sickness*, *Cast in Doubt* – all published by Serpent's Tail – and *The Madame Realism Complex*. Her story, 'Reveal Codes, or Life is a Joke', appeared in the 1995 Whitney Biennial catalogue. Recently she wrote the text for *The Velvet Years*, a book of Stephen Shore's photographs of Warhol and the Factory, 1965–7. She lives in New York.

William Trevor was born in Mitchelstown, Co. Cork, in 1928, and was educated at a number of Irish schools and at Trinity College, Dublin. He is a member of the Irish Academy of Letters. He has been awarded the Hawthornden Prize, the Royal Society of Literature Award, the Whitbread Book of the Year Prize, the *Yorkshire Post* Book of the Year Prize and the *Sunday Express* Book of the Year Prize. He is the editor of *The Oxford Book of Irish Short Stories* (1989) and has written plays for the stage, radio and television. In 1976 William Trevor received the Allied Irish Banks' Prize, and in 1977 he was awarded an honorary CBE in recognition of his valuable services to literature. In 1992 he received the *Sunday Times* Award for Literary Excellence.

ABOUT THE AUTHORS

Elizabeth Young was born in Lagos, Nigeria, and educated in London, Paris and York. A literary journalist who also writes fiction, she is co-author of *Shopping in Space: Essays on American 'Blank Generation' Fiction* (published by Serpent's Tail in 1992).